Sparks Fly

By Bec Weekes

Author Bio

Bec is a new, independently published author from regional NSW, Australia.

Her love of writing began at a young age but mostly consisted of poetry, until like many others, during Covid, she rekindled her love of reading. This quickly blossomed into a dream of writing her own love stories and in 2024, she released her debut novel, Sparks Fly.

When she isn't writing, or reading, Bec enjoys spending time with her husband and seven-year-old son.

You can follow along with all of Bec's new release on her socials

Instagram: @bec.weekes.author
Tiktok: @bec.weekes.author

Contents

Playlist

Highway to Hell – AC/DC

Missin' Someone – Dan & Shay

Scared to Start – Michael Marcagi

Am I Okay? – Megan Moroney

How Do I Do This? – Kelsea Ballerini

I Don't Dance – Lee Brice

Amazed – Lonestar

Shake It Off (Taylors Version) – Taylor Swift

Never Not Remember You – Cooper Alan

Life with You – Kelsey Hart

Sparks Fly (Taylors Version) – Taylor Swift

To all the hard-headed, fiercely independent girls out there.

It's okay to accept help every now and then.

Who knows, it might just lead to the best sex of your life.

Chapter 1

BETH

'Dearly Beloved, we are gathered here today to Farewell a loving Husband, Father, Son and Friend, Griffin Adams.'

'Highway to Hell' by AC/DC plays loud and proud over the speakers as we all regress from the parlor of the funeral home. I'm flanked by my two brothers, Will and Nate, followed by my dad Hank, and Nate's girlfriend, Olive, who are hand in hand with my four-year-old son, Logan.

I've been dreading this day for months. We knew Griffin's time was coming. He was diagnosed with terminal pancreatic cancer a year ago. He planned his entire funeral service, the verses that were read, the music, the photos. My larrikin of a husband even wrote his own eulogy. He thought of everything, I didn't have to lift a finger. He planned his own send-off, and it was just perfect.

After the service, our closest family and friends reconvene for a few drinks at the local foodie hotspot, 'Just In Thyme' a trendy restaurant/bar which is co-owned by my youngest brother Nate.

I'm absolutely exhausted from accepting condolences from the seemingly endless line of mourners, so I grab myself a glass of wine from the bar and take up residence at a high-top table in the back corner. Even in the early evening, it's dimly lit, so I'm hoping this buys me a few moments to myself.

With the formal part of the day over, I feel a sense of relief wash over me. As I sit quietly at my table, I watch Logan as he tries to rough house with his uncles and of course they play the part and let him think that he's getting some good shots in. Usually when this kind of chaos kicks off at any family gathering, Griffin would be the ringleader, egging on Logan, and it would eventually turn into some kind of WWE inspired tag team match with the 4 boys. Logan always came out victorious, obviously.

Everyone has always told me Logan is so much like me, but it's funny, in the last 6 days since Griffin left us, I see so many uncanny resemblances between Logie and Griff. And now, watching as he makes light of an otherwise somber occasion, he is his father's mini. The class clown, the life of the party. Just as Griffin always wanted. It's been my lot in life to be surrounded by strong willed men. Although, if you asked them, they would probably all tell you that I made them that way.

With the exception of my sister, Bella, who couldn't make it to the funeral, due to just having moved interstate with her new boyfriend, some corporate type that none of us have had a chance to get to know properly yet. It's always been me and my boys.

Our mother suffered some pretty serious mental health issues just after the twins, Nate and Bella were born. By the time they were two years old, she signed away her parental rights to all of her kids, packed up and left, just days before my twelfth birthday. Leaving my dad to raise the infamous 'Philips four' all on his own.

My dad was thirty-four when he became a single dad. Ironically the same age as I am now when I've just become a single mother. We have always been a tight-knit family; I'm just not used to being the one receiving the support. I'm usually the strong one, it's always been a bit of a running joke that 'I'm a strong independent woman that doesn't need a man to survive.' But since losing Griffin, I've felt a massive shift in me, now that not having a man in my house is my reality it sinks in that I have some much to teach Logan, to make sure he remembers his dad in a positive way, not for the sick man that he was in his last few months.

Just as I begin to get lost in my thoughts, I feel the bar stools on either side of me pull out. I shake my head, willing away the tears that are threatening to fall. I honestly don't know how I still have tears left. I look around and see my dad, Hank, and my boss, John, coming to sit on either side of me.

"It was a beautiful service, Beth, so fitting for Griffins final bow." John begins. I've worked as an office assistant for Johns contracting firm for my entire working career, he and my dad have been friends since they were in high school, so he is pretty much considered family.

"You take all the time off you need; you've had such a hard few months making Griffins final days perfect. We will manage without you for as long as you need."

"Thanks John, I appreciate it, but if it's all the same to you, I really would like to get back into some form of normality. The house feels so lonely now, and you're right, it has been a long few months, I've had enough time, it will be nice to be surrounded by familiarity, once I get everything cleared out."

"If you're sure, and if you need any help moving all of that big medical equipment you've acquired, or any little odd jobs that need fixing around the house, you be sure to let me know and I will send some of the boys around to help you."

I guess that's the perks of having your own contracting company, having handy guys at your disposal whenever needed. John stands, gives me a sympathetic smile, and a couple of soft taps on the shoulder, before shaking my dad's hand and walking away.

My dad puts his arm around my shoulders and my head instinctively falls into him, burrowing into his neck, I let out a big exhale that I didn't even realize I was holding.

"It will be alright, darling girl. As a twelve-year-old kid, you helped me figure it out all those years ago, I reckon as a couple of fully grown adults we can help you figure it out." He pushes to stand, plants a light kiss on the top of my head, and then goes to join my brothers and my son in the middle of the room.

Logan is clearly getting tired because he has climbed up into Wills arms and has cuddled into his neck. That's my cue to leave, so I drain my glass of wine, take my son into my arms and we walk out to face our new reality.

****

Two weeks later, I take a deep breath in as I walk through the door. "Oh my goodness, Beth! You're back!"

Of course, my coworker, Abi is the first to greet me. Abi is the payroll and accounts officer, and as the only two female employees at the firm, naturally, we have formed a close friendship in the 3 years she has worked here, we also share an office space. She almost feels like a bonus little sister to me, at 26 years old she is 8 years my junior, and although she is damn good at her job, it's fun for me to witness her naivety around life sometimes.

"Yeah girl, couldn't stay away from you any longer." She rounds her desk and almost gets up to a jog before she launches herself at me, throwing her arms around me in one of the tightest hugs I've ever experienced and that's saying something because in the last three weeks, I've experienced A LOT of hugs. But this one, this is one of the most sincere.

"It's so good to see your face, I really needed some estrogen back in this place to break up the sausage fest around here." Abi breaks out in a schoolgirl style giggle.

"Let me go make a coffee and then you can fill me in on everything I've missed." I set my bag down at my desk, running my fingers over the photos I keep of Griffin and Logan. I fire up my computer, before heading across to the kitchen to make a coffee.

I'm mindlessly stirring the sugar into my coffee when I hear another set of footsteps enter the kitchen. "Beth? Oh my God, it's so good to see you, I didn't expect to see you back so soon."

I immediately recognize that voice and I turn to be met with the most piercing pair of blue eyes peeking out from under that familiar baseball cap that I've come to know so well, I see it day in and day out around here.

Mason Clarke is the lead contractor here, he is one of those guys that could build you anything you wanted to build and fix just about anything that was broken. He is about five years older than me, but I had seen him around town before I started working here. I remember him playing football with Griffin over the years, they were respectable opponents on the field in their younger days.

I guess that's what happens when you live in a small town, everybody knows everybody in some capacity. I grew up in Rosewood, and so did my parents, so I've lived here my entire life.

It's a small town, with a population of about 2000 people, although in summer that almost doubles as a lot of tourists converge on town because of both the Rosewood River and the lake in town as well. So, we get fisherman, and boating families here for the summer, if you enjoy anything water based, Rosewood is the place to be. There truly is something for everyone here.

"Mason, hey. Yeah, I, uh - couldn't sit around the house wallowing in self-pity any longer, and I knew this place would be falling apart without me so figured I should get back on the horse sooner rather than later."

I was prepared for today to be full of awkward silences, working with almost all men, I knew some of them wouldn't know what to say or how to act around me, and treat me with kid gloves. But Masons face breaks into a wide grin at my poor attempt at a joke.

Mason approaches the counter and begins to fill his mug from the coffee pot. When he isn't out on a building site, we quite often meet here in the mornings, completely coincidentally. Our routines just seem to match up, but I enjoy our little morning chats.

"I was sorry to hear about Griffin. I'm so sorry I couldn't make it to the funeral, we had a big project running behind for a strict deadline, so it was all hands-on deck around here, you know how it goes."

"Yeah, some things will never change. God, I feel like I've been gone forever. How are things going with you? How's the family?" I pass him the sugar, before taking a few steps back and leaning against the far wall, while he stirs his coffee before turning to face me, leaning against the counter, we both take our first sips of coffee and for me, I feel it hit my soul.

I feel a weight lift. This feels like normality returning. This feels easy.

"Good, good. I'm good, Rosie is really good. She's getting so goddamn big now, four years old and apparently needs nail polish and lipstick for every occasion. I'm going to have a real little diva in a few years."

Rosie is Masons daughter, and she is the most beautiful, sassy little firecracker I've ever met. Rosie and Logan go to preschool together, so I often see her at drop off or pick up time.

He eyes me over the rim of his coffee mug and our gazes lock for probably a second too long, "How are you, Beth? Really, how are you coping?"

My breath hitches at the genuine tone in his voice. He continues to hold my gaze for a moment longer and I swear his stare almost rips through me. I offer him a weak smile. Those icy eyes could extinguish a forest fire, I'm sure of it.

"Better than I thought I would, if I'm honest. Logan has had some trouble sleeping. He misses his dad, obviously. But we're doing okay. My dad and brothers have been an absolute godsend helping out with him, the only thing I can't seem to manage on my own is the goddamn lawn mower, because Griffin insisted on keeping his vintage model mower instead of upgrading to something from this century. The man made sure to teach me how to change the oil in my car, and how to file a tax return before he left. But apparently, he had to take the mower skills to the grave with him." I say it with a smirk.

I used to joke that Griffin loved his lawn as much as he loved me. The man was obsessed. He had the greenest thumb, and his lawn and garden were his pride and joy. It's the one aspect of his life I fear I absolutely will fail him at. If his thumb was green, mine is as black as the night sky.

"I could take a look at it if you like, see if I can show you how to use it. Or you know, I could just do the lawns for you. I must agree with Griffin here, yardwork is somewhat therapeutic for me, it's like my happy place, and at the moment, we are in a small rental, so I don't have much yard to keep me occupied. I'd be happy to come and help you out around the place every couple of weeks."

"That's - super generous of you, Mason, but I can't ask you to do that."

Why can I feel tears starting to prickle behind my eyes? The entire towns generosity in the past few months through Griffins Illness and passing has had me in tears more times than I have cried in my entire life.

From homecooked meals, to babysitting, they even set up a crowd funding page to send us on a few holidays, so Griffin got to see out his 'Bucket list' and now this, I feel like I'll be indebted to this entire town for all of eternity.

"You're not asking me Beth, I'm offering. And before you say anything else, the only payment I will accept is in the form of a cold beer when I'm done."

He shakes his head and flashes me a smile, as he begins to walk out of the kitchen. He stops at the doorway before turning back to look at me. "It really is good to have you back, Beth."

Chapter 2

BETH

6 Months later

It's late in the winter, and when I was at the hardware store this morning, I saw they had the most beautiful, apricot-colored roses on a clearance sale. I stopped to look at them and almost caught myself crying right there in the garden section. Son of a bitch, they were called 'Adams Rose.'

Griffin always used to groan about the price of roses around Valentines Day and vowed that one day he would grow his own, so he could sell them and make a killing. Plus, our house has serious country cottage vibes, and our entire street is lined with little white picket fences, the real small town country stereotype.

When we bought it almost ten years ago, as a bit of a fixer upper, we both agreed some gorgeous roses would be a beautiful finishing touch and really compliment the whole aesthetic.

We never did get around to clearing the garden beds before he got really sick, I took it as a sign that these roses shared his last name, so I bought all 4 of them, and got to digging out the garden bed as soon as I got home.

Mason should be coming around this afternoon. He taught me to use Griffins ancient mower months ago, but as much as I insist, he doesn't need to keep coming around, without fail, every other weekend, he is here.

If Griffin could see our yard now, he might even be a little bit jealous because, truthfully, I don't think it's ever looked this good.

I must look a treat, covered head to toe in soil. Logan decided to help me dig, which involves more dirt being flung around the place than anything else. I wear most of it, but he is proud of his efforts.

"What in the world are you two attempting to do?" I hear Mason say as he steps out of his truck. He rounds the front and approaches the back door where Rosie is strapped into her booster seat. "We're being excavators!" Logan exclaims excitedly.

As soon as Mason opens the back door, and Rosie and Logan see each other, it's like nothing else in the world exists, Rosies feet barely hit the ground before they run for each other screaming and wrap each other in a big hug, almost knocking each other flat. If that doesn't make a person smile, I don't know what would.

They have become the best of friends over the last six months. Mason brings Rosie around almost every time he comes. The kids play, and Mason and I work around the yard, or I take the opportunity to get some housework done inside, while the human hurricane is distracted. Rosie seems to bring Logan an immense amount of happiness. Which is a relief for me because her father seems to be having much the same effect on me.

We have formed a really close friendship over the last few months and these afternoons outside of work have become like a form of therapy.

Every time he does any work for me, I never fail to come through on his request for payment in the form of a cold beer when he is done.

Except since the weather turned cold, we have changed to hot drinks around the outdoor fire. So once he has finished mowing the lawns, Mason starts to gather some kindling to start the fire in Griffins old firepit in the backyard. Rosie and Logan play on the back porch, while I sweep up the last of the garden debris.

"Daddy!! I need to go potty!" I hear Rosie yell from the porch down to her dad who is crouched down next to the fire, blowing into it, trying to get the kindling to ignite.

I chuckle to myself because in that moment, I'm glad it's not just my child that feels the need to announce himself every time he needs to tinkle.

"Hurry Daddy, I'm BUSTING!" She yells as she starts to shuffle back and forth on her feet. Mason comes up from the back yard at a jog, clearly exasperated that the four-year-old waited until the very last minute to tell him she needed to go. In one swift motion, he scoops her up and heads for the back door, disappearing into the house.

A moment later Rosie comes back out, and resumes playing without missing a beat. I hear Mason walk down the steps of the back porch and he pauses as he levels with me as I exit the tool shed beside the house.

"Your bathroom tap is dripping." He says, shooting me a glare with those glacial eyes.

"Yeah, I know, I meant to call a plumber, but – "I look up at him and his mouth is open in shock, he grabs his chest as though I've mortally wounded him.

"Beth, don't you dare insult me by calling someone else, I can fix your leaky taps. I'll get the tools from my truck, and it will be done in ten minutes. You go finish the fire, and I'll be done by the time it's lit… Call a plumber, my ass."

He walks away shaking his head and I turn to hide my small grin. Truthfully, I knew he would fix it, but he has already done so much for me that I hated to ask.

The four of us sit around talking as has become our routine on the afternoons Mason comes around. It's been comforting having a male presence here. I've never been a girl's girl. I'm used to having that masculine energy around me all of the time, so it's been especially comforting having him hang out.

We spend the afternoons just sitting and chatting about work, about parenthood, about life in general.

Mason has told me all about his childhood growing up on a farm just outside of town and how he goes back out there almost every spare moment he has to help his parents who are ageing but can't stand the thought of giving up life on the land just yet.

Mostly though, Mason has supported me through all of the stages of my grief. Never once belittling my feelings or making me feel like I'm being silly or overreacting. Constantly reassuring me that all of my feelings are completely normal and valid. It's been six months now, and I feel like he knows me inside and out.

"Daddy, can I have one more marshmallow, pleeeease? Mama lets me have 3 when I'm at her house, please Daddy?" Rosie is putting on her best puppy dog face and her hands are clenched in front of her dad begging.

Mason clears his throat and shifts his weight in the garden chairs we arranged around the fire. "Yeah Honey girl, I guess that's fine. Just one more."

"I'm sorry, did she just say mama's house? Did I miss a chapter? Mase, is there something you're not telling me?"

Mason shifts in his chair again as though he is suddenly uncomfortable, raising his hand to his jaw and giving his day-old stubble a rough rub.

"Fuck..." He mumbles into his hand. "I wanted to tell you but there was just never a right time. Uh, well, I guess... yeah, um, Hannah and I split up about 3 months ago."

"WHAT IN THE WORLD!? Mason Clarke, you've let me drone on and on about some of the most insignificant problems, all while smiling and nodding, meanwhile you're going through a divorce and didn't think you could mention it? What the hell, man? I thought we were friends?"

I playfully lean over and give him a shove to the upper arm. He knows I'm not actually pissed at him, but in reality, I am a little bit put off by it. I've told him all of my deepest darkest fears and feelings over these last few months so it hurts a little bit that he didn't feel like he could do the same. Typical male, I guess…

"Beth, honestly, I'm fine, she's fine. It's probably the most amicable split in the history of divorces. The writing was on the wall for a long time before we decided to finally call it. We are still very good friends and will remain that way, especially for Rosie. We split everything 50/50, including custody so there has been no bitterness, or arguing. Honestly, I feel… at peace with it all. Theres nothing more to tell, honestly. I'm fine."

"Still, I wish you had've told me. Instead of letting me go on and on about myself. Are you sure you're ok? You guys were together for a while, huh?"

"Yeah, since we were seventeen. So just over twenty years, married for about thirteen of them. I'm okay though, seriously. It was best for everyone. One day, I'll tell you all about it. Maybe over a drink or five, because I refuse to get into my emotions over a cup of cocoa with two kids on a sugar bender hopping around us." He lets out a humorless laugh.

At the mention of kids being hopped up on sugar, he glances at his watch, then gets up from his seat. "Rosie, it's time to go, start packing up, and say goodbye to Logie and Beth please."

While the kids groan in protest and start to pick up their array of toys. Mason looks down at me still planted firmly in my chair, staring blankly into the fire. I actually feel like I'm in a bit of shock at his revelation coming out so casually.

"Hey, now we can be a couple of lonely hearts together, yeah?" He nudges my upper arm with a playful fist and turns to begin helping the kids pack up.

"Hey Mason." I say as I stand from my chair, finally comprehending what he has just told me. I walk over to meet him about halfway across the yard, and I wrap my arms around his neck, pulling him for a friendly hug.

After a few seconds of hesitation, his arms wrap tightly around my waist, and he lets out a deep breath into my neck. I slightly release my grasp, only to hold him at arms length so I can look him in the eyes.

"Thank you for everything you have done for me, even while your world has been completely altered. I'll hold you to that drink, we can have a proper debrief."

He just smiles his trademark wide smile, before huffing out a silent laugh "I'd like that" he says, before turning his baseball cap backwards and bundling up his daughter like she's a football. He holds his fist out for Logan to bump on his way out, "See ya, Pal" Logan pounds it, then Mason ruffles his hair. And then they are gone.

What the fuck just happened... And why did it mess with my emotions so much?

Chapter 3

MASON

I'm so fucked… I've known Beth forever, I had always seen her around town, at my football games when we played against Griffin, and we've worked together for so many years, and have always got along well.

We bonded when she found out Hannah was pregnant at the same time as her, we were both to be first time parents, and our babies were due just a month apart.

Then we bonded even more when we were both trying to work through the 'baby phase' and were both basically walking zombies for a solid year.

She's so incredibly funny and always makes me laugh, even on the worst days. Sometimes when I'm having a bad day or week, I find excuses to go into her office, just so I can see her.

I loved my wife, but things hadn't been right for a while. We had a lot of stressors in our marriage that we definitely didn't handle properly. And somewhere along the way, we simply fell out of love. I feel horrible admitting it, but it felt like such a relief when we finally talked it out and decided that separation was best for all of us.

But now here I am, six months after Beths husband died, feeling like I'm sporting a schoolyard crush on the office girl. I feel like such a dick.

She has told me so many times that she can handle her own yardwork now, she feels like she is using me. But it's quite the opposite. I know she can handle it, shit, this woman would strap up and go to war if she thought she needed to. I'm the selfish prick that just likes spending time with her, but don't really know the protocol about doing that when for one, we are coworkers and oh, did I mention her husband just died?

She has confided so much in me over the last few months, and I don't even know how to navigate this. So, I will just keep mowing her lawns and fixing her dripping taps. And watching the clock of a morning, so I know to make my coffee at exactly 9.05am, because that's when she is usually in the break room making hers. I know, I'm pathetic.

It's early Sunday morning, and Rosie has slept in for the first time in, well, ever. The poor thing didn't even make it the 10-minute drive home before the sugar crash hit her after all of the hot cocoa and marshmallows at Beths yesterday. Add that to the hours of running around that she and Logan did, and I would be surprised if I see her before 8am. She was exhausted.

I get up and make myself a cup of coffee to bask in the extra peace and quiet. I put my phone down on the dining table and head into the kitchen and turn the pot on.

From across the room, I see my phone light up with a text message. I wonder who on earth is messaging me at 7am on a Sunday. When I get to my phone, I can't help but smile.

Beth: Hey Mase, hope you slept well. Not sure what we laced that cocoa with, but Logan is still out like a light, so weird. Anyway, I was thinking about our conversation yesterday. Logan is having a sleepover at my dad's house next Saturday night, I'd love to go for that drink, if you're up for it? Completely understand if you have plans or don't want to. Let me know either way.

I have to rub my eyes and re-read the message about ten times. Am I dreaming? She actually wants to grab a drink? Fuck... How do I say yes without sounding too keen?

I type out at least four different responses and immediately delete them. What the fuck is wrong with me? She's not asking me out on a date. We are friends, she is obviously just trying to return the favor like I've been here for her through her grief and mourning. She's just trying to be here for me.

Yeah, tell that to the fucking butterflies in my stomach and the semi erection I'm now sporting. What am I, fifteen years old?

Coffee. I need coffee, maybe that will make me be able to form a sentence like an almost 40-year-old man.

Mason: Mornin'.. Is it kind of depressing that even though they sleep in, we are still awake at the ass crack of dawn? Sure, a drink sounds good, I'll be out at the farm most of the day, does 7pm work for you? Did you have anywhere in mind?

Theres only two bars in town, O'Reilly's, which is a bit of a dive. Or Just in Thyme, which will no doubt be crowded as all hell because it's become such a hotspot since it opened about a year ago. It will probably be impossible to get a table with less than a weeks' notice. But if that's what she wants, I'll do my best to make it happen for her.

Beth: 7pm is fine, I have all night, so no rush. You ok with Just in Thyme? They have the most amazing cocktails there. They are all themed like everyone's favorite childhood characters.

Mason: So I've heard, I haven't been able to check it out yet. It's always so hard to get a table there. I'll give them a call when they open and try and book us in?

Beth: Leave it with me, I know the owner and he owes me a favor or two. Enjoy what's left of your peace and quiet!

* * * * * * * *

Six. That's the number of times I've changed my shirt. And after all that, I've settled for a plain black button up. I changed from my ratty farm jeans into my nice wranglers. I live in jeans, there was never a question of what pants I'd wear but I just can't decide on a shirt.

Why am I even putting so much pressure on myself? It's just a drink with a friend. I am riddled with nerves, and I shouldn't be. This is no different than us chatting while I'm at her house or at work. I just need to keep telling myself that.

I thought I was getting over this silly crush, but then she hugged me goodbye last weekend and I haven't stopped thinking about her touch, the smell of her shampoo. Ugh, I truly am pathetic.

We agreed to meet at the restaurant at seven, but I'm so nervous I can't sit around home watching the clock, so I decide to head in a bit early. I sent Beth a text to see if she had eaten and she hadn't so now it's dinner and drinks. Glad I didn't know that too far in advance, so I didn't have time to stress on that.

I arrive at Just in Thyme a little after 6.30pm and the hostess tells me our table isn't ready yet. Beth pulled off a miracle being able to get us a reservation here, it's usually booked out at least a month in advance, which is massive for a town this size. I'm told I can wait at the bar and honestly, thank God. I'll order a Beer and hopefully have my nerves calmed a bit by the time Beth arrives.

The bar area is separate from the main dining area. It gives the venue flexibility to have a rowdy club environment while also maintaining a classy dining venue as well. It's the best of both worlds.

"Hey buddy, what can I get for you?" The burly bartender approaches me. I'm tall, about 6'2. But he is slightly taller, probably 6'4. He's built like a tank too and gives off that nightclub bouncer vibe.

I can see why this place never seems to have any trouble, no man alive would be game to stir anything up with this mountain of a man in their presence.

"Uh, just a beer please" I say. He puts it down on the bar counter in front of me. And I can feel him lingering, looking at me.

"Let me guess, first date nerves?" He says as he points at me with a single finger gun.

"Uh, not exactly, no. Just dinner with a… friend." I reply, but he must catch the slight hesitation at labelling our relationship.

"Oooh, but you want it to be a date?" Who is this guy, Dr Phil? He is staring at me waiting for my reply.

Thank God for small mercies, because before I start bumbling to come up with an answer, a waitress taps me on the shoulder to let me know the table is ready. Just as she leads me through to the dining area, I lock eyes across the room with Beth.

She looks absolutely stunning, and I swear the world feels like it's moving in slow motion. I take her in as she walks toward me. Her long, dark brown hair falls past her shoulders, it's rare to see her with her hair down, it's usually tied up out of her face, but tonight it's down in gentle waves, The way it frames her face so perfectly has me swallowing down, hard.

 She's rugged up against the cold weather in a thick red coat, that falls just above her knees, and she's paired it with tights and boots with a slight heel. She is on the tall side too, probably 5'9.

As she shucks her coat off, she's wearing a simple white long sleeve shirt and a tight leather look skirt that falls mid-thigh. I don't think I've ever realized just how long her legs are, but this outfit.... Damn, it hugs every perfect curve and highlights every gorgeous inch of her body.

She finally makes it to stand in front of me, I slightly shake my head, waking me from my daydream and while I can't be certain, I hope I didn't just stand here in front of her with my mouth agape.

"Hi, look at you, almost didn't recognize you, not covered in dust or grass. You scrub up good!" She says, as she leans in and gives me a gentle peck on the cheek.

I know it's friendly, but my ENTIRE body reacts to it. The way it rolled off her tongue so naturally. I hold her chair out for her, because I was raised right, and she peers back at me over her shoulder with a smile. I offer to get her a drink and when she decides which one she wants I head back out to the bar.

The bartender smirks as he sees me approaching. "Your lady friend made it, huh? Dude, take a few breaths, you're radiating nervous energy, I could feel you coming from the other room. She must be someone special huh?"

"Yeah, something like that... I'll just get a lime and Soda, and I'll get a Mad Hatter cocktail for my... Friend"

"Coming right up. I can bring them to your table if you like?"

"No, no that's ok, I can wait... Apparently I could use a minute to take a few breaths." I say with a smile and a slight chuckle.

When I return to the table with our drinks, the waitress approaches and takes our order for food. Beth flashes me a smile and I ask how her week at work was.

I didn't see her much at all this week, I was mostly out on job sites, we are super busy at the moment, so I haven't had a lot of spare time to stop in and see her.

"Nuh uh uh... We aren't talking about me tonight. Not for a second. C'mon Mister, tonight is all about you."

"Damn, I should've known this night was a trap. Okay, well my week was good. We finished up the old church project. And started demolition on the Nixon house. So overall, pretty productive. Am I really not allowed to even ask how you are?" I smile as I take a sip of my drink.

"My week was fine. Thank you for asking. Seriously though. I'm a little hurt you didn't feel like you could tell me about your separation. Are you sure you're okay?"

"Yeah, I mean. I've taken some time to process it. Honestly, we had been having some problems for a while. But I'm ultimately really proud of how we handled it all. I think we both just knew we had fallen out of love. There was no bitterness. Our marriage was just a victim of circumstance, I guess."

"That can't have been an easy conclusion to come to. Or an easy conversation to have. It's such a big part of your life to lose. Over two decades."

"No, it wasn't easy. But that doesn't mean it wasn't the right decision." I drop my gaze to the table. I take a sip of my drink to choke back the emotions I can feel creeping up my throat.

How does this girl have this kind of effect on me? I haven't felt the least bit upset about my split this whole time, but now, spilling my problems to the woman who had the love of her life taken from her way too soon?

That's what gets me choked up. Maybe it's guilt, feeling like I maybe didn't fight hard enough for what she would probably kill to have back.

"Mase, you know there's absolutely zero judgement at this table, right? I can tell you're not as fine as you say you are. Look, I'm not going to push you into talking about it. Trust me, I know how shitty it is to have everyone constantly in your face asking if you're okay and expecting you not to be. But I do want you to know that if or when you are ready to talk about it, you can come to me. I know you men like to think there's some unwritten rule about not talking about your feelings, but I want you to know that rule doesn't apply when it comes to me and you okay?"

She has the most sincere look on her face. She reaches across the table and rests her hand on top of mine which has been mindlessly, and probably nervously playing with a napkin since I sat down. She lingers there as her thumb rubs gentle strokes against the back of my hand.

At that moment, I hope I've bought her even a fraction of this level of comfort over the last few months. I give her a gentle smile.

"Okay… I'll talk, but I hope you know what you're asking for, it's a lot."

She pulls her hand away abruptly just as someone approaches our table with our food. Because *timing…*

"Heyyyy. I heard we had a VIP in the house tonight! Had to come and check it out for myself. Hope I'm not interrupting. What's up, Beth? Haven't seen you around in a minute."

She stands and hugs him in greeting, this is obviously the guy she called in a favor with to get us the table on such short notice.

"Zee! Oh my God. Yes, as usual, you are absolutely interrupting, but you're 100% forgiven. It's so good to see you." She gives him another quick hug and I don't know why, I have no right, but a massive rush of jealousy washes over me, who is this guy?

Right on cue, she turns to me with a smile to introduce us. "Zee, this is my good friend Mason. Mase, this is my brother's best friend and co-owner of this place, Zealand West."

He reaches out to shake my hand and fuck me, there must be something in the water in this place because he is another big dude, just like the bartender.

"Hey man, nice to meet you. Thanks for getting us in here at such short notice. It's a really nice place, you've done a really good job here."

"Thanks man, I really appreciate it. It's a real dream come true. Anyway, I've gotta get back to the kitchen. Have a good night kids." He shoots us a wink and walks back to the kitchen stopping at almost every second table to accept compliments from the other patrons.

I can see what everyone raves about. This place really is amazing, such a welcoming environment.

"Sorry about that, anyway, where were we?" She takes her seat back across from me and picks up her knife and fork to start eating. And I start talking.

I spend the best part of the next hour telling her everything about my marriage breakdown. I don't leave a single detail out.

I tell her all about how we went through years of fertility struggles, both before and after having Rosie. I tell her how we had several miscarriages, which we didn't handle well, and drove us apart instead of bringing us together. I tell her how we both gave everything we had into a fight to get what we knew we wanted, but somewhere along that line, we forgot to look after each other. And we just fell out of love.

I tell her that the separation conversation came because Hannah shoulders a lot of the guilt of not being able to give me any more kids, and she felt like for me that should be a deal breaker. In a way she decided for us. But there's no blame, if the shoe was on the other foot, I know I would feel the same.

By the time I'm done talking, we have finished our dinner, had dessert, Beth had another cocktail, I had another beer, and we have finally moved onto a lighter conversation. I feel lighter getting everything off my chest and knowing I don't have any secrets from Beth anymore.

Well, except for the fact that I feel even more attracted to her now.

We just about close the place down. I can feel the wait staff trying to give us the move along, so we finally decide to call it a night. Beth excuses herself to use the bathroom, and I head to the bar to fix up the tab, and see the guy from earlier, Zealand and the big bartender having a laugh behind the bar.

"Ah, here's the lover boy. You look heaps more relaxed now big guy, everything turned out okay then?" I hear Zealand let out a quiet chuckle behind him. I'm not sure what that is about but I'm glad my personal suffering has kept someone entertained tonight.

I thank them both for their hospitality and turn to find Beth back in the dining area. I only had two beers, so I offer to drive her home. It's late and freezing cold out.

As soon as we walk out the doors of the restaurant, the cold air hits us both, so we walk as quickly as we can across the parking lot. As we get to my truck, I crank the heat and within seconds, the condensation from our breath disappears.

The drive back to Beths house is only about ten minutes from the restaurant, and it goes so quick it feels like about two.

It's almost midnight, but I don't want this night to end. I can't believe how nervous I was a few hours ago. When this, here and now, feels so easy, so natural.

I pull up out the front of Beths house, she removes her seatbelt, and I jump out and round the car to open her door for her. I know it feels a little bit like a romantic gesture but fuck it. This whole night has started to feel like a date. Or at least something that could lead to a date eventually.

"I had a really nice night, Mason. Thank you so much for opening up to me. And I'm glad we could end the night with a few good laughs. I know you said we could be a couple of lonely hearts together. But, after tonight, my heart feels a lot less lonely. Thanks to you."

She hops down from my truck and starts to walk up the path to her front door.

As she passes by me, I grab her by the elbow and pull her into me. Her hands wrap straight around my waist, her head falling into my chest. One of my arms wraps around her shoulders and the other hand cups the back of her head.

I take a big breath in, like I'm trying to memorize the smell of her, or the feel of her in my arms. I lay a light kiss on the top of her head, hoping I'm not overstepping any boundaries.

"Thank you for tonight. I needed it probably more than I realized." She pulls away, looks up at me with a smile. "Goodnight Mase. I'll see you Monday."

CHAPTER 4

BETH

I slept like a baby last night, I had such a good night and came home feeling so at ease and honestly, the happiest I've felt in a long time.

Unfortunately, I'm woken up by my phone pinging like mad beside me. I open it up to see it's my sibling group chat. This should be good.

Nate: So…. Mason, huh?

Will: Did you stay for drinks after work last night, bro? you still drunk? Who's Mason?

Nate: No, no, I'm not drunk… but one of the Phillips Four was a little bit last night. Beth... care to chime in, or should I continue?

Bella: Oh, I have no idea what's going on but I'm invested.

Will: Makes two of us. Beth, wake the fuck up.

Nate: I'll give her 2 minutes to enter the chat or I'm spilling.

Will: Fuck it, spill now, we can compare stories when Beth surfaces.

Bella: Beth I'm sorry, but I gotta side with the boys here. Please forgive me.

Beth: I knew I should've risked my life by going to O'Reillys. But no, stupid me had to be loyal to the family business.

Bella: Don't avoid the question, Beth. Who's Mason? He sounds hot.

Will: Spill it, Beth.

Nate: Oh, he was definitely a good-looking dude. I'm straight enough to admit it. But that's not the best part...

Bella: Do you people not know how to tell a story?! Someone better start talking right now!

Beth: You absolute pack of morons, I had dinner and a couple of drinks with a FRIEND. Theres nothing to tell.

Nate: Ok, well thanks for half of the story... But Zee told me he walked up and saw you stroking his hand. How very scandalous of you Beth...

Will: That's it? I got this excited because my sister touched a man's hand? Are we 5? Did you get your cooties shot afterwards Beth?

Beth: Thank you. At least you're old enough to agree, it is NOTHING. Mason is a friend, he has been there a lot for me over the last 6 months and now he is having a hard time, so I just wanted to repay the favor.

Bella: Aww. Still so worth it to me. I hope you had the best night out xo

Nate: Now entering: The town of Denial, population: Elizabeth.

Beth: Oh, you wanna full name me, Nathaniel? You wait until I see that little gossip Zealand again. Theres a reason I steered clear of your bar room last night, and this is exhibit A. Unless one of you Dipshits want to bring me a coffee, I'm going back to my sleep in before I have to pick up Logan. Go live your own lives children.

Will: Can't wait for dinner Friday night, Beth. I wonder how long it will take for dad to find out you held a boys hand?

****

Friday nights have been a highlight of my week for as long as I can remember. My dad dubs them 'Philips Fridays' and it's been a tradition pretty much ever since we all started leaving home.

We all gather back at dads, which is our childhood home. The typical country house, an expansive open living room, a huge open plan kitchen and dining, with a massive dining table that my grandfather made when my parents moved in here after they first got married.

He said he knew one day there would be a handful of kids here and wanted to make it big enough that we could eat around this table all our lives. So, the table would comfortably seat about twelve adults.

Some might think it's overkill, but dad is still convinced one day, it will be full.

This house holds so many memories, early childhood memories of when it was just Will and I, we are only two years apart, so we were either best friends or mortal enemies, there was no in between.

Then a few years later when the twins were born, the table finally felt like it was filling up.

I remember our dad sitting Will and I down and sitting across from us, telling us our mother had left. It was one of the few times I've ever seen him cry. I remember the first time I bought Griffin around. I remember the first time Nate bought Olive here, and the array of girls Will has graced us with over the years. I remember everyone sitting around the table when I told them all I was pregnant with Logan.

I remember much the same formation when we told them of Griffins diagnosis. And it was where we all sat in silence in the wake of his passing.

Who knew a piece of furniture could hold so much emotion.

Fridays are usually my late day at work, while everyone else at work finishes early, I like to stay back and finish up any loose ends that have carried over from the week. I get so much more work done when I'm alone and the office is quiet. So on fridays, Will picks Logan up from preschool.

Will has spent the last fifteen years in the Army, with multiple deployments to the Middle East. He returned from his final deployment just before Griffin died and has been spending his time mentoring and caring for other veterans who are injured or disabled.

Eventually, he wants to set up his own care service providing all kinds of supports for our returned Vets, but for now, he is only working part time while he readjusts to small town, country life. And thoroughly enjoying his uncle duties.

Will always plans something fun for their Friday afternoon boys day. He takes Logan to the park, or the bowling alley, out for ice cream. Whatever it takes to outdo Nate in the favorite uncle stakes. Griffin was an only child, so my brothers have always fiercely competed for the number one uncle.

By tradition, a Philips Friday means everyone dresses super comfy. I'm talking pajamas, slippers, sweaters, whatever requires the least amount of effort. We come together, eat whatever feast my dad comes up with, and then settle in for a game of cards or a board game.

We used to play Monopoly every week, but we gave that up when we decided that Olive must be cheating as she was unbeatable. Most times now we opt for cards and I'm sure we have invented several of our own games.

This Friday night is pizza night. When I walk in, it looks like a bomb has gone off in the kitchen. There is flour absolutely everywhere, I'm not sure what these boys were doing to get it on the roof, but they managed it. It's times like this I wish I was here to cook.

The fact that my dad cooks, and Will watches Logan, means Nate and I are on clean up duties, and Nate usually dips early to go to work for the night.

Owning a restaurant means Friday night is one of his busiest nights, but he still makes time for Philips Fridays.

I'm the last one to arrive, which is not unusual, Logan runs to the door and launches himself into my arms, covering my front in flour. Thank God I haven't had time to change yet.

I scoop him up in a cuddle, before propping him on my hip and heading to the kitchen, I give my dad a kiss on the cheek, scrape my finger through his homemade pizza sauce and lick it off, moaning as the flavors hit my tastebuds.

I worked through lunch today so I'm absolutely starving. Will slaps the back of my hand and tells me to wait like everyone else has to.

I head to the back patio and find Olive and Nate sitting on the love seat, beside dads' outdoor fireplace. It's so cozy out there on a winter's night, I decide I'll get changed first and then join them for a while until dinner is ready.

Walking out the back door, I take a seat opposite Nate and Olive. They are so good together, polar opposites in the looks department, where Nate is well over 6 foot tall and looks like he's bulking for a body building competition. Olive is one of the most petite women I've ever met. She's about 5 foot 3, with almost white blonde hair. He looks like he could throw her across the room with no effort. They have been dating for about three years, and I know Nate is keen to propose to her sometime in the not-so-distant future.

"Were your ears burning or something? We were just talking about you." Nate says with a shit eating grin on his face. "Nate, don't..." Olive nudges him in the side, he's obviously up to something.

"It's ok, Ol. I've been expecting his grilling all week. Surprised he is doing it out here in private, not in front of dad and Will so everyone can pile on, so I'll take the little victory, I guess. C'mon, lay it on me, little brother"

I raise my eyebrows, giving him a challenging look. Lowkey hoping it would be some kind of reverse psychology. Like if he thinks I'm coming into this prepared for him, he might get scared off and not want to fight me.

A girl can hope.

Nate takes a long pause. He is really seriously considering his words. I don't think I've ever seen my outgoing, outspoken, little brother lost for words before.

Wait, is this actually going to be a serious conversation? I was prepared to cop more smart-ass comments like I did on Sunday morning. But he looks like whatever he has to say is causing him physical pain. Maybe he is just constipated. That must be it.

Nate doesn't do serious, it's why he and Griffin got along so well.

"Beth, I don't even know what I want to say exactly. I know it's not my place to say anything at all. I'm just your comedic, handsome little brother" Olive smacks him in the side harder this time.

"Ow, save something for later, baby." He says flicking Olive a wink, she blushes and lets out a little giggle. I screw my nose up and look between the two of them.

"Ew. Never thought I'd ask you to carry on speaking when you were clearly just stroking your own ego, but please, go on..."

"Right. Well, I just thought I'd tell you my side of the story from last weekend, in case you didn't know." He adjusts himself in his seat, leaning forward with a look of sincerity on his face, he meets my gaze across the fire.

"I know you said you're just friends with Mason and that's really amazing, I'm glad you're getting out of the house and having a social life. But Beth, the guy has feelings for you. And I just thought you should know because obviously, you've had a tough couple of years, and I didn't want you to be in any awkward positions. Especially when you work with the guy. I don't want your life to be any harder than it's already been."

"Did he... tell you he has feelings for me?" I thought I would hate this conversation, but now I'm interested to hear my brother out.

"No, he didn't. But he didn't have to. Trust me Beth, I've been working in bars and restaurants for six years, I've seen a lot of people come through with the first date jitters. And the guy was dripping in them. And then later in the night when you two were still in the dining room chatting, and laughing, Zealand came out and told me he could see sparks flying between the two of you. It wasn't until Mason came to pay the tab and left that Zealand told me that he was who you were there with. I hadn't put two and two together that you would be there with 'Lover boy' as I had dubbed him. Zee thought that was hilarious when I found out he was with you, by the way."

"Nate, I appreciate your concern. But Mason and I are just good friends. I'll be really honest here and say this, I do feel a connection with him. And if or when I'm ready to explore that, then that's up to me and him to decide. He has just separated from his wife, and you obviously know my situation. So this 'thing' is the very definition of complicated. For now, I'm enjoying his company. But thank you for handling this like an adult, not just throwing me under the bus in front of everyone. Especially Logan. He has become really good friends with Masons daughter, Rosie. So, we have even more to be careful about than just our own feelings."

"Wait, THE Rosie is Masons daughter? Beth, that little Casanova in there hasn't stopped talking our ears off all night,

Rosie this, and Rosie that… Will was about to start taking notes from the kid, he seems to have so much game when it comes to this girl. They already have a whole imaginary family, kids and all, he's got it made."

I giggle at my brothers for being jealous of my four-year-olds imaginary family dynamic. "Yeah, that's my boy." My smile drops and I chew the inside of my cheek.

"Look Nate, You guys have all been an amazing support network for me, you know this. But this isn't just about me. Mason and I are both new to this single parenting thing, having someone who knows what that's like has been so good for all of us. So yeah, I do feel a connection with him. But it also feels too soon after Griffin for me to even be thinking about the possibility of moving on. My emotional scars are so raw. And so are Masons. So, we will just take things day by day and if that leads somewhere, someday down the road, then I guess that was meant to be. But in the meantime, I need friendship, and good company. And he gives me that."

"Okay, yeah, I understand. Well, while you're just hanging out, can you keep bringing him to my bar because I really enjoyed riling him up. If I had've known it was you he was there with I could've really had some fun." I hear Olive scoff from beside him. She is so small I almost forgot she was there, she is pretty much eclipsed by Nates big frame.

I stand from my seat, ready to go inside and see the rest of my family, but Nate stops me at the door.

"You know we just want you to be happy Beth. No one deserves complete and utter happiness more than you."

Is this guy having a stroke? It's the only explanation for him saying nice things to me.

Tears start to well in the corners of my eyes, but before they can fall, I tip my head back to stop them.

"Ughhh, enough of this soppy love fest, get inside so I can kick your ass at Poker... or is Go Fish more your level?"

Chapter 5

MASON

Its Saturday afternoon, and today is the day that I would usually go to Beths, but it's pouring rain out, so if I showed up there today it would be pretty darn obvious I was there for more than the lawns.

I'm going stir crazy in the house, and trying to keep Rosie entertained is a full-time job. We have already had three separate tea parties, finger painted for an hour, played fairy dress-ups and she had me pretend to be her husband while she acted out going on a shopping spree. This kids sense of imagination never fails to amaze me.

It's only lunch time and I'm quickly running out of ideas to keep her occupied. I head to the kitchen to start making us some sandwiches for lunch.

I'm buttering the bread when my phone chirps with a message.

Beth: Hey, are you being driven as insane as I am? How do their teachers do this with 10 times as many kids every day? My house looks like Jurassic Park threw up in here. I didn't even know my kid had this many dinosaurs.

Mason: I've never felt as relieved as I do now, hearing you say that. Rosie has already had me dressed up as a fairy princess, and I can't drink anymore pretend tea. I fear next she will want to paint my fingernails, and that just won't go over well on the job site on Monday. Send help!

Beth: I'm sorry, I can't help right now, too busy laughing at the thought of you dressed up as a fairy princess.

Mason: I thought I could trust you.

Beth: I'm really sorry. I actually do have a very important question to ask you though.

Mason: Shoot.

Beth: What color were your fairy wings? *laughing face emoji*

I put my phone down and return to making our lunch. I can't wipe the smile off my face. Only a week ago, this woman was making me so nervous that I felt like I could vomit and now here we are texting back and forth like it's the easiest thing in the world… maybe even a little bit, flirtatious?

Beth: Okay, I'm sorry. I've stopped laughing now. I was thinking of setting up a movie afternoon for Logan soon. Was thinking of making a bit of a blanket fort, but then I thought... I might need a contractor for that. Do you happen to know where I could find a good one of those on this short notice?

Mason: Woman, you wound me. You really just woke up today and chose violence, huh?

Beth: Rub some fairy dust in it, it will heal in no time. I'm kidding. But if you want to bring Rosie over to chill out in this second rate, DIY blanket fort, you're more than welcome. I have more than enough popcorn to go around.

Mason: If you promise to drop the fairy talk, we would love to come. We are just having some lunch and then we will head over. Thanks for the invite.

Am I crazy to think she was missing the routine as much as I was?

My hands feel clammy and all of a sudden, the nerves have crept back in. I've never known a woman to have this kind of effect on me.

I tell Rosie that we are going to go to Beth and Logans house as soon as she is finished her lunch, it makes me smile that she is as excited as I am. She hoovers her sandwich down in record time.

I head into the bathroom to make sure I have zero traces of glitter on my body. As much as I love to see Beth smile, I don't need her laughing AT me.

We arrive at Beths about an hour later. Of course, Rosie had to pick a different Princess dress than the one she has been wearing all day. Most days with Rosie require at least three costume changes.

"There's my favorite fairy princess! Oh, and Rosies here too!" Beth exclaims as she opens the door, she bends down to give Rosie a hug, but when she looks back up at me, she can't contain her laughter anymore.

Dammit, if she wasn't so goddamn beautiful when she laughs, I'd be annoyed at her for that comment.

"I'm going to regret telling you that for years to come, aren't I?" I walk past her shaking my head, but I can't hide my smile.

I help Beth finish building the best blanket fort these kids have ever seen, I pour the kids each a cup of juice and a bowl of popcorn fresh from the microwave, while Beth sets up the TV for the kids.

Beth and I sit side by side on the couch, and of course, we can't see the TV past the extravagant fort that takes up most of the living room, but it doesn't matter. It's a kids movie we have both seen approximately a million times anyway, and I'd much rather sit here and chat to her all afternoon.

"So, we seem to have become the victims of some of the small-town gossip that goes on around here." Beth says, she has opted for black leggings, with a comfy oversized pink sweater, and thick woolly socks, she sits with her legs tucked up underneath her, and she looks so cozy and comfortable. I just want to wrap my arms around her and hold her here all afternoon.

Down boy, control yourself before you have a problem.

"Oh? How so?" I say raising an eyebrow at her.

Small town gossip always gives me a good laugh because 90% of it is utterly ridiculous.

"My friend Zee, from Just in Thyme the other night? He co-owns the restaurant with Nate, my youngest brother… Who happens to be the bartender who apparently had to give you a pep talk of sorts?"

That cheeky smile of hers is back but she's looking at me cautiously, like she isn't sure if she should've said that out loud.

"I'll admit, I had some nerves about us meeting up. We haven't really spent any time just the two of us, outside of work and kids. I wasn't sure how things would go, and yes, I wanted things to go well... Of course, if I'd known that was your brother, I might've tried to be a little more discreet, or just gone thirsty all night"

I chuckle, mostly because I feel a bit embarrassed and I'm not sure how much her brother might've told her.

"It's okay, I was only mad that the little smart ass felt like he needed to blow up our sibling group chat so early the next morning, ruining my child free sleep in. I swear he is a vampire that never sleeps. So then my other two siblings had to get in on shit talking me as well. They really thought they were all clever."

I smile at the chance to get to know a bit more about her. The Philips Four are a bit of a local legend around here. Everyone knows at least some of them in some way. "You sound like you have a really close relationship with your siblings."

"Yeah, I mean, we were kind of bonded in a way that no kids should be. Our mother had some health issues and up and left us just before my 12th birthday, so I pretty much had to step up and help my dad raise them, particularly Nate and Bella who are almost ten years younger than me, they were still just babies when she left." I watch her face sink as she recalls her childhood trauma.

"Beth, that's some heavy stuff, I can't imagine having your childhood taken away so suddenly like that. No wonder you're all so close, and your dad too, that must've destroyed him." She nods her head silently.

"It was really hard for everyone. I don't think any of us came out completely unscathed. My dad has never been interested in finding love again, even though he admits the loneliness gets to him. Nate and Bella have both had their struggles with abandonment. I think Will is the only one that's using the whole situation to try and change the world. Building on that and his experience in the Army to change peoples lives on the other side."

Far out. You hear so many stories about the Philips family around town. How happy they all are, how close they all are. It's easy to see why. I look at Beth and although there is a sadness in her eyes, the corners of her mouth are slightly tipped up, like she is proud of how far her siblings have come from such rough times. "And you?"

"I think it's made me a better mother, I remember enough of my mothers' good days to see how she was with us when she was good. I just have some rough days, that make me angry with the world.

"Something I really struggled with, was at Griffins Funeral I heard one of Griffins Uncles tell Logan that he is the man of the house now. I know it was just a passing comment, he probably didn't know what else to say to the little boy who just lost his dad, but something in me snapped, it was lucky that my other brother was beside me and heard it as well, because I saw red.

"No kid should have to step into their parents shoes, ever. I had no choice, there were three kids younger than me that needed caring for. But I won't let that happen for Logan. He will keep his childhood if it's the last thing I do."

Damn, She's pretty when she's feisty. At this point it's safe to say, I like her in every way.

"Ugh, anyway, again with the emotions." She swats away at the tears forming, "What about you, do you have any annoying siblings?"

"Just a sister, Leah, but we aren't that close. We used to be, but she wasn't cut out for farm life, so as soon as she was old enough to move out, she moved to the city and we really only see her around the holidays now."

Beth reaches out and grabs my hand that's resting on my knee. She strokes her thumb across my knuckles, similar to the way she did at the restaurant the other night.

My breath hitches at her touch. Gently I curl my thumb around her hand, this feels intimate. I'm mindful of freaking her out because I have no idea how she feels about this, or me.

Fuck, I know we need to talk about it. But I don't even know how to approach that. And with our kids right in front of us isn't the right time.

Right on cue, there's movement in the fort. The popcorn has run out which means, we have mere seconds left until the four-year-old monsters are bored. Beth removes her hand before their inquisitive minds bust out on us and ask questions.

I never know how much a four-year-old might understand, but given that I'm not even ready to have a conversation with Beth yet, I can't have that conversation with a four-year-old.

The movie finishes so we help Beth pack up the blankets and pillows and head home. I have a lot of new proposals to do this week, so I will be seeing Beth a lot around the workshop, and nothing has made me more excited to go to work.

❋❋❋❋❋❋❋❋❋❋❋

49

Its Friday night and I've dropped Rosie back to Hannahs, I'm looking forward to a decent sleep tonight. I think Rosie might be going through something because she won't sleep in her own bed, which means I've spent the last week with four-year-old feet in my ribs, hips and back.

I'm awoken by the sound of my phone ringing. I open my eyes and realize it's still dark. I pick up my phone and through bleary eyes, look at the time; 2:07am. Then the name of the caller catches my eye. *Beth*

I clear my throat, willing away the sleepiness "Hello?"

"Oh god, I'm so sorry to wake you. I was honestly hoping to get your voicemail." I let out a chuckle. Only she would call in the middle of the night and not want me to pick up.

I hear her hiccup on the other end of the line. "Beth, are you okay?"

"I'm fiiiine." She drags out the middle of the word, adding about three syllables to a four-letter word.

"Yeah, you sound just great."

"Whiskey is disgusting. Did you know that?" another hiccup escapes.

"I did know that. It's certainly not my drink of choice. Did you have some Whiskey tonight?"

"Shhh. My dad is in the guest room, he might hear you." She lowers her voice to a whisper, Damn, she is hammered.

"Beth, I don't think it's me you have to worry about. Are you okay?" I rub my hand along my jaw.

"My idiot brothers bought a bottle around, and they said they could drink more than me, but I said they were liars. I drank them under the table easy."

"Sure sounds like you did. Let's see how victorious you feel in the morning, huh?"

"It's after midnight, it is morning already." I sense as the tone in her voice changes. It's hard to say over the phone, while Beth is clearly intoxicated, but I think I detect a little bit of disappointment, maybe?

"Beth, is everything okay?" She doesn't answer me for a minute, I know she is still there because I can hear her breathing. After a moment she sniffles into the phone. Is she crying?

"Beth, what's going on?"

"It's nothing, really. It's just… Well, it's now officially my birthday and I guess, I was just feeling a bit lonely. I shouldn't have called. I'm sorry, it was stupid. I just had such a nice day with you and Rosie on Saturday, and then the night with my brothers here got out of hand and I'm a chatty drunk and then I had to come upstairs to an empty bed for the first time on my birthday and I just…. "

"Beth, stop talking. Do you want me to come over?" Another hiccup.

"No, no. That's okay. My dad is here, I'll be okay, I just needed to talk for a minute. Thank you for listening."

I huff out a bit of a laugh. "Anytime. Now try and get some sleep, but maybe chug some water first." I hear the tone in her voice pick up again and I know she is back to smiling, even just for a second.

"Goodnight, Mase."

"Goodnight, Beth. And hey, Happy Birthday."

Chapter 6

It's only Wednesday, but this already feels like the longest week in history. We are so busy at work, I feel like I haven't had a spare moment to breathe.

A lot of my job is data entry, which can be mind numbing at times, so I'm always happy when one of the guys come in with any purchase requests or even needing to talk to Abi about payroll requests or anything. It's like a little brain break, and we love hearing about what's going on, on the front lines of the company, outside of our four walls.

We have a really good team here and everyone gets along and loves to have a laugh. Of course, lately there is one particular contractor that I enjoy seeing more than the others, but being the lead contractor, Mason also has a team of other people he can delegate tasks to when he needs.

Thankfully, today is not one of those days. He has just received the approval for two more large projects, so he will need to spend some time with me so we can work out what materials we need to order in.

He walks in with his clipboard tucked under his arm, carrying two cups of coffee. It takes a minute for my eyes to adjust and realize he's carrying my coffee mug. I left it on the sink to drain this morning, so he obviously saw it and filled it up for me.

"Thought you might need that to get through this next little bit." He says and this mother fucker winks at me. He pulls up a chair to my desk, spins it around and straddles it backwards, so his legs are spread wide either side of the back of the chair.

He sits so close beside me that his knee is slightly brushing up against my thigh. He has been in his office all morning, So I can smell his cologne, but also the faint smell of freshly cut timber. The man is always covered in sawdust.

"Beth, are you all good?" I hear him say

Huh, what? Oh my god, I totally blanked out.

"I'm sorry, I spaced out there for a minute." I say as I glance down at where our legs are touching. I like the feeling of being this close. It feels comfortable, but man, it caught me off guard. Both the contact and how much I like it.

Mason lowers his voice to a whisper "Do you want me to move?" I look up at him to hold his gaze for a moment before shaking my head.

"I'm all good, let's get this done."

We sit like that talking for about an hour and once we are both positive we have all our procurements sorted, he reaches across me to borrow a pen, even though there is a perfectly good pencil tucked behind his ear.

I'm beginning to think he is just finding excuses to be close to me. I wouldn't put it past him, especially if Nate is right and he does have feelings for me. This certainly feels like he is stalling, trying to soak up every second of being nearby.

He signs off on the ordering section of his checklists, before thanking me for my help, saying goodbye to Abi, and leaving. I finally let out a deep exhale.

"What in the ever-loving fuck, was all of that?" Abi says from behind the partition that separates our desks. She stands to peer over at me.

"What was what?" I play dumb, trying to avoid the question, because I don't even know how to answer that.

"Oh excuse me, but next time Mason Clarke walks into this office, I'm going to go and borrow a welding helmet to shield me from all of the sparks going on between you two. Care to share?" She is looking at me with doe eyes, she's such a hopeless romantic.

Wait, did she just say sparks? Has she been talking to my brother and Zee?

"I don't know what you're talking about Abi." I say while rolling my eyes, but I have to hide my smile, which is so wide it's actually hurting my face.

Yeah yeah, I know, Denial, population = Me.

****

The next morning, I pull into the carpark at work, and I notice Mason's truck isn't here. I guess it's not unusual, a lot of the times he is already on the job site by the time I make it to the office. Although he had said he was going to be at the office all week and truthfully, I have been enjoying seeing him around the place every day.

I figure something must've come up at one of the current job sites and I can't question his absence now that Abi thinks she is onto something. So I go and make my morning coffee, and settle into my desk to start my day.

When I go to clock out for my lunch break, I see his name on the staff board, and noticed he never clocked in for the day. So, I decide to check in and make sure everything is okay.

Beth: Hey, missed you at the coffee pot this morning, everything okay?

Mason: Hi, just caught Rosies stomach bug that she had earlier this week, So I'm basically dying. *laughing emoji* *Vomit emoji*

Beth: Oh no, you poor thing. I'm on my lunch break now, can I bring you anything?

Mason: No I'm good thanks. Just the thought of food makes my stomach feel like it's twisting. Besides, I don't want to expose you to this, it's awful.

Beth: If a four-year-old can survive, then so can you. Rest up, please let me know if you need anything. Is Rosie with you this week?

Mason: She was, but when I started to feel sick, Hannah came and got her, she was supposed to go back to Hannahs tomorrow anyway, so it's fine. Hopefully I can just sleep this off.

Beth: Not gonna lie, a whole day in bed sounds pretty good. Minus the vomiting, of course. Enjoy your sleep, I'll check in with you later. xo

Shit, was the xo a bit much? Too late now it's sent. Oh god, what have I done. I'm such an idiot.

I can't concentrate for most of the day, I don't know why Mason has consumed so many of my thoughts. It's just a stomach bug, it will probably be over in twenty-four hours. But I just want so desperately to be there for him. To help in any way I can. Hell, I even want to risk my own wellbeing to just sit with him for a while and comfort him. Maybe rub his back or scratch his head. I know that makes me feel better when I'm not well.

What is this man doing to me? Surely it's too soon for me to be having these feelings for another man? Am I just attracted because of all of the good things he has done for me? That must be it, surely. A hero complex, that explains it.

The minute I finish work, I get to my car, and I hover my fingers over the keyboard, wanting to type out a message to see how Mason is going. But I also need to pick Logan up, and then the evenings are usually hectic by the time we do dinner, bath, book and bedtime.

I decide I will pick Logan up, treat us to some takeout for dinner, to buy me some time.

It's Thursday, which means it's Nates night off from the restaurant, so I call him and see if he is interested in earning some uncle points by helping me with bath and bedtime. Since he wants me to be happy, I'm sure he will understand and be happy to help.

"So, let me get this straight, your 'friend' is sick, and you want me to come and babysit, while you sit by his bedside and rub his back until he is better... and you still expect me to believe he is just a friend?" I can hear Nates grin through the phone. He thinks he is right about Mason and I having a relationship.

"Nate, I'm asking you for an hour tops. If you can't do it, I'm sure Will could. Or dad. I'm asking you because I thought you understood that Mason and I have a special… friendship."

Shit, I didn't mean to hesitate on that last word, and that's definitely not going to help deflate my little brothers big head.

"Over my dead body you will call Will. He gets every Friday afternoon to be the favorite Uncle. Of course, I'll come and hang out with my favorite little guy, I just had to make you sweat for it first. And don't think I'm not bringing extra treats for dessert."

"Whatever you want, thank you so much. I'll see you soon." I smile and start the car to go and pick Logan up.

When Nate arrives, Logan has had his bath and is ready for his dessert, book and then bed. Nate gives me a wink as I'm walking out the door, and says "Go get him, Tiger."

I roll my eyes at him and groan "How on god's green earth did I end up with YOU as a brother?"

I sent Mason a text as I finished dinner checking in, and he said he was feeling a little brighter, but hadn't attempted to eat anything as yet.

I head to the supermarket and pick up some dry, salted crackers and some Gatorade. Also grabbed some ginger lollies, which honestly taste like shit, but they work a treat for nausea.

The cashier puts everything in a bag for me and I jump back in my car and drive to Masons. When I pull up in front of his house, I see his bedroom light is on. So I text him.

Beth: I have something for you.

Mason: Intriguing. Hopefully, I'll be back at work tomorrow, I'll pop into the office and see you then?

Beth: Maybe you should open your door right now.

I wait for a minute, then the front porch light comes on. I'm standing a few feet back from his door, keeping my distance as he requested, but I've dropped the bag of goodies right on his doorstep. He opens the door and Oh my God.

I take a deep Inhale at the site of him and begin to chew on my bottom lip. I know the man is sick and all, and he does look awfully pale. But he answers the door wearing nothing but grey sweatpants. Grey. Of all of the sweatpants he could be wearing. He's wearing grey. And that's it, no shirt, nothing else.

I shouldn't be surprised by the fact that the man has the body of a God. He works a physical job and when he isn't there, he is on his parents' farm doing more physical work. Or at my house, doing, yep, more physical work. And it shows.

He isn't overwhelmingly ripped, like you get from spending hours in the gym, he is just naturally sculpted to perfection. Maybe it's just because my lady bits have been closed for business for a long time now, but man, I feel like I'm on fire.

Fuck I want to touch his Abs. With my tongue. Christ, where did that thought come from?

He leans against the doorframe, while crossing his ankles over one another and runs his hand across his jaw.

"I don't remember ordering any home deliveries tonight." He flashes me a smile and I have a feeling I just made him feel infinitely better.

"I couldn't help myself. It's nothing really, just a few things that always help me feel better when I'm nauseous. I've kept my distance, so hopefully I won't catch your germs. But I just felt like I really wanted to see you and try to make you feel a bit better." I return his smile, because I can't help it.

"You didn't need to bring a bag of groceries with you to help me feel better."

Chapter 7

MASON

2 Months Later

This is getting out of hand. What I thought was a little schoolboy crush that would pass, has continued to grow into a full on infatuation. I'm still going to Beths every other weekend, sometimes not even to do any yardwork. Sometimes we just sit and chat, while the kids play.

A few times Beth has asked us to stay for dinner, which is always an offer I can't refuse, the girl can cook.

We have also been out for dinner without the kids a few more times since that first night. I might be crazy, but I feel like she might be feeling at least a few of the same feelings as I am.

I just need to find a way to talk to her about it.

I swear over the last couple of months, if I didn't know any better, I'd say she has been teasing me a little bit.

I walked into her office the other day, intending to talk to Abi about an issue I was having with my company credit card. The minute I walked in, I locked eyes on Beth, who just happened to be reapplying some lip balm at the time. What should have been such a simple thing, especially for women, they probably do it one hundred times a day. But she swiped the balm over her lips, ever so slowly, rubbed her lips together and then pursed them as though she was blowing me a kiss.

I couldn't hide the fact that I was blatantly staring at her lips. I can't even be sure I didn't start drooling a little bit. But I do know when I managed to drag my eyes back up to hers, she winked at me. She fucking winked at me.

She is almost definitely flirting with me. And I am not arguing with that one bit. I just wish I could get a handle on my self-confidence and return the favor instead of blushing and running away like a coward

Somedays when I'm working around the office, I will try and take my lunch break at the same time as her. But this feels like torture now that I know she brings a banana just about every day. I swear, I am no better than a teenage boy, having to excuse myself because I got hard watching a girl eat a fucking banana. It was the fact that she never broke eye contact with me the whole time that did me in.

There is no way in hell she doesn't know what she is doing to me. The things she is making me imagine.

I'm already dreading receiving my next water bill because I've needed some long, cold showers recently. And some long, warm ones when I really can't get her out of my head and resign myself to imagining she is in there with me. I really need to put myself, and my right hand, out of our misery and just talk to her.

It's not a conversation we can have at work, obviously. But when the kids are around there are always so many distractions that I'm worried I won't be giving the conversation my full attention. And then when I finally do get her alone. I chicken out, or I'm so distracted by her smile, or her laugh or her big green eyes that I can barely form a sentence, let alone hold a deep and meaningful conversation.

I sit on the couch at home, I usually pick Rosie up for my week on Friday afternoon, but it's Hannahs birthday, so Rosie is staying with her an extra night.

I'm glad Hannah and I have been able to maintain a positive co-parenting relationship, where we can just swap and change days without feeling the need to 'owe' each other days. It has made everyone's life so much easier.

I miss Rosie, and the house feels empty. I figure getting out would be a good idea, but to be honest, there's only one person I want to see.

Mason: So Rosie is at Hannahs for an extra night, and I'm at a complete loose end. What do all the childless people do with their spare time?

Beth: You do know who you texted right? How should I know? *laughing face emoji*

Mason: Have you finished work yet, or are you still trying to earn that employee of the year title?

Beth: I'm almost finished, just a couple more things to do and then I'm out of here. What a week, I'm exhausted.

Mason: Would you like to grab a drink on your way home? I have some things I really need to talk to you about.

Fuck that probably sounds bad.

Beth: Um, that sounds ominous. Mase, I'd really love to grab a drink with you. But Friday nights are the one night of my week that I can't. My dad does these dinners, Philips Fridays, and I know it sounds lame, but it's tradition, and I can't skip it. I'd never hear the end of it. But you'll come round tomorrow? We can talk then?

Mason: Yeah... Yeah, absolutely. Philips Fridays, huh? You guys really are just the cutest little family unit, aren't you?

Beth: Aw, you think I'm cute?

There she goes again. Fucking flirt.

Mason: That's not my first choice of word to describe you, no. *winking emoji*

Beth: I'm going to need a list, in order, of all these words you would use to describe me.

Mason: Someday. Go enjoy your night with your family. I'll see you tomorrow. x

I still always second guess sending the little x on the end of messages to her, but she does it to me all the time when she knows she is ending the message thread.

Over the last couple of weeks and months, we have gotten quite comfortable showing each other some physical touches. We have hugged on occasion, which of course, my body always reacts to. But still could be platonic for all I know. And the gentle hand strokes whenever we start talking about topics that are hard to talk about.

Beth just doesn't hesitate to offer comfort in any way she can, even though I know her losses in her life have been far greater than mine. It's probably her most attractive quality to me.

I make my personal favorite pasta carbonara for dinner and decide I'll just put a movie on and chill out in my bed with a beer and some snacks for the night.

My movie finishes around 9.30pm, and I reach over to turn my bedside lamp off to get some sleep. When I hear my phone buzz beside me.

Beth: Are you still awake?

Mason: Just turning in. Everything ok?

It's unusual for Beth to message so late. I'm immediately put on edge, I stare at the screen, waiting for those three little dots to pop up and tell me she is replying.

The dots don't come, but my phone starts ringing. "Hello?" I answer, sitting up on the edge of the bed.

"Hey Mase, I'm sorry to call so late. I just got home and got Logan into bed. I just sat down and then started to feel a bit guilty for turning you down tonight. You sounded like you really needed a chat."

"Oh god damn, woman. You had me worried something was wrong. You don't need to feel guilty Beth, we aren't attached at the hip. If I'd known you had standing Friday night plans, I never would've asked. Especially knowing it's made you feel this kind of way."

"I'm sorry, I just had a bit of a rough night, Logan is going through a bit of a rough patch, I think he's just missing Griffin extra lately. My dad even commented tonight that Logan seemed a bit withdrawn, he even declined going out for ice cream with Will this afternoon. And on top of that, my sister is acting really distant. She usually FaceTime's every Friday but she has missed the last two. It's really out of character for her. I'm sorry, bit of a trauma dump for your Friday night."

I can hear the sadness in her voice, and it kills me. God, what I wouldn't do to make her smile again.

"Beth, do you want me to come over? I can't do anything about your sister, or Logan, but I can be there for you."

"No, no, it's late. I'm already in my pajamas, in bed. And you said you were about to turn in as well. It's fine. I just… I guess, I just needed to hear your voice."

She raises her tone at the end of that like it was a question. Maybe she thinks she will scare me off with that comment, or maybe she wasn't sure if that's what she needed.

"And has hearing my voice made it any better?"

"Yeah, surprisingly, a lot better."

"Well, I've got all night, I'll be here as long as you need me."

We talk for another hour. I get a good rundown of her week, she tells me more about her family, and we talk about things that might help support Logan. By the end of the conversation, Beth is definitely smiling, I can hear it in her voice.

Her happy voice gives me chills sometimes, especially when I know it's me who has put her in that good mood. I'm glad I could get happy Beth back tonight. I probably would've chickened out of the conversation I'm planning on having tomorrow if she was still upset.

I feel good about tomorrow. I still have no idea what I'm going to say, but I'm not leaving her house until she knows how I feel about her.

Chapter 8

BETH

After Logan had a bit of a rough day yesterday, I ask him to choose what we do this morning. He wanted to bake Griffins favorite cookies. So that's exactly what we do.

We make a double batch because I know Mason and Rosie are coming over this afternoon so we will no doubt polish a few off then. I'm certain more chocolate chips go straight into his mouth than make it into the cookie dough, but who am I to argue with him.

Once the cookies go into the oven Logan sits cross legged in front of the oven door and watches them cook. I take a seat next to him on the floor.

"Hey buddy, Grandpa and Uncle Will said you were having a hard day yesterday, do you want to talk about it?" He looks up at me, and it's like looking directly into Griffins eyes.

"Not really Mama, I just miss Daddy sometimes. I wish we could visit him."

He rests his chin in the palms of his hand and huffs out a sharp exhale.

"I know buddy, me too. But you know what? We still have each other, I'm not going anywhere. And when we really start to miss Daddy, we can always do things like bake his favorite cookies or go to his favorite spot at the lake. We can still do all of those things to feel like he never left, okay?" He looks up at me, with tears in his eyes.

"Benji told me I was weird because I don't know how to go fishing, but Daddy never got to teach me." He has tears falling now. God kids can be assholes.

I make a mental note, find out who Benji's parents are.

"Oh come here big boy. Let me tell you a secret." I pull him into my lap and hold him tight to me.

"The secret is, even if your Daddy was still here, he was really bad at fishing, he couldn't catch anything, no matter how hard he tried. But guess what? We actually know some of the best fishermen in the world, do you know that?"

He swipes at his cheeks, clearing the falling tears and looks up at me with so much hope in his eyes. "We do?" I cradle his face and give him a reassuring smile.

"We sure do. Your Grandpa and Uncle Will are the best fisherman I know. Uncle Nate is pretty good too. I'm sure if you want to learn, they would love to teach you. Then you can go to school and tell Benji that you know everything there is to know about fishing! How does that sound?"

"You're the best Mama. I can't wait for next Philips Friday, I'm going to ask Grandpa to go Fishing." I ruffle his hair.

"Okay kiddo, I think these cookies are just about ready, and Rosie will be here soon." That perks him up straight away and he bolts out of the kitchen in a flash, no doubt to drag out all the toys he wants to play with.

****

It's only early in the season, but Spring has definitely sprung. It's unseasonably warm out today, so after we have all pitched in and done a bit of yardwork, we set up the Slip ' N Slide for Logan and Rosie, I know this will give Mason and I some uninterrupted time to talk about whatever it was he wanted to talk about when he messaged yesterday.

I was kind of glad for the distractions yesterday, so I didn't have time to overanalyze what he might've wanted to talk about.

I grab Mason a beer from the fridge, and I pour myself a glass of wine, I sit up on the deck chairs on the back patio while Mason has a couple of turns on the slide showing the kids how it's done. It looks like he is having as much fun as they are, and it's equally as entertaining for me.

He looks up and sees me laughing at them all and stops to smile at me like I'm the only girl in the world.

When I raise his beer and tip it at him, he comes jogging up the yard stops just in front of me and does possibly the hottest two movements I've ever seen.

First, he removes his baseball cap with one hand, while the other reaches behind his head and pulls his wet T-shirt off with one swift movement. Then secondly, he puts his baseball cap back on... backwards. I literally feel jolts of desire pool between my legs.

Yeah, I really need to get laid.

He drapes his wet shirt over the railings of the patio to dry, and then sits in the deck chair next to me in just his gym shorts, exposing a lot more of his muscular thighs than I've ever seen before.

Why am I all of a sudden finding a man's thighs hot? Fuck me, I hope this conversation he wanted to have isn't too serious because right now, there's no way I can look him in the eyes.

He grabs his beer and takes a long pull. I watch his throat bob up and down as he swallows. And have to physically shake my head to bring me back to reality.

Ok Beth, it's time to get serious. If you want this man, all you have to do is say the word. Why can't I just say the word?

He clears his throat and that really drags me out of my daydream. "You okay there? Do you need a hand picking your jaw up off the floor?" He says with a smirk and a glint in his eye.

"Oh someone thinks big of themselves. But seriously, can you warn a person before you do that next time? I thought it was common knowledge that toned bodies and backwards caps were one of the biggest turn-ons in the world... and it's been a long, long time for me. Maybe wait until my back is turned next time."

I feel my face go a deep shade of red. Not sure where that streak of boldness came from, but I'm not mad about it. The man is doing things to me.

"And miss that priceless reaction? No thanks. I think I'd like to keep surprising you whenever I can."

I giggle like a little girl, and if it's possible, feel like my blush goes a shade deeper.

"Logan seems to be a bit happier today." He says as he scrubs his hand through his hair, sending water droplets flying everywhere.

"Yeah, we had a good little chat about it this morning. Some wiener kid at school made a comment about how he was weird because his dad didn't teach him to fish." I roll my eyes but he must hear the hurt.

Logan was barely old enough to know what a fish was when his dad began the fight for his life. It wasn't exactly top of the list of life skills to teach him.

"Are you fucking with me right now, which kid? I oughtta rough him up a bit" Mason says, trying to coax a smile out of me.

"Some kid named Benji, I've never really even heard Logan talk about him before."

"Oh, Benji Willis? That tracks, the apple doesn't fall far from the tree there. We did a renovation job on their house a few years ago, just before Benji was born. His mother was one of the worst people I've ever met. Nothing was good enough for her. Always screeching at the top of her lungs about something. Try not to let her kids comments get to you, the kid will probably end up on a milk carton someday."

I let out a little chuckle at that, Mason always knows how to bring a smile or a laugh to my face.

"And hey Beth, I don't know if I've ever told you this, but the Rosewood River runs right through my parents property. Maybe one day you guys could come out there and I could show him a thing or two about fishing. I'm not the best at it, but I've been doing it since I was about Logans age. I'd be happy to take you out there if it's not overstepping any boundaries. Rosie isn't super keen on the farm life, gets that from her mother, but maybe having you guys there might change her mind a bit."

"Mase, that sounds amazing. You know, if you're going to teach my son to fish. I will admit I'm overdue for a mani-pedi. Tell Rosie to bring her stuff, she can paint my fingernails anytime."

I look over at him and smile. I see pure appreciation in his eyes. I just know he has been coming up with an endless list of reasons why Rosie can't paint his fingernails, it's only a matter of time before he has to give in.

We sit in silence for a few moments, I feel like we are just soaking in each others presence as we have done so often. He shifts in his seat a little and lets out a shaky exhale, if I didn't know any better, I'd say he is nervous about something.

He breaks the silence by saying something that catches me completely off guard.

"God, if Hannah was a fly on the wall here today, she would be having a field day." I just about spit out my sip off wine.

I'm not sure what his ex-wife has to do with our recent exchange but I'm curious to know now. I slowly turn to look at him and arch an eyebrow at him.

"Sorry, what?"

"Oh, lower your hackles, it's nothing like that. It's just that, Rosie has told her how much time we have been spending together and how much fun we have. So Hannah approached me about it, which was terrifying by the way. And she said she had a feeling we would end up getting closer. Even as coworkers she had seen us interact at work functions and just always knew we had a lot in common and a bit of a., Spark, I guess." He says with a shrug of his shoulders.

"Huh, son of a bitch." I say, as I take a sip of my wine, in an effort to hide my smile.

He tilts his head and raises an eyebrow at me. "Well, I'm not sure what reaction I was expecting from you, but that didn't even rank in the top ten" He says with an amused smile.

"No, I'm sorry, it's just that, that's the third time I've heard someone say that they see sparks between us. Zealand said it the first night we went to Just in Thyme, and then Abi said it a few months ago on the day you bought me in a coffee while we went through one of the big purchase orders. And now from your ex-wife of all people. It's just a bit crazy, don't you think?"

"Yeah, it certainly feels crazy." He says as he averts my gaze. I don't know if he was expecting me to confess my feelings in that moment, he almost seems disappointed.

I keep staring at him, trying to analyze his demeanor and judge how he is feeling. I feel like I have so many butterflies I can feel them floating from my stomach all the way up to my throat. Might also be the wine talking, who's to say.

"And what about you?" I don't drop my stare from him for a second.

"What do you mean?" He turns his head back towards me and finally meets my gaze again.

"Do you.....uh, Do you feel a spark, between us?"

Mason gets up and closes the distance between us, we weren't sitting that far apart, so with two steps he comes to stop in front of me.

He crouches down so we are at the same level and he makes sure I'm looking him dead in the eyes.

"Beth, I'm going to be very honest with you here. No. When I look at you, I don't feel a spark."

Oh.... Fuck me, my stomach just dropped. How did I read this so wrong.

For the first time since this conversation began, I finally drop his gaze. I stare down at my lap and I feel my body begin to betray me because I swear, I feel the prickle of tears beginning to form in the corners of my eyes. I knew it was too soon.

God, I'm such an idiot. I take a deep breath and try to blink back the beginnings of the tears when I feel his fingers below my chin lifting my gaze back to his.

"Hey, get out of your head for a minute and let me finish." I look up at him and he is smiling, that trademark, cheek splitting grin of his.

I give him a puzzled look because what the fuck is he talking about, can he just spit it out already?

"Beth, when I look at you, I don't feel a spark, because I feel the burn of the whole fucking forest fire. For me, I'm way past a spark."

Fuck Me, don't worry about a forest fire burning, with words like that... It's me, I'm the one on fire.

"Beth, I need to get this off my chest, and I don't expect you to say anything in return. In fact I'd even prefer it if you didn't say anything. Over the last few months, I've developed feelings for you that go deeper than just friendship, or coworkers. At first, I thought it was just a bit of a crush, and it would pass, but months later, it has only deepened. And I've put off saying anything because I couldn't gauge where you were at, and I didn't know the appropriate amount of time to wait, and there just never felt like there was a good time to say anything. But I can't hold it in anymore. Every time you share another detail of your life with me, and I get more of a glimpse of you as a person, my feelings just seem to grow more and more and if you've taught me anything in the last few months it's that life is just too damn short. So I'm telling you. And as I said, you don't have to say a word back to me. I just needed you to know."

He lets out a big exhale, and he looks like the weight of the world has just been lifted.

"Mase, I.."

"No Beth, you don't have to say anything if you're not sure. I just needed to say my piece. And I want you to know there is absolutely no pressure on you here. If you don't feel the same, then I will be fine continuing on as friends and coworkers. If you feel like it's too soon, and you need more time, I will wait for you. I will take whatever you want to give me in any capacity because I've felt happier in the last few months of getting to know you than I have in years. And this feels like it could be something really special, if we just give it a chance. But only if you want to."

At this point he sounds like he has got word vomit coming out. Like he has been stewing on these feelings for so long and now they are all just coming out at once. I raise my index finger and put it across his lips to stop him talking for a second.

"Hey, get out of your head for a minute and let me finish." I say, throwing his earlier words back at him. I continue to hold my finger over his lips, and I see it now, what everyone has said about sparks, because having his lips on any part of my body, I feel it. There isn't a single part of my body that doesn't feel like it's sparking with heat right now.

"Mason, I hear what you're saying. I've felt a connection between us too, for a while now. I've been so conflicted with myself for weeks now, because I would love nothing more than to see where this goes. But I don't know if I'm ready. Maybe I'll never know. I honestly wasn't expecting to feel this way about another man, ever again. And then you came in, swooping to my rescue when I didn't even know I needed it and just -- turned everything on its head. I'm almost certain I can't dive right into another full-on relationship right now. But if it's okay with you, and you can bear with me while I learn to do this again. Then yes, I think I want to see where this could go."

I lower my finger, and I notice his breathing has increased, he looks like he has just ran a marathon. He cups one of my cheeks with his hand and holds my gaze.

"I don't want you rush into this decision Beth. I can't imagine what it must be like in your mind at the moment. It's a huge step. So It's completely fine if you need more time, if we're doing this, I want to do it right. Why don't you take a week to think it through? Do you think you could get a babysitter for Logan next weekend? Let's have dinner Saturday night, and we can talk some more about it then."

I can't even speak, I just nod. I can feel the tears starting to well up, but they don't feel like sad tears. Maybe a little bit of relief, because I know now how he feels about me. Maybe a little bit of fear, because I still don't know if this is too soon, or if I'm ready for this.

I don't know how Logan will feel about this. Or whether my family will be okay with this, Griffin was part of the family, it might be too soon for them as well.

Mason rises to stand, grabs his shirt from the railing and puts it back on. "It's getting late, we better get going. Think about it but remember…. Theres absolutely no pressure, right?"

He grabs my shoulder and give it's a light, reassuring squeeze before grabbing Rosies towel and wrapping her in it. They say goodbye and leave.

I take Logan inside and put him in the bath, he looks up at me with bubbles all over his face "We had a fun day today Mama. I like it when Rosie and Mason come over. Mason is funny." I smile at his approval.

"Yeah buddy, he is funny. I like it when they come over as well. And guess what? Mason asked if we want to go to his farm one day soon. I'm sure he has lots of animals to see, but best of all, he can take you fishing right there!" I watch as his eyes go wide and light up with the excitement of learning a new skill. I think Mason just won massive brownie points in my sons' eyes.

Maybe Logan would be ok with this after all. Am I worrying about nothing?

Chapter 9

BETH

Friday comes around way too quickly. I haven't been sleeping very well all week, thinking about all of the pros and cons of getting into a new relationship.

Yes, I'm worried that it's too soon, and it will affect more than just me. But I'm also so incredibly attracted to Mason who has now openly admitted that those feelings are mutual. It feels ridiculous to let that go to waste.

3pm comes around and everyone is starting to pack up for the day. One of the last ones to leave is Mason, I haven't seen or spoken to him much this week, I think he has been purposely keeping his distance, trying to give me the space to think things through.

He sticks his head into the office door, greeting me with that wide, cheeky grin, "Still on for dinner tomorrow night?"

I just nod my head silently, I'm excited to spend time with him again. I just need to work out what I'm going to say to him first.

"Perfect, I'll pick you up at seven. Goodnight, Beth." Before I can even say anything else, he is gone. So it just leaves me to finish up my work for the afternoon before I head to my dads' for Philips Friday.

I sit at my desk and stare blankly at my computer screen, and before I know it twenty minutes have passed, and I haven't completed a single task.

I can't get Mason out of my head. I decide it's a pointless exercise being here, so I pack up early and head out.

I consider going and sitting by the lake. It's where I feel closest to Griffin, he loved it there, it bought him peace. In the few months before he died, I remember we were sitting on one of the benches beside the lake while Logan threw some food to the ducks. Griffin was joking about me bringing another man here one day.

We actually spoke about me moving on in the future several times. I said I don't think I ever could, and he would always tell me not to be ridiculous, that I shouldn't waste the rest of my life being alone.

I'm sure he is looking down on me and having a good laugh at me feeling so conflicted about this right now.

Even thinking about Griffin has made me feel even more at war with myself. I know there is one person who will know what to do. So I head to Philips Friday early, for the first time ever.

"Hello?" I say as I walk through the door into my dads house. It's awfully quiet in here, usually when I get here it's utter chaos. But Will and Logan won't be here for at least another hour. The house smells amazing already, so I know my dad is here somewhere. It's roast dinner night, so he has already started cooking.

"Dad?" I hear some fumbling coming from upstairs, and my dad calls down "Beth? You're early. Give me a minute, I'll be right down."

I kick my shoes off and go to put them on the rack when I look down and notice a pair of ladies' boots.

Weird, they definitely aren't mine and they don't look like Olive's style either.

I put my bag down on the hall table and then notice a set of keys that I've never seen before. Before I even have time to process that, my dad walks down the stairs. With a lady following two steps behind him.

Oh my god what have I walked into. Note to self, never show up anywhere unannounced...

My dad clears his throat and is avoiding my gaze at all costs. "Beth, this is my uh, friend... Sadie. Sadie, this is my daughter Beth." She reaches her hand out offering for me to shake it.

"Uh, is it safe to touch that, or should we all maybe wash our hands first?" I try to hide my giggle. I can't help it, I make inappropriate jokes when I'm uncomfortable.

"Elizabeth!" My dad scolds me. I might be thirty-five years old, but dads angry voice still scares me straight.

"I'm sorry, it's really nice to meet you, Sadie. I'm sorry for... interrupting. Are you here for dinner?" My cheeks feel red and hot, and I have to physically bite the inside of my cheek to hold in my laughter. I can't wait to tell my siblings about this.

"Oh no, that's ok, I was just leaving. It was really nice to finally meet you, Beth. I've heard so much about you."

"Oh? You have, have you? Dad, why haven't we heard a thing about Sadie?" My dad just scowls at me and tries to smack me over the shoulder, thankfully Sadie is standing in the middle of us so he misses.

Sadie turns and gives my dad a peck on the cheek.

"It's fine, I'll talk to you tomorrow. Bye, Hank." She grabs her keys and puts on her boots and leaves.

As soon as the door latches shut, I double over in a fit of laughter. It doesn't feel like that long ago that my dad busted in on Griffin and I in a similar scenario. I was mortified back then. It kind of feels like sweet revenge now that I get to be on the other side of it. But honestly, it just feels good to laugh after a whole week of stressing myself out.

"Oh, grow up, Beth. When you've calmed yourself down enough to tell me why you're showing up to my house two hours early, unannounced, I'll be out in the backyard, watering the grass."

"I'm sorry Dad, I truly am. I actually did come here to talk to you in peace before the chaos arrives. I've uh, been having a bit of a tough week, actually. And although that interaction has gone a long way at cheering me up, I could actually use a bit of advice. If you think you have any to spare?"

That sentence sobers us both up pretty quickly. My dad knows I don't ask for advice lightly. I'm usually the one dishing it out, not asking for it.

"Okay, don't worry about the lawn. Do we need tea or Wine?" I smile, because I already feel a whole lot better just being here. Being home.

Dad fixes us a cup of tea and we sit next to each other at the giant kitchen table. I start at the very beginning. Of course, Nate and Will couldn't keep their mouths shut so dad knew that I was friends with Mason, outside of work. Add that to the fact that Logan talks about Rosie and Mason non-stop and it was no secret. But I've never openly mentioned him in front of my family, as far as they are concerned, we are just friends and beyond that, it's none of their business.

"Last weekend, Mason told me he had feelings for me, and Dad, the things he said, the way he poured his heart out to me, was some of the most romantic things I've ever heard and in the heat of the moment, my heart was ready to jump out of my chest and run head long into a relationship. But then my head kicked in and said hang on a minute, it's too soon, and what if Logan isn't ok with it, and what if you guys aren't okay with it, and all of a sudden I was having all of these big thoughts and feelings, and I was caught in this big tug of war between my head and my heart. And I just don't know what to do. We agreed to have dinner tomorrow night to talk about it some more. And I'm still so unsure."

"Darling girl you know what I just heard? Your head is stopping you jumping into something because you're worried about Logan, you're worried about us, and you're worried it's too soon. Well guess what, from where I'm sitting, Logan adores Mason and Rosie, and I'm sure he would be thrilled to spend more time around them. Us? Beth, we just want you to be happy, whatever that looks like for you. And is it too soon? I don't think there's ever a way to know that. But I know for a fact, Griffin wouldn't want you sitting around wasting your life away wondering. He wouldn't want you to miss out on something really great, because you were worried about how everyone else feels. When was the last time you put yourself first and did something because YOU wanted it? Look at me Beth, I've wasted years of my life being alone, always too busy working or with you kids, now I'm almost sixty years old and I'm just now opening myself up again and wondering why the hell I didn't do this years ago. Worrying about a problem doesn't solve a problem, Beth. If your hearts telling you to take a chance, then it's a chance worth taking." He pulls me in to give me one of his fatherly hugs. I let out a big exhale.

"Also, I need to meet this Rosie girl that has my Grandson wrapped around her finger. She sounds like a real gem." I smile up at him.

"She is, and her dad is pretty cool too. Maybe I could invite them around one day? Preferably when Nate and Will aren't here so I can ease them into the Philips lifestyle."

"Might be a good idea. Those boys will be like a dog with a bone when you tell them about your potential new relationship" He stands, collects our mugs and takes them to the kitchen.

"Not if I tell them about yours first." I wink at him then run away to grab my bag and go change into my pajamas before everyone else arrives.

****

79

For the first time all week, I fall asleep with ease. I know what I need to do now. The nerves are gone, the internal conflict is at rest. And so am I.

I drift off to sleep excited for tomorrow to tell Mason exactly how I feel. I sleep like a log. At least until one AM when I'm awoken to the sound of Logan coughing.

I go into his room to check on him and I can hear him wheezing from outside his bedroom door. Shit.

He had juvenile asthma when he was a baby, but he hasn't had an asthma attack since he was two years old. I thought he had finally outgrown it.

I run to the bathroom and dig through the medicine cabinet looking for an inhaler, but I can't find one. It's been so long since we needed one, and with all of the medications we needed for Griffin, the cabinet has been overrun with other things. Double Shit.

Hot steam always used to help him, so I run the shower and close the doors, so the room gets nice and steamy.

We sit in the bathroom for twenty minutes doing some deep breathing exercises, but he is still wheezy and struggling with some of the exercises.

I don't like this. Not at all.

Thirty minutes after I first heard him cough, I call the paramedics. They get here in record time, and have him attached to a nebulizer, so he can breathe a bit easier. His head is covered in sweat, and he is so restless, saying his chest is hurting. This is a bad one. He has never had chest pains with an asthma attack before.

We arrive at the hospital, and he is immediately transferred to the pediatrics department. Logan is given a few doses of steroids to help ease the inflammation in his lungs and given an oxygen mask to wear while he rests.

In between, he is given more of the asthma relievers through the nebulizer as well. I don't let anyone see how terrified I am.

I've only done this a couple of times, but always had Griffin with me. I am so scared for my helpless little boy. I feel like I'm constantly fighting back tears.

Once he is stabilized, a nurse rolls in a fold out sofa for me and returns shortly after with some blankets and a pillow. There's no way I'm sleeping for the rest of the night. Even though I know he is in good hands, my adrenaline hasn't worn off yet and I can't take my eyes off his little chest. Watching it gently rise and fall, and gradually come back to a normal respiratory rate.

I see every hour on the clock. I think I drift off somewhere between 4am and 5am, but it would only have been for twenty minutes maximum. Even if I wanted to sleep, these fold out Sofas are not made for adult bodies.

I send my dad a text to let him know what has happened, and then text the sibling group chat to let them know we are in the hospital. They will no doubt filter in as soon as visiting hours begin. Logan is the center of all of their worlds.

I get the usual responses from my brothers, competing over who is going to buy him the biggest stuffed toy. But then my phone pings with a separate message.

Bella: Hey Sissy, please give little man the biggest cuddle from Aunty Bel. I'm so sorry I can't be there to visit him and cheer him up. I might not have my phone on me for a few days, Brad has organized for me to go to some fancy fitness camp thing with some of the other partners of guys from his office. Apparently, there is a big charity event coming up and they all want to look their best. I have put on a bit of weight since moving here, so will be good for me to get my butt into gear. Please keep me posted with how Logie is going but just don't be worried if I don't respond, I will as soon as I can. Love you guys xx

Beth: He signed you up for a fitness camp, without asking you? Sorry, but, red flag, Arabella. I'm sorry, but I'm worried about you. You've been skipping Philips Fridays more often than not, I'm not sure what you've got going on, because you don't talk to us, but whatever it is, don't shut us out, okay? We love you, and miss you heaps. Talk soon. x

I really need to set aside some time to shake some sense into my baby sister. What the fuck has she gotten herself into?

Just before lunchtime, I hear a commotion coming from the front doors, and I just know it's my brothers and my dad. Logan must know as well, because he sits up in his bed. He is still wearing the oxygen mask but has perked up a lot in the last six hours. All that remains is a bit of fatigue, and a slight wheeze when he takes a deep breath.

My brothers are both carrying ridiculously oversized stuffed animals, Nates is a bear and Will's a giant blue Rabbit. They are a sight for sore eyes, but you couldn't wipe the smile off Logans face the minute he laid eyes on them.

Its times like these I'm grateful for my family, they always drop everything and rush to be here for us.

Just as the morning visiting hours are ending, and my family are saying their goodbyes to Logan, Nate punches Will in the arm, and says "I call shotgun." Before they take off running out of the room towards the car.

How old are they again? My dad shakes his head, but he lingers for a minute and says "I guess this puts a bit of a spanner in your works, huh?" I look at him a little perplexed, before it hits me.

Holy shit, I almost forgot. Oh my god, I haven't slept a wink and I've been so preoccupied. Shit.

"Yeah, never a dull moment in my life. Maybe it's a sign that now is just not the right time. You better go before those two kill each other over the front seat. Love you Dad."

He starts walking but stops when he gets to the door, he turns to look back at me and with a sympathetic smile he says, "Elizabeth, there might never be a perfect time. Doesn't mean it isn't right. Love you, keep me posted."

Chapter 10

MASON

The sun is blaring today, I'm out in the field with my dad, checking our perimeter fencing. The one downfall of owning a couple hundred head of cattle, is they are thick as nails.

You know the saying the grass is always greener on the other side? I think that was written by someone who was watching cows graze, they are always trying to bust through fences to get to the neighboring properties.

We have stopped to fix one section of fence, I'm half-way through digging the post hole, one of the many physical jobs my dad just isn't able to do anymore, when I hear my phone ping from the front seat of my dads truck.

I'm sweating up a storm so I tell my dad I need a quick water break and I go and check who it's from.

Beth: Mase, I'm so sorry to have to do this, but I'm going to have to cancel our dinner plans tonight. I'm so sorry.

Well, I guess there it is. I've tried to leave her alone this week, to give her some space to think about things without me being in the way. I guess that's the confirmation that she doesn't want the same things.

I know I said I'd be okay with just being friends, but fuck, I really thought she was in the same place I was. I feel like I've been kicked in the gut.

I shake my head and throw my phone back down on the seat, take a gulp of water, swish it around my mouth for a second and then spit it out. I let out a quiet groan.

Apparently, while my dad is physically ageing, his hearing is working just fine. "Everything ok over there, son?" He tips his old worn cowboy hat up off his head so he can look me straight in the eyes.

"Yeah, fine. Was just looking forward to catching up with a friend tonight and she just cancelled." He narrows his eyes at me.

"We talking like a friend, or a FRIEND? You seem mighty disappointed for just any old person…"

"It's nothing old man, really. I thought she was going to turn out to be more than a friend, but the fact that she just cancelled on me, tells me she doesn't feel the same. It's kinda complicated and I really just want to get these fences done, so can we please not talk about it right now?"

I turn to go back to the section of fence we were working on, but I know he isn't about to drop this that easily.

"It normal for your lady friend to cancel plans out of the blue like this?" He leans on the fence post, crossing one of his ankles over the other.

"No, not at all, over the last few months we have basically made any excuse we could to see each other. She has never cancelled plans, especially on such short notice. But dad, you've got to understand. I gave her a lot to think about. Tonight was supposed to be the night she decided whether or not we take things further than just friendship. Obviously this means she doesn't want that, but couldn't tell me to my face."

"You ask her why she was cancelling?" He raises an eyebrow at me.

"She didn't give a reason, and honestly, I don't know if I want to hear it."

My dad shakes his head and while looking down at his boots, lets out a chuckle. He takes two steps and closes the distance between us before he slaps me around the back of the head, causing my hat to fall off. "Hey, what the fuck was that for?"

"Because you're a dummy. This girl means that much to you, and she gave you reason to think those feelings were mutual. She aint cancelling for no reason, dummy. Get back on that phone and ask her why."

I pick up my hat and put it back on my head, then let out a groan like I used to when I was ten years old and my parents would ask me to muck out the horse stalls.

Mason: You've kind of got me worried now, is everything okay? Do you need more time? I said no pressure, and I mean it. Whatever you need. Can we at least talk it out? Remember what you said on our first night out? Theres zero judgement when it comes to me and you and talking through feelings. Whatever is going on, you can tell me, I can take it.

Those three little dots appear immediately. I don't take my eyes off my phone until Beths response comes through.

Beth: Mase.. Logan is in hospital. He had an asthma attack in the middle of the night. He's okay now, but we will be in here at least until tomorrow.

Mason: Oh shit. Beth, I'm so sorry. I didn't even know he was an asthmatic. Do you guys need anything? I'm at the farm, but should be back in town by about four o'clock if you need anything dropped in.

Fuuuuckk. I take my hat off and run my hands through my hair. Then I turn and face my dad who is wearing the biggest shit-eating grin I've ever seen.

"I was right, wasn't I, dummy?"

"Her kid is in the hospital. Had an asthma attack during the night. How did you know?"

"Son, you been walking around here with your head in the clouds for months. Your mother and I knew there was something going on. I don't know if you know this, but you have a tell. When you're happy, you whistle, any song, any tune, but you don't stop whistling. Been doing it ever since you were about twelve years old. Stopped for a few years there, so imagine our surprise when not six months after your marriage breaks down, you're out here chirping like a bird again… Dummy."

He shakes his head and returns to unrolling the fence wire. I guess that's the end of that conversation. Good, because I feel like a fool enough without him rubbing it in anymore.

****

When I get home, I shower and change and sit on the edge of my bed. I can't believe I thought Beth was going to just cut me down in a text message. My old man was right, I am a dummy.

I just wish there was something I could do to help Beth out. I remember when Rosie was admitted to hospital about a year ago with a viral infection. It was horrible, so sterile and boring, horrible food, and that's if you even get fed. Sometimes in the pediatric department, they only feed the kids, the parents don't get a meal, they might just get some cheese and crackers or a day old, leftover, stale sandwich. I shiver just thinking about it. At least when we went through it, it was Hannah and I and we could tag each other out to eat and shower. Beth is doing this alone.

Mason: Hey, just checking in to see how you guys are?

Beth: Thanks for checking in. Logan is breathing heaps better. He is just really tired, which isn't unusual following an attack. He has just been sleeping. He is probably out for the night I'd say.

Mason: Hopefully he sleeps it off. And you? How are you feeling?

Beth: Truthfully, exhausted. I haven't slept since the attack started at 1AM. I haven't eaten all day, haven't showered,

87

I'm still in my pajamas from last night because we left home in such a hurry in the ambulance. Hopefully we will be home in the morning so only a few more hours.

Mason: I'm going to ask one more time, do you need me to bring you anything? I had my whole night blocked out for our dinner plans, so it's really no trouble.

Beth: That's ok, I'll be fine until morning when the doctors round. If we aren't discharged then, I'll call you begging for some coffee at the very least. I should probably try and get some rest. The pull out sofas are not made for sleeping. Good night Mase. Talk tomorrow. xx

Theres that xx. She's ending the conversation there. Selfishly I could sit and talk to her all night, but I can imagine how exhausted she is.

Fuck it. When I was sick, she showed up on my doorstep with a bag of groceries to help me, even though I told her not to. My girl is hungry and in need of a shower. I can fix that.

Huh.. My girl feels good – Feels, right.

I head to my kitchen and put on a pot of pasta to boil. Lucky I make a mean creamy, cheesy pasta. Perfect for when you're starving hungry and need a whole lot of comfort. It's quick too, so I won't be getting it to her too late.

I put it in some Tupperware, pack it in a bag with some snacks and a couple of juice boxes, unfortunately the only drinks I have in a to-go container. Dad life.

I also fill up my Thermos full of coffee. I grab one of my backpacks, and shove in one of my old football training shirts and a pair of my gym shorts. They will no doubt be way too big on her, but at least they are clean. I grab the goodies and jump in my truck.

On the way, I stop in at the late night store and grab the sour worms I know she loves, a toothbrush, toothpaste and some soap. And a coloring book for Logan, it's like winning the lottery when I see they have a dinosaur one.

Then I head to the hospital. I pull into the parking space, and sit in the front seat of my truck staring up at the building that stands about five stories high. It's only a small town so it's not a huge hospital. As I stare up at it, I wonder how I should play this thing. Do I just walk in there, even though I'm not family? Should I call her?

Just then, while looking up at the building, I see the most beautiful woman in the world, sitting in the window of the fourth floor.

It's one thing I do remember about the Pediatric rooms, they were high enough to have spectacular views out over town. I know how I'm going to play this. If I can see her, it means she can see me.

Mason: The best thing about the pediatric rooms is the view over town, especially at night. Am I right?

I watch as she looks at her phone, then out the window, taking in the view. She looks back down at her phone, just as those three little dots appear. I type fast so I can beat her to a reply.

Mason: Look again, a bit lower this time.

She glances around the general area of the entrance to the hospital and the parking lot, and we lock eyes the minute she spots me.

I hold up the bags of goodies I'm holding and I can see her smile and tilt her head. Then she is shaking her head like she can't believe I'm here.

That makes two of us.

My phone rings so I put a bag down to answer it. "I know, I know, you said you didn't need anything. But I also said that to you once, and you showed up anyway. You need food. If you want, I can leave this at the front desk and you can grab it from there. But I can also come up and sit with Logan while you shower. The choice is all yours. I don't want to overstep."

I'm still watching her at the window, I think she might be wiping tears from her eyes. "Please, come up." I nod and hang up the phone.

I laughed at Beth when I get to their room and watch her struggle to decide whether to eat first or shower. The poor girl is so exhausted, she looks like she's a bit of a zombie walking around.

I tell her freshening up might wake her up enough to actually be able to feed herself. So she takes the toiletries I bought with me, and the clothes I bought for her, and heads into the shower.

She is so tired, I wish I could get in there with her and wash the day away for her. What I would give to run my fingers through her hair or down the length of her spine, across the curve of her perfect ass.

I snap myself out of that thought when I remember this is a hospital, and I don't even yet know how she actually feels about me. So, instead I sit beside a sleeping Logan so she can soak for as long as she needs.

When she emerges from the bathroom, fuck me. I know it's inappropriate because of where we are but dammit if I don't get half hard watching her walk out wearing my clothes.

With her long dark hair hanging down, dripping wet. She looks so much better now that she has cleaned up a bit.

I grab out the dish of pasta and the cutlery I bought from home. I give her the choice between juice and coffee. She takes the juice, knowing the coffee will stay warm until morning in its insulated Thermos.

As she raises the first bite of pasta to her lips she lets out a long moan and well, if I was half hard before, there's no hiding that I'm fully hard now. I shift on the sofa and fuss with pulling a pillow over my lap.

She obviously notices the tent in my jeans because she giggles before hiding it behind her hand. "Oh my God, I'm sorry, it's just so good to have food after over twenty-four hours without eating."

"I'll take it as compliment. Don't start apologizing now, it's not the first time I've had that reaction to you." Her eyes widen like she can't believe I just said that.

Fuck it, she knows how I feel about her. I've opened a flood gate and I won't hold anything back anymore.

We chat for a while, she explains all about Logans history with his asthma, and she won't stop apologizing for ruining our dinner plans, no matter how many times I tell her it isn't her fault.

She is about halfway through her pasta when she looks at me and says "It's not fair you know."

I raise an eyebrow at her. "What's not fair?"

"You're this superstar dad, an amazing friend. You're good at your job. You can fix just about anything that's broken. You're ridiculously good looking. And to top it all off, you can cook. How do I stand a chance?" She smiles at me, and I glance down at my lap, where I'm still holding the pillow.

Fuck me, hearing her say all of that, I'm surprised this pillow hasn't been torn clean in half yet.

"Hopefully, you don't." I shoot her a wink, and she blushes the deepest shade of red I've ever seen on her, just as a nurse comes in. "I'm sorry to interrupt, but visiting hours are over, I'm afraid you'll have to go."

Chapter 11

BETH

The next day drags on. During the doctors morning rounds, we are told we will be able to go home that afternoon, but Logan would need another dose of steroids first, just for good measure. So we hang around the hospital all day.

Logan is still exhausted and I can't wait to get him home to his own bed, in a quiet house, not being woken up every hour for the nurses to do their observations on him.

I slept slightly better on a full stomach and in a comfy T-shirt that Mason is definitely never getting back.

Mason said he was heading back to the farm today, so I haven't bothered him, even though I've been dying to text him all day. He got his feelings off his chest a week ago, and now I need to get mine out. If I was unsure before, last night really convinced me that this is the right thing to do.

Around six pm, we are finally given the all clear to go home. I call Will to come and pick us up. He already has a booster seat installed in his car, for when he picks Logan up from preschool. And he was the genius that wanted to compete with these god forsaken oversized stuffed animals, so now he can help me haul them home.

When we pull up to my house, I see my dads car in the driveway, he has a spare key for emergencies. He has let himself in to fill my fridge with some food for dinner.

Logan is out like a light, he is so exhausted and still suffering through a little bit of fatigue, so Will carries him straight into his bed, before helping with the bags and toys.

My dad gives Logan a goodnight kiss and tells him he is glad to see him home. Will does the same but ruffles his hair gently before they both leave.

I'm so glad to be home. I get changed into some fresh pajamas. Just some silk boxer shorts, and a cami top with lace trim on the bust. I throw my hair up in a messy bun. I'll deal with it later when I shower before bed.

I heat up some of the lasagna that my dad put in my fridge and sit on the couch to eat it. I realize I haven't let Mason know we are home, so I fire off a quick message.

Beth: We are home! Logie is exhausted so is already out for the night. Can't wait to sleep in my own bed. I now have the back of an 80-year-old.

Mason: Welcome home. The poor little dude. Hopefully a solid nights sleep will put him right, and your back. Have you eaten?

Beth: Yeah, my dad dropped over a lasagna big enough to feed an army, so we are set for about a week.

Mason: Good, good... Do you need anything else?

Before I can respond I can see the three little dots appear again, he is typing another message, so I wait to see what he is going to say before typing out my response.

Mason: P.S I'm really looking for an excuse to see you, so would really help if you could throw me a bone here and say yes.

Beth: Now that you mention it, there is something I need...

Mason: Anything, I'm all ears...

Deep breaths, Beth. This is your shot - Shoot it.

Beth: You.

I wait for the three little dots to appear. They don't. Have I stunned him speechless? Maybe I freaked him out, came on too strong. The suspense might kill me. After a few minutes, I haven't heard anything. So, I fire off another text.

Beth: Mase? You there? I didn't mean to freak you out.

Still no dots appear. After a few more minutes, I'm really stressing. It has been almost ten minutes since my message, and I am starting to get really worried I've put my foot in it.

I put my phone down and am just about to eat my feelings when I hear a knock at the door.

I open the door and the sight of the man standing on the other side of it takes my breath away. He is breathing so heavily; I have to question whether he just ran all the way here. There is pure fire in his eyes.

He grabs me by the waist and pushes me backwards inside, kicking the door shut behind him, a couple more steps backwards and my back meets the wall of my entryway.

I loop my arms around his neck, look him in the eyes, his eyelids look heavy, and his hair is a mess, like he has been running his fingers through it. Like he has been conflicted about doing this.

With his forehead resting on mine, still breathing heavily, he says "Beth, I'm trying to be respectful here, but you've been driving me crazy for a long time. If you don't want this, say the word, and I'll stop. Otherwise, I'm going to kiss you now. Do you want me to stop?"

I open my mouth to speak, before I realize that he is the one that has stunned me speechless. So I just look up at him and shake my head. "Please, don't stop."

I don't even finish that sentence before his mouth is crashing into mine. His hands both still have a tight grasp on my hips. His kiss is hungry. I know he has waited so long to kiss me.

His hands reach around me, slide across my lower back and down over the curve of my ass. He stops when he has a perfect handful of my ass before he lifts me up, so that my legs wrap around his waist.

Holy shit, Mason was right. There are no sparks here. This is way beyond sparks. Kissing Mason Clarke is like Times Square on New Years Eve. Or a thousand forest fires all at once.

Our mouths haven't broken contact once. We spend the next couple of minutes kissing like it's both the first and last time we will ever kiss again. Happy just exploring each others mouth. I groan when his tongue sneaks its way past my lips. He pulls back to look at me in the eyes.

"Beth, you can't be groaning like that, unless you want to snap what little is left of my self-control. I'm hanging on by a thread here." He runs his mouth along my jaw before stopping briefly just below my ear. He doesn't kiss me there, instead he simply blows out a hot breath, dragging it down the length of my neck, before pressing a gentle kiss on my collarbone.

My legs are still wrapped around his waist with his hands firmly cupping my ass. I can feel his erection pressing into me, I'm scared to break this position because my shorts are definitely wet through, it's quite possible his jeans might be as well.

"God dammit Beth, you have no idea how long I've wanted to do this. When you said you needed me, I couldn't drive here fast enough." I laugh as he gently plants kisses up and down the column of my throat, and over to my shoulder.

"I'm sorry it took me so long to admit it." He shakes his head and breathes out a bit of a laugh, but before he can say anything else, Logan calls out to me from his bedroom.

I close my eyes and let out a big exhale that no doubt carries enough disappointment for both of us. I rest my forehead against his for a second as he lowers me down, my body slides against his until my feet hit the floor again. I straighten up my shorts and shirt and tell Mason to wait for me in the living room while I get Logan resettled. It's definitely time we had a conversation.

****

It takes me a little while to get Logan resettled, he gets a bit clingy when he is sick. Usually Griffin was the best at cheering him up. Something else I need to learn how to do.

I've been laying next to him rubbing his back and singing to him for about twenty minutes, and as he drifts back off to sleep, my heart begins to pound. I haven't been able to wipe the smile off my face, since I opened the door and saw Masons face.

I sneak out of Logans bed, and close the door over. Before heading out to the lounge. I find Mason on the couch, his muscular arm resting along the back of the three seater couch, long legs in a wide man spread, his gym shorts have ridden up slightly to reveal those thighs. Yep, there they are again.

Who am I kidding, literally anything about this man would be a turn on for me right now.

He looks more relaxed than I've seen him, maybe ever. I guess the relief of finding out your feelings have been reciprocated will do that to a man. As soon as I enter the room, I can feel my nerves starting to waiver.

"How is he?" He says, as he sits up and rests his elbows on his knees. I sit at the other end of the couch, trying to keep a little bit of distance between us, because after the way he just touched me, I don't trust myself to talk to him without trying to recreate that scenario.

"Yeah, he's back asleep. Just restless, I think." I give him a weak smile, I'm exhausted too, but I wouldn't trade this for the world.

"I'm sorry, I should've checked that it was okay to come over instead of just barging in like that."

"Mase, you asked for a reason to come over. I gave you one. I told you I needed to see you." He sits back and places his arm back over the back of the couch.

"Since you're here. Do you want to talk, like we were supposed to at dinner?" I place my arm over the back of the couch as well, just so my hand is resting on top of his.

"Only if you're up for it. You've had a big few days, you're probably just as keen to get to bed." He starts to gently stroke my knuckles.

"I'm afraid I won't sleep until I tell you all of the things that have been going through my mind in the last week, so if it's okay with you, I'd like to say my piece now."

He gives me a brief nod and I can tell he is still nervous. Like he still thinks I'm going to turn him down.

"I spent all week going back and forwards in my brain. One minute I want to move forward and the next minute, I can't let go of the past. I've worried about how everyone else would feel about me moving on. I've done a lot of soul searching and revisiting memories, and conversations with Griffin just hoping that somewhere I might find the right answer. Looking for some kind of sign that this is the right time for me to move on.

"Then I visited my dad, and he told me a few home truths, and I told myself I was ready. But then when Logan got sick, and again my doubts crept in, and I thought that was a sign that it isn't the right time after all." I pause briefly.

I think I've worded this all wrong because I can tell I'm not putting him at ease any here. His gaze has dropped to where our hands are touching, like it's the only thing grounding him right now.

Wrap it up, Beth. Put him out of his misery.

I continue, "But then yesterday when my dad came to visit us in the hospital, he said something that made me think. He said it might never be the perfect time, but that doesn't mean it isn't the right one." That gets his attention. He looks up at me like he is questioning If he heard that right.

"So, what are you saying?" I can hear the hope in his voice.

"I'm saying, some days I might have doubts, and fears. Lots of them. But, in spite of those, I want to give this a go. If you'll have me."

His eyes twinkle and his face splits in a smile, He tilts his head back, resting it on the back of the couch and lets out a chuckle, he rolls his head to the side to look at me "Are you fucking with me right now? This feels too good to be true."

I crawl across the lounge and sit on his lap, facing him, my legs straddling either side of his. His hands go straight to my hips and run gently up and down my side, I cup his face in my hands.

"Would it help if I pinched you, so you know you aren't dreaming?" I lay a soft, gentle kiss on his lips., before coming back up to look in his eyes.

"This feels really scary to me. But life is too short, right?" I lay another gentle kiss on each of his cheeks and the tip of his nose. He reaches up and cradles my face in his big hands.

"Beth, we take this at your pace, ok? If you aren't comfortable, at any time. You just say the word."

I move to sit next to him, with my head laying on his chest and his arm around my shoulder, rubbing gentle strokes down my arm. I have a hand resting on his thigh and we just sit there in silence, like it's the most natural thing in the world.

No background noise, no talking. Just being in each others company.

I can hear the sound of his heart beating in his chest and it must be like some kind of white noise, because next thing I know I'm in his arms, and he is carrying me to my bed. He pulls my blankets up and lays a kiss on my forehead.

"Goodnight, Beth." I hear the front door lock and then his truck drive away a moment later, I fall back to sleep with a smile on my face.

Chapter 12

MASON

I walk in my front door and throw my keys on the side table. Then lean my back flat against the back of the door. I close my eyes and take a few deep breaths in and out.

On the third exhale, I break into a smile, and I fist pump into the air. Both my stomach and my heart are doing backflips.

I can't believe any of this, I feel like at any moment I am going to wake up and realize it has all been a dream.

I was glad Logan woke up and cockblocked us a little bit. Beth seems very cautious, and things were heading in a dangerous direction if she needs to take things slow. I am going to need to find a fuck ton of self-control if I'm going to maintain my composure around her. The last thing I want to do is let Beth see that I'm no better than a horny teenager.

I lay in my bed going over everything that happened tonight. I read her text messages over and over.

There is one thing I need…. You.

That will live rent free in my head for years. Everything she said, seeing her battle between her fears and her hope for happiness. Sounds like I owe her dad a beer when I meet him.

The taste of her lips when I devoured them. Just thinking about that now has my dick springing back to life.

She looked so at ease as I tucked her in to bed. And I know in this moment, I will do whatever it takes to continue to help her ease her fears and doubts. I smile to myself before turning my bedside lamp off and turning in for the night.

My alarm sounds on Monday morning and I let out a long groan. I really am not ready to get up. I was having the best sleep of my life. I grab my phone to switch my alarm off and see I have a text.

Beth: Good morning, I'm sorry for falling asleep on you last night. Thank you for coming over. I never would've asked but I needed to tell you everything. I'm glad it's all out in the open.

Mason: Morning gorgeous, I'm glad too, but please stop apologizing so much. You'd had a big few days. Will I see you at work today?

Beth: Yeah my brothers are going to take turns watching Logan around their work schedules so I'll be there. Busy week this week, Abi and I have a Spring Fling to finish planning *laughing face emoji*

Uggghhhh not this again. Every year, John and his wife, Caroline put on a staff function around this time of year.

We don't usually get to have a Christmas party as work is usually too hectic at that time of year with all of our clients wanting work wrapped up in time for the holidays and then a lot of our colleagues are busy planning or travelling with their families. So John and Caroline decided to make a tradition of a midyear function instead.

It's usually a good night but every year is a different theme, and everyone is expected to dress up accordingly. This year is Spring Fling, so I'm expecting it to look like a high school prom. As if one of those wasn't enough.

Beth has booked out the bar area at Just in Thyme for the night, so that should also be interesting. It's only two weeks away so I guess I'll have to find out how we are going to handle our new relationship in front of our colleagues.

I'm not even sure if our company has a policy on employees dating, I can't imagine it's been an issue in the past given that probably ninety per cent of the staffing body are married, and the amount of males far outweigh the amount of females.

I should probably ask about it though. I like to lead by example so can't be seen to be breaking the rules.

Mason: Out of interest, do you happen to know if there are any fraternization rules at work? Just something I thought about, and should probably know the answer to before Spring Fling,

Beth: Is that your way of asking me to be your date, Mason Clarke? *winking face emoji*

Mason: No, I was planning on just throwing you over my shoulder and carrying you in with me. It eliminates the risk of being rejected or stood up.

Beth: Look out Hallmark, there's a new romance expert in town.

Mason: Oh, it's romance you want? Well, just you wait Beth. You won't know what hit you. Seriously though, do you think I should ask John? Or Abi?

Beth: Leave it with me, I'll do some investigating.

****

The week goes by in a flash. Beth and I haven't had much of a chance to be together outside of work, and I have been in and out between job sites and the office all week, but I managed to sneak in two lunch breaks with her, met her at the coffee pot one morning, and we have been texting pretty much non stop since last weekend.

We have made plans to go out to my family farm this weekend so I can show Logan a thing or two about fishing, Beth

102

has planned a picnic lunch, and some activities her and Rosie can do while they sit back and watch.

We also wanted to talk to the kids and gauge their feelings on us being in a relationship. I know it will be a deal breaker if they aren't okay with it.

It's Friday so as soon as I finish work, I get in my car, excited to go and pick Rosie up. She is a handful, but I miss her when she isn't around. I don't take for granted how lucky I am to have 50/50 custody though. I know a lot of dads lose out in divorce settlements these days.

'Daddyyyyy!' Rosie comes flying out the front door and crashes into me, her little arms wrapped around my thighs. I pick her up and throw her over my shoulder and tickle her sides while she kicks and screams in fits of laughter.

I put her down when we reach the front porch steps, I crouch down at the bottom of the steps and with her standing two steps above me we are as close to being eye to eye as is possible. She looks me in the eyes as she puts her little hand on my cheek and says "You look extra happy today, Daddy."

"That's because I am, Honey girl. I get to see you!" I wrap her up in my arms again, and my hand engulfs her tiny little head. She has my dark hair but the cutest little ringlet curls that are all Hannah.

And as though I've summoned her with one thought, I look up to the front door to see Hannah standing in the doorframe watching me reunite with our daughter, a smile on her face. "Hi."

"Hey, you coming in? I've just got a couple more things of Rosie's to pack and then she will be all good to go."

Hannahs parents helped her to buy me out of my share of the house we owned together. It's always bittersweet coming here, we had some good memories, but we also had a lot of really dark times. I'm glad Rosie gets to keep her childhood home though.

"Hey Rosie girl, I need to talk to your mama for a minute, do you think you could go upstairs and make sure you have everything you need from your bedroom?"

She gives me a puzzled look, because she is a smart kid and knows that's a bit out of the ordinary, but takes off running up the stairs a moment later. I take my hat off and run my fingers through my hair a few times before putting my hat back on.

"Uh oh, that sounds ominous." Hannah says as she is sizing me up trying to get a hint at what I might need to talk to her about.

"I uh, I know what the rumor mill is like in this town, so I just wanted to make sure you hear this from me first… I'm seeing someone."

I bite the inside of my cheek as I wait for her reaction. Truthfully, I keep waiting for our amicable split to turn sour like most of the other divorces you hear about.

She can obviously tell I'm a bit nervous, she crosses the room and give me a hug. I definitely wasn't expecting that. She pulls away and takes a few steps back, then flops onto the couch.

"Thank you for telling me. I appreciate you considering my feelings like that. Am I allowed to ask who?"

"I think you already know the answer to that, Han." I say as I sit down next to her on the couch. I look over at her cautiously, this all feels so awkward.

"I hoped I knew the answer to that. I swear to God if you had've said anyone else's name right now, I might've smacked you. I'm happy for you Mason. You two are good for each other." I smile at that.

I don't know why I felt like I needed her approval. But it helps. And it feels good to know it won't affect anything between us.

"We were thinking of talking to Rosie, and Beths son Logan about it tomorrow. I think she will be okay, I just want to be honest with her. And Beth and I both agreed, if the kids have any issues, then that's it. They come first."

"Mason, I'm sure she will be fine. She talks non stop about Logan and Beth, she adores them both. But listen, while I appreciate you wanting to put her first. She is four, and gets upset if you give her the wrong colored plate for dinner. Don't end your brand new relationship. If she isn't fine with it straight away, she will be with time. If she isn't fine with it, we can talk to her together and I'm sure she will come around. But lets cross that bridge if or when we get to it."

She lays a hand on my shoulder and gives it a reassuring squeeze. Just as Rosie comes barreling down the stairs carrying a purple, polka dotted horse. "Daddy, can I bring Sparkles?" I let out a laugh and shake my head.

"500 stuffed toys in my house already.. Sure, what's one more?"

✳✳✳✳✳✳✳✳✳✳✳✳✳✳

I put an extra booster seat in my truck so I can pick Beth and Logan up and take them out to the farm for the day today. Rosie is dragging her feet, she has never been keen on going to the farm, she thinks the animals smell funny, but when she sees the second booster seat, and finds out Logan is coming, she changes her tune a little bit, apparently she will do anything he wants to do.

When I'm done installing the seat I stand back for a minute, because damn, two booster seats look real good in my backseat. Beth is organizing us a picnic for lunch so I pack us a cooler with some drinks, I tell Rosie to pack her stuff, and of course she grabs her makeup and tiara.

I grab our swimming gear and towels, because it's warm enough today at least for the kids to splash around a bit.

105

We arrive at Beths, Rosie takes off into the house to find Logan and I find Beth in the kitchen, she looks amazing as always. She is wearing denim cut off shorts, which make her legs look like they go for miles. She has paired it with a long sleeve, pink linen shirt that is loosely tucked in to the waistband of her shorts, and the sleeves are slightly rolled up.

I told her to bring their swimming gear as well and I can see she is wearing a bikini top underneath. What I wouldn't give to see her take that shirt off right here, right now and give me a peek of what's underneath.

Her hair is tied up in an effortless, loose messy bun with a few strands pulled out to frame her face and she has her sunglasses perched on top of her head.

It takes everything in me not to pull her in and kiss her, but the kids are here. Hopefully by this afternoon, I can kiss her whenever I want to.

"Hey you." She says as she looks me up and down. I'm wearing boardshorts and flip flops, and a plain white cotton T-shirt.

"Hi. Need help with anything?" I stand right beside her, so to the kids it looks like I'm lending a hand, but I just needed to be close to her.

"No we are just about all set. Wait till you see Logie, he's so excited" She turns her head and calls out to Logan. I haven't seen him since he was sick last week but Beth said he hasn't stopped talking about going fishing today.

He comes running into the kitchen and this kid is dressed head to toe in camouflaged mossy oak, looking like he is ready for a full on game hunting trip. He is carrying a net and bucket.

I hold back a little chuckle, God I hope we catch something. I don't think I can handle letting him down.

"Looking good little dude." I crouch down to his level and hold out a fist for him to bump, as we usually do every time we see each other, but today he looks at my fist, and then pushes it aside and steps into my arms, wraps his hand around my neck and says

"Thank you for taking me fishing Mason."

Damn, this kid…. I wrap one arm around his back, pulling him tighter as I push to stand, lifting him up with me, I sit him on the countertop so he is at my eye level. "Anytime buddy. You look like you might be the one teaching me how to fish."

"Grandpa told me that the fishies shouldn't be able to see me, or hear me. So I have to hide and be quiet."

"That's good advice right there. Alright, are we ready to do this?" He nods his head with so much enthusiasm and kicks his feet like he could run on thin air.

I look over at Beth and she is staring blankly at me, watching me interact with her son, and I swear I see tears in her eyes.

I put Logan back down on the ground, he picks up his net and bucket, and runs out to find Rosie. I take a few steps to stand in front of Beth and reach out to tuck a strand of hair behind her ear.

"Ready?" She looks up at me with those big green, watery eyes, and nods her head. So I grab the picnic basket and she rounds up the kids.

****

As we drive down the dirt roads heading towards the river, we pass the field that currently has our breeding herd in it, there are a few calves that have been born so far this season, Logan gets excited at seeing the babies, so we stop and get out of the car.

I watch his eyes light up as he squeals with glee at the sight of watching a couple of calves kicking and bucking around the field. Even Rosie is giggling at them, which makes me smile even harder.

107

I'm determined to get her to see the good things about farm life and that's when I remember one of my favorite things to do when my sister and I were young. Dad would drive the truck while we sat in the bed of the truck. Of course he only ever went slow, but he hit every bump in the road and we always had an absolute ball. So I tell Beth to sit in the bed, and hold onto the kids.

It's only a few minutes drive to the banks of the river, especially at this low speed. I think this is going to be a core memory for all four of us. They are all laughing, having the time of their lives, bouncing around the back, kicking up the dust. I've never heard Rosie laugh as hard as she is right now. Yeah, this feels right.

I stand on the banks of the river, I've shown Logan how to bait and cast his line, he is a natural, I only had to show him once and now he looks like he has been doing it for years.

Every few minutes, my eyes glance up further into the grassy field where my girls are chilling out having a tea party. I never thought I'd get to enjoy time like this on the farm.

As I glance up at Beth, she catches me staring and holds my gaze for a moment, from my right hand side I hear Logan scream "I got one, I got one! I got a bite!"

I take a few steps over to him and son of a bitch, he has a fish on. I help him reel it in, and he grabs his net to land it. Beth and Rosie come running down to see the fruits of our labor.

When we bring the fish to the bank, I am actually impressed, it's a decent sized fish. I grab it out, take the hook out, and ask Logan if wants to hold it. He grimaces a bit, and then the fish starts to flop around, he lets out a squeal.

"I need to take a photo to show Grandpa. Can you help me hold it, Mason? Mama, take a photo, quick!"

I crouch down behind him and bring him into my arms, while I hold this fish in front of his body like a prized trophy. He doesn't hold it, but he puts one hand on the fish and his other hand covers the top of my hand that is in the fish's mouth. Beth pulls out her phone and we both smile for a quick photo before we put it back in the water and he waves as it swims away.

"How was that, bud?" Beth says, I look up at her and again, she looks like she has tears welling in her eyes, at least this time, she is smiling with it so I know they are happy tears.

"That was the best Mama, I can't wait to tell Grandpa and Uncle Will, and Uncle Nate." He is jumping up and down with excitement.

"Don't forget to tell Benji too, pal." I add. Beth chuckles, looks at me and mouths "Thank you." She smiles and nods as she takes Rosie by the hand and they walk back up the slight hill to where their picnic blanket is set up.

"Well, I don't know about you Logan, but all this fishing has made me hungry. What do you say we go and check out what we've got for lunch?" He grabs my hand and we follow a few steps behind Beth and Rosie.

We all sit down on the picnic rug and Beth starts unpacking the food she has made, sandwiches, trays of fruit, cheese and crackers, a few little chocolates for after. She covered all bases.

We talk and laugh over lunch and when we are all finished eating, we all lay down on the rug, watching the clouds go by, Rosie is sprawled out like a starfish, Logan has his head resting on Beths stomach.

Beth lays flat on her back with one hand stroking Logans head, and I lay beside Beth with one hand under my head. With my other hand I reach down and discreetly loop my pinky finger in hers.

We lay there for what feels like hours trying to make shapes out of the clouds. Rosie thinks everything looks like a fairy or a princess, Logan argues that they are all dinosaurs or dragons. Beth and I just laugh at both of their imaginations.

We sit up and look at each other, both giving each other a slight nod. Our sign that we are ready to talk to the kids.

"Hey guys, can you sit up for a second, we have something we want to talk to you about..."

Chapter 13

BETH

I take a deep breath in, because I'm not even sure how to approach this with them. How to explain a new relationship when there is kids involved.

"So you guys know how we have all been hanging out and having lots of fun lately?" The kids look at each other and then nod, looking back and forth between Mason and I.

"Well, as adults we have been having lots of fun getting to know each other better and becoming really good friends over the last few months as well. And well… together we have decided that we want to try and be more than friends. So that might mean that you might see us holding hands, or hugging, maybe kissing. But we wanted to know how you guys would feel about that?"

Rosie stands, pops her hip out, extending one leg and tapping her toes. She props one hand on her hip, while bringing the other hand's index finger to tap on her lips which she has pursed in a thoughtful expression.

"So, you're saying you want to be my dads girlfriend?" she narrows her eyes at me and I'm instantly nervous about where she is going with this.

"Yeah Rosie, that's exactly what I'm saying. Do you think you would be ok with that?" She taps her foot a few more times.

"Hmmm. I guess that could be okay. He is still my husband though, and still has to take me on shopping trips. But I guess he could be your boyfriend too."

She shrugs her shoulders and I let out a little giggle. Mason grabs her and pulls her into his lap, giving her a slight tickle as she lands.

We both look up to Logan who has been sitting quietly, not saying anything, just staring blankly down at his lap.

"What about you Logie? Do you have any thoughts or feelings you want to share?" I say while I gently pinch his cheek.

He looks up at me with tears in his eyes and my stomach sinks. I knew this was too soon.

"Does this mean you don't love my daddy anymore?" His tears start to fall and I immediately grab him and pull him into my lap. Rosie comes over and gives him a gentle hug as well, crouching next to us.

"No buddy, not at all. I will always, *always* love Daddy. He was very, very special to me and no one can ever take his place." I wipe his tears away and he nods gently. This must be so much for him to take in.

"Buddy, do you remember how daddy was always laughing, and being silly, and goofing off all of the time?"

That brings a hesitant smile to his face, and he nods again. "Well, he used to do that because all he cared about was making us happy. But you know how since Daddy went to heaven, we were both really sad there for a while? Do you remember what things made us feel better?"

He looks up at me through his tears and finds a sheepish grin. He silently points at Rosie. "Yeah, that's right. Rosie made you feel better. And Mason has helped me to feel better. I think that's pretty special, don't you think?"

"I like when Rosie and Mason come over."

"I think Daddy wouldve loved to see us happy again, don't you?"

"Will I have to call Mason daddy, like Rosie does?"

Holy shit, I wasn't expecting him to say that, That catches me out and feels like a sucker punch. I wasn't expecting his mind to go that far ahead. Mason sees me struggling to come up with an answer to that one.

"Logan, you don't have to call me anything you don't want to. You can call me Mason, or your friend, or hey, you can even call me a stinky butthead if that's what you want." Logan and Rosie both break out in fits of laughter at the mention of the word butthead.

"Can I call you stinky butthead?" Rosie says.

"NO!" Mason and I both say in unison. We all giggle. That seems to have lightened Logan up a little bit. But Mason continues to add

"Logan, I will never be able to replace your dad. Trust me, I'm nowhere near as funny or as cool as he was. I really like spending time with you, but we aren't going to do anything that makes you feel uncomfortable okay?"

Well, I'm officially being blinded by the hearts in my eyes. This man couldn't be any hotter right now if he tried.

Logan looks between the two of us and then over to Rosie who has clearly lost interest in the conversation and is twirling in circles singing a made up song.

"Rosie is happy about it, so I guess it's okay with me too. But Benji said girls have yucky germs." His face has immediately changed into one of disgust.

"Don't worry about that buddy, I've had my shots." Mason says as he leans over and kisses me on the cheek.

Rosie stops twirling and both her and Logan look over and say "Ewwww" in perfect unison.

"Right, who's going to be first to get thrown into the river?" Mason says as he stands up and chases the two screaming kids down towards the water.

****

Beth: Good news, I looked through all of our employee handbooks this morning, there's no written rule against employees dating. I'm sure John will be fine with it, but If it makes you feel any better, we can talk to him about it together tomorrow if you want to.

Mason: Yeah, I think that's a good idea. I'd rather just be transparent. I have to set a good example.

John is beginning his transition to retirement, it's part of the reason Mason has recently taken over doing the proposals and a bit more of the client facing tasks. He is poised to take over when John eventually does retire. He is only in the office on Tuesdays and Thursdays now, so Mason pencils in some time to be in the office so we can talk to him together.

John is like an extension of my family. He has been friends with my dad since they were in high school, he and Caroline own the house across the street from my Dad, and his daughter, Maggie is around the same age and Nate and Bella so they pretty much grew up together.

John also had a massive soft spot for Griffin so I'm worried it will be a bit awkward. I feel like I'm more nervous to talk to John than I was to talk to my dad.

I knock on his office door, and peek my head in from behind it as I open it slowly. "John, do you have a minute?"

"Beth! For you, I will always have a minute. What can I do for you?" He moves to shut the door behind me, and then realizes Mason is two steps behind me. He gives me a bit of a confused look, like he isn't sure if it is a coincidence that Mason is here at the same time.

114

"Actually, Mason and I would like to talk to you together, if that's okay." He ushers Mason in and we each take a seat opposite Johns luxury desk chair that looks more like a rocking, reclining armchair that belongs in a living room, than an office chair.

"I'm just going to come right out and say this John, no beating around the bush. Mason and I have started seeing each other. I have read through the staff handbooks and can't find any written rules against it, but if it's going to be an issue for you or the company, we need to know sooner rather than later."

Mason sits with a stunned look on his face, like he can't believe I just blurted it out like that without trying to sweet talk our boss a little bit first.

John just says "hmm." And then sits back in his chair, tapping his fingers on the giant, cushioned arm rests. He looks between the two of us and then lets out a deep exhale.

"Did you two honestly think that you had been hiding your feelings up until this point? Honestly, I'm only here two days a week and even I can see the spark between you."

Why does everyone keep saying that?

Mason and I look at each other, and I can't help but smile. "Beth, after everything you've been through. You deserve happiness. If this is where you've found it, then grab onto that with both hands. Besides, even if I wanted to, your father would never let me hear the end of it if I got in his little girls way. Mason, you'll do well to remember that. You don't fuck with the Philips'. Hank will have your balls if you mess with his girl here."

He stands from his chair and I know that's our cue to leave. He shakes Masons hand, and he leaves. John stops me just before I walk out and says "I'm happy for you Beth. Truly, you deserve all the happiness, and he is a really good guy." He gives me a gentle pat on the shoulder, and I walk out as well.

✶✶✶✶✶✶✶✶✶✶

Going down the checklist of people we wanted to talk to about potentially pursuing a relationship with Mason, we have checked off every single one… Except my siblings, the one I've been dreading the most.

I know I'm going to cop so much shit from my brothers. At least I have my dad on my side. I have his little secret to hold over his head if he doesn't have my back with them.

It's Friday afternoon and everyone else is leaving for the day. I've spent all day trying to prepare myself for telling my siblings about Mason. I have backed myself into a corner now because the Spring Fling is tomorrow night and it's being held in the bar room at Just in Thyme so unless I want to spend the entire night watching Mason from afar and not touching him, then I need to tell them. And I'm done fighting my physical attraction to this man.

I'm working late as usual, trying to get through my pile of data entry I wanted to get finished when I hear the door to the office open. I thought everyone would've left by now.

When I look up, I see Mason walking in. He has bought me in some invoices that I will need to process for Abi. More work, how generous of him.

"Nervous for tonight?" he says as he sits on the edge of my desk, right beside me.

"I am, but not because I don't feel good about us, just because I know how much shit I'm going to cop. Nate has thought from the very first night we went to Just in Thyme that there was something there, so it's going to be painful hearing him gloat about being right."

He looks down at me, grabs my chair by the arm rest, taking advantage of the fact my chair is on wheels, he slides me over so I'm sitting between his legs.

116

"What are you doing?" I look up at him with a smirk. He leans down, with an arm on each of the arm rests of my chair, completely caging me in.

"Just thought I could maybe, make you forget about some of that for a minute." His eyes wander down my face, stopping at my lips. His tongue darts out and runs along his bottom lip, leaving it shiny and wet.

I bite my bottom lip and then say "And how do you plan on doing that?"

He runs the back of his index finger down my cheek, before gripping my chin between his finger and thumb, dragging my gaze up to meet his. "Unfortunately, I can't do the things I'd like to do to you while we are in our place of work, but since we are alone… I can do this."

He crashes his mouth down on mine, while lifting me up to stand so I'm at his eye level, his tongue is immediately flicking into my mouth, tasting and exploring.

He wraps his hand around my lower back and pulls me in close so our bodies are flush against each other. I can feel him hardening against me and I get an instant rush of heat between my legs. I'm not sure how I'm going to pull away from this.

"God Beth, I've loved watching you walk around in this tight skirt for so long, just teasing me, begging me to take it off you. I don't think I can wait much longer."

I pepper him with kisses down his neck and he lets out a long groan that sends shivers down my spine. As our mouths meet again in another deep, passionate kiss, I feel his hand rub up the side of my hip, then over my ribs, before coming up to palm my breast, ever so gently like he is expecting me to freak out. Not today, I need the extra motivation.

I grab a handful of his shirt as though I have to brace myself. His touch feels electric. I can feel my arousal building and if I'm not careful, it will be running down my legs before long.

It's Mason that breaks our kiss. He holds me at arms length, we are both panting for breath. "We can't do this, not here. Fuck, but I want to." He runs his fingers through his hair.

"I know, not the time or place." I smooth down my skirt and straighten my shirt.

"How are you feeling now?" he says as we cups the side of my face.

"Well, you took one pain away, and replaced it with a whole other type of pain."

"Tell me about it" He says as he glances down at his worn, dusty jeans that are noticeably tighter than they were moments ago.

I don't think I've ever wanted anything more than I want to see those jeans on my bedroom floor.

"Call me tonight, and let me know how things go. Good luck with your brothers." He places his hand around the back of my neck and brings me back in for one last, deep kiss before he turns to walk out.

He stops at the door, turns back to me, raking his gaze up and down my body and says "Tomorrow, that skirt is mine."

Chapter 14

BETH

My concentration is shot now, thanks to the tall, denim clad contractor that just strut his way in and out of my office for a little bit of Friday afternoon torture.

I start to shut down my computer and pack up for the day, I know it's pointless trying to get any more work done when I'm not sure I even know my own name, my brain is so fried. My body feels like it's quite literally on fire.

I decide today I'll go home and get changed before going to Dads, instead of rushing around there and changing in to my comfy clothes there, as usual.

It wouldn't hurt me to freshen up a bit after that kiss anyway, splash some water on my face, maybe I should just go all out spend some quality time with the massaging shower head. Relieve some of the tension I feel creeping back in.

Almost an hour later, I'm clean and refreshed. I've given myself a pep talk in the mirror and I'm ready to go.

Beth: I'm on my way to dads now. 15 minute warning to Facetime in. Please, Bel. I need everyone together x

Bella: Yes, sir. I'm ready when you are. Love you x

Ah, so my smart ass baby sister does still exist.

I walk in and it's chaos as usual. Will, Nate and Logan are wrestling on the living room floor. Dad is running around the kitchen, doing five things at once. Olive is clearing logans dinosaurs off the dinner table. I don't think the boys even notice when I walk in, they certainly don't question why I'm early and already dressed. I give Olive a smile and a nod as she walks down the hall with an armful of my kids toys.

"Hi Sweetheart, you're early. Making this a habit?" my dad says while smiling joyfully at me, as I approach him to plant a kiss on his cheek.

"Just not too early this time." I waggle my eyebrows at him and he nudges his elbow into my side while jolting his eyes around to make sure no one heard.

"I actually wanted to talk to everyone together. Bella is waiting for me to Facetime her. Do you think you can spare a second away from cooking?"

"Anything for my girl." I clear my throat loudly enough to pause the wrestling match in the lounge room. They truly hadn't even heard me walk in because that makes Logan run and jump up into my arms. He wraps his arms around my neck and squeezes my cheek into his chest.

My two brothers follow him into the kitchen, both with confused looks on their faces, no doubt now just clicking on to the fact that I'm here almost an hour earlier than usual.

"Who died? Surely that's the only reason Beth leaves work early." Will Says.

"Haha, very funny." I say back as I roll my eyes back at him.

"Its okay Mama, I kept our secret all day!" Logan beams with pride.

That grabs everybody's attention. Wills head snaps around so fast I'm surprised he didn't slip a disk. Nates jaw hits the floor, he is rarely rendered speechless, but this seems to have done it. Dad drops the metal spoon he was holding onto the floor with a loud crash, and Olive reappears out of nowhere "Secret, who has a secret?"

"So close, buddy. So close." I ruffle his hair as I put him back down on the floor.

"Can you go pack up the rest of your toys and wash up for dinner please? The grown-ups need to talk for a minute."

"Ok, well, sorry to disappoint you. You aren't about to catch me out in some scandal, I'm actually here early because I wanted to talk to you all together. Can someone dial Bella in please?"

Nate takes out his phone to dial as we all take our regular spots around the table. Nate props his phone up at the end of the table so Bella can see everyone. After a quick round of greetings to our sister, I start talking.

"Yes! I knew it! Pay up, William. I win." Nate stands abruptly from his chair and starts dancing obnoxiously around the table while chanting "I win, I win, You lose, You Lose" Somethings will never change around here. Nate will always act like a ten year old.

"Seriously? You guys were betting on whether I'd date this guy?" I give them both an unamused look.

"No Beth, we knew you'd hook up with him. The bet was on how long it would take. See, Will here thinks you're some kind of nun, and would've waited two years. I know some women just can't wait that long. Right, Ol?" Nate says as he winks at Olive.

"Eewwwww." We all say in unison. Olive looks like she wishes the ground would swallow her whole at that moment. I've never seen her blush so deep.

"So when do we all get to meet him?" Olive asks, clearly trying to change the subject.

"Technically, I've already met him. But, he's going to be at your work thing tomorrow, I'm assuming? So this time, I get to really have some fun with him." Olive and I both roll our eyes at him now.

"Nate, leave her alone. Would it kill you to just be serious for one moment. Think about how scary this is for Beth." My sister chimes in, Who knew? One of the youngest and most wise. And right now, my favorite of the Philips siblings.

"Relax, Bella. I'm sure our Bethy has a new found way of calming her nerves." Will decides to add, while poking his tongue into his cheek. I hear Bella scoff at him and I move to punch him in the shoulder.

"Oh hey guys, I've got to go, I'm so sorry. Brad just pulled up, so I've got to make a start on dinner. I'm happy for you Beth. Love you all."

Bella hangs up abruptly, but it seems no one else is worried, so I don't let it bother me too much. "Pops, you're awfully quiet on this matter. Don't you have anything to add?"

Nate looks at our dad and then back to me, the same way he used to when he was a kid and he had just dobbed on me for no reason.

"I'm happy that Beth is happy. And that's all there is for it. Now if you'll excuse me, Dinner isn't going to cook itself." I see Nates head immediately deflate. Sucker. That plan backfired.

"Oh and Nathaniel, before you think about any methods of torture for tomorrow night. Mason and I have an agreement that the more you annoy either one of us, the more handsy I will allow him to be in your bar. So be careful, because you are right about something. I'm certainly no Nun." I give him a couple of gentle slaps on the cheek and his smug smile quickly falls off his face.

＊＊＊＊＊＊＊＊＊＊＊＊＊＊

I get home from Philips Friday and get Logan into bed. He is exhausted after eating his weight in chocolate pudding and then beating us all at Uno, and then Go Fish. His new favorite game ever since Mason took him fishing.

I make myself a cup of tea and then sit up in my bed and call Mason as I said I would. He answers on the second ring.

"Was beginning to think you'd forgotten about me." His voice sounds gravelly, like he was either almost asleep, or he was asleep and I just woke him up.

"Oh babe, I could never forget about you." That came out as a joke but.. It felt right.

He chuckles at that and I can hear how tired he is. He is definitely in bed. "How did dinner go?"

"It was every bit as painful as I expected. Nate was hellbent he is going to have some fun with you tomorrow night, until I told him about our little deal, that shut him up pretty quickly."

"For my own selfish sake, I hope he does it anyway. I can't wait to have my hands on you." I can hear the smirk in his voice, and I like it.

"Is that so? And where exactly are you planning on having your hands?" I'm shamelessly teasing him now. I don't even care.

"Oh baby, this time tomorrow night, I hope there isn't a single inch of you that my hands haven't been."

Checkmate. Game, set, match. Stick a fork in me, because I am done.

"Was really hoping you'd say that." Tomorrow night really can't come quick enough.

Mason and I talk for almost an hour. We make plans for tomorrow, Logan is staying with Will for the night so I can enjoy the night and not have to wake up at the crack of dawn the next morning.

Mason is going to pick me up, he isn't much of a drinker, he usually only has one or two beers so is happy to be the driver for the night. It works out okay for me, because him picking me up, means he will also drop me home. To my empty house. That will definitely feel lonely if he doesn't come in.

The next afternoon I start to get ready. I am so incredibly nervous about tonight. The fun, flirty confident Beth from yesterday is gone and has been replaced by the nervous Beth who has just realized she is planning on officially moving on with her romantic life tonight.

I usually love the opportunity to get dressed up. I never really get much of a chance to anymore, so I love the Spring Fling idea, to get really dressed up and have some fun with it.

I have four dresses to choose from, but I can't decide, nothing feels quite right for this occasion. Probably because I didn't buy these dresses thinking 'Hmm, what would be best to convince a man to have sex with me after having zero action for close to two years.'

God, has it really been that long?

I have decided I want to wear my hair down, in curls, which I also never get to do because Logan always plays with it and messes it up anyway, so it's easier just to pull it back out of my face. I do my hair and makeup while I mull over the choices of my dress.

I try all four on and narrow it down to two. A baby blue, silk wrap around dress that falls to about the middle of my shins. Or a red off the shoulder number that is skin tight and falls just above my knees. One is elegant and classy, and the other is hot as fuck. I can't decide which look I want to go for tonight.

I grab my phone and dial Bella. I've never been a girls girl, so apart from Abi, I don't really have any girl friends and I honestly have missed my sister so much since she moved.

The phone rings for so long I'm just about to hang up when she answers "Beth? hey, what's up?"

Immediately my skin prickles with concern, something is really off. "Why are you whispering?" I ask her, it comes out a little more harsh than I had intended.

"I just didn't want to disturb Brad, but I'm in the other room now, so I'm all good to chat. What's going on?"

"I need your help, picking an outfit for my work function tonight. I've narrowed it down to two, but they are very different vibes and I can't decide. Do I go elegant or slutty?"

"I mean, firstly, I need to ask. How do you want the night to end?" I huff out a breathy laugh.

"You're my little sister, I'm trusting you not to tell our meat head brothers this, but I'm pretty sure which ever dress I wear, it's ending up on the floor." Bella lets out a girly scream and I can hear rustling in the background so I just know she is kicking her feet in the air like a teenage girl.

"I'm so excited for you. Switch to facetime and show me the options."

I try on both dresses while we both talk like old times. I miss having my sister around all the time. We have always lived within a ten-minute drive of each other our whole lives, and now she has moved interstate, she is at least a twelve hour drive away. It sucks big time.

We share a special bond, given that I practically raised her. We have always just been able to talk about anything and everything with no judgement, and now it feels like she is a world away.

"The blue. I think it's classy given it's for a work function, but because it's the wrap dress with the uneven hem it still shows enough leg to be sexy as well. And it will be effortless to take off." She lets out another girly squeal.

I have poured myself a wine to calm my nerves. I get dressed while still chatting away to my sister.

Mason said he would be here at five thirty and it's just after five now. This is the longest I've spoken to Bella in months, so I'm not ready to hang up yet, so we decide to keep chatting.

I put the phone down on the bathroom counter while I do a few last looks, and touch up my makeup.

"You've got this Beth. You look amazing."

"Thanks Bel." I'm startled when I hear a loud bang, followed by yelling coming from the other side of the phone. I look down at my sister who's giggly, happy face from moments ago has dropped into something I don't quite recognize on her… Fear? Shame?

"Bella, is everything ok?" My tone is dripping with concern.

"Uh, yeah, it's just Brad watching the game. He has a fantasy league type thing with some guys from his office, it's kind of high stakes, so he has a lot riding on it. It's fine. I guess the game is over and things didn't go his way. He will cool off eventually."

There's a knock on my door. Shit, he's early. "Bel, he sounds really mad. Are you sure you're ok?"

I open the door and my breath is instantly stolen. Mason is wearing black dress pants, a simple black button up shirt, long sleeve with the sleeves slightly rolled up showing off his corded, toned forearms. The top button is undone, Leaving just the right amount of chest showing to look classy yet sexy as hell.

"Beth, I'm fine, I promise he will cool off and it will all be okay, And by the looks of your face right now, I think you need to turn me around and introduce me."

I look back down at my sisters face on my phone. Then back up to meet Masons gaze I mouth the words 'I'm sorry' to Mason as I slowly spin the phone around. "This is my sister Bella. Bella, meet Mason."

"Hi, Bella, I've heard so much about you. It's nice to meet the sensible Philips first. I hope you don't think I'm being rude, but I'd really like to kiss your sister now."

"I'd think you were rude if you didn't. I'll leave you to your night. Have fun kids"

"Thanks Bel. Hey, listen. If you need anything. Night or day. You call me. You hear?"

"Yes, mother. Go. Enjoy your night. Love you." I smile slightly as I hang up even though she has given me some things to worry about. That boyfriend of hers is a walking red flag. Thank God the best distraction I could think of just walked in my front door.

<h1 style="text-align:center">Chapter 15</h1>

MASON

Fuck, do we really have to go to this thing? I've never seen a more beautiful sight than the minute Beth opened her front door. This shade of blue. This is her color. It compliments her beautifully.

Her long hair is in gentle curls framing her gorgeous face. Her makeup looks like it was done by a professional, she usually wears light makeup to work but this is next level. Shimmery silver eye makeup that makes her green eyes really pop. And her lips. Fuck, I want to devour those lips.

Id also like to see them devour me in more ways than one.

"Hi" I say to her because I don't think I can form a full sentence right now. I'm still taking her in, I don't even know if I've managed to look her in the eyes yet. I'm too busy committing the rest of her to my memory. And my spank bank. Fuck me.

She has finished off the look with some silver heels which make her almost as tall as me, but fuck do they make her legs look fucking amazing. And the way that dress rises and falls in all the right places.

Jesus Mason, snap out of it before you bust the zipper on your pants.

"Hey, you. You look so god damn good." I don't miss the way she also runs her eyes down the length of my body either.

"You're one to talk. You are absolutely stunning." I grab her hand and lift it to my mouth and press a gentle kiss to her knuckles, before meeting her gaze.

"Seriously, I almost forgot how to breathe for a few seconds there." She chuckles at that.

"I'll just get my bag and then we can go."

The whole drive to the restaurant, I keep my hand on Beths thigh, rubbing small circles with my thumb. The act of climbing into my truck made her dress fall to the sides so her thighs are exposed from about midway, giving me complete skin on skin contact with her and fuck, her skin is so smooth, exactly how I expected it to be.

I don't miss the way her breath hitches every now and then, and she lets a few small moans escape as well. This is going to be a long night.

We arrive at Just in Thyme and everything looks amazing. Beth, Abi and Caroline did an amazing job organizing this, as usual. It's always a great night out.

Every one eats, John gives a speech and thanks everyone for their hard work. Then the fun stuff really starts, it's an open bar and some of the guys can get pretty rowdy after a few beers.

There is a DJ setting up beside Just In Thyme's rather large dancefloor so I know this night is only just beginning.

I've been getting a mixture of both daggers and cocky grins from Nate who is working the bar tonight, since we walked in and he saw my hand resting on Beths lower back.

We have been back to Just in Thyme since that first night but Beth always coincidentally planned it so he wasn't working when we were here. I know he is going to give me and Beth a heap of shit tonight, so I approach the bar for the first time. Might as well get it over with.

"So I hear you are officially lover boy now." He reaches out his hand, and waits for me to shake it. "Nice to officially meet you, I'm Nate."

I shake his hand. Although he comes on strong, I think he is trying to assert some kind of dominance.

"Yeah, glad it's finally official. Can I get a lime and soda, and a glass of the house white, please?"

"Oh she's starting off slow. I thought she would go straight for the hard stuff. Pacing herself, smart girl."

"She said something about needing her wits about her tonight, with you in the room." He chuckles before turning to pour Beths wine.

I return to Beth who is talking to a couple of the guys wives and girlfriends, I'm sure Beth could make small talk with a brick wall and make it look like interesting conversation.

As I hand her her glass, she grabs my bicep, looks over at me and smiles. She taps her glass to mine in a 'cheers' motion and takes a sip. I lay a gentle kiss on her temple. It comes so naturally. She leans into me so I slip my arm around her, my hand coming to rest on her lower back, I rub gentle circles.

Fuck, this dress feels almost as good as it looks.

As the night goes on, and everyone gets more and more tipsy. The dancing begins. I'm a wall flower, from way back, so I'm happy to sit at the bar and watch.

I watch as Beth dances with John, and with Abi, and anyone else that comes near her. She is clearly having the time of her life.

I'm absolutely taken by her, the way she throws her head back laughing at Abi's dance moves. I've never been much of a dancer. But now that I know it makes her smile like *that*. Hell, I might just have to start.

"Whatcha lookin' at?" I hear from over my shoulder. I turn to see Nate grinning at me like the fucking cheshire cat.

"The most beautiful girl in the room." I turn my attention back to Beth because I don't want to miss a minute of looking at her.

"Gag." I hear him say as someone approaches the other end of the bar. I feel the stool on the other side of me pull out and look over to see Caroline, John's wife.

"You're absolutely captivated by her, aren't you?" She says as she sips the last of her drink.

"Like fireworks on New Years. Is that pathetic given everything that's happened in the last year?" She puts her empty glass on the bar, then comes to stand right in my line of sight.

"It's only pathetic if you don't do anything about that feeling, Mason. It's because of both of your pasts, that you two deserve all of the happiness this life has to offer. Don't let it go." I smile and she pats me on the shoulder before turning to order another drink.

I've moved halfway across the room, talking to one of my guys and his wife, and I sense her before she even gets to me. Before I can even look up and find Beth, I feel her hands on my back, rubbing a straight, slow line from my shoulders and down to my ribs, before I feel them slide around to my front, wrapping me in a hug. "Dance with me." She whispers as I feel her press the front of her body into my back.

"Beth, I haven't danced in public in... Well over 15 years, at this point, I'd be a risk to public safety." She spins me around so I'm facing her. She leans her face in close to mine, stopping when she is just an inch or so away from my ear.

"One drink, and then one dance. And then maybe we can get out of here." Pulling away from me, she gives me a wink with a cheeky grin, before taking me by the hand and leading me to the bar.

"She's making you dance, isn't she?' Nate says with that trademark shit eating grin he always seems to have. I can tell he is enjoying this way too much.

His stare bouncing between us. "She only dances when she is happy, so take it as a win." He reaches over and gives me an encouraging tap on the shoulder. He hands Beth another drink.

I need to have all of my control tonight, so I wasn't going to drink at all, but fuck it, I need a drink for this. Nate surprisingly hasn't been talking to much smack, but I suspect he might be taking notes to use against Beth in the morning in front of their other siblings.

Beth downs her drink in two huge gulps. I watch her throat bob up and down with every swallow. *Damn.* She puts away liquor with the best of them. And she is perfectly fine, I think this is about her fourth drink, and she could pass every sobriety test with ease. If anything, it's made her more flirty. God help me.

"C'mon big boy, it's dance time." Her brother stands there with his mouth open, clearly wanting to say something to that, but also, obviously being caught off guard.

"Yeah, go get her, Tiger." He says as he mimics cat claws and makes a meow sound. I know he is going to blow up their sibling group chat with gossip tomorrow, anyway, might as well give him something to talk about.

"Fuck it, let's do this." I say as I down the rest of my beer and follow her blindly onto the dance floor.

Abi and a few of the other guys and girls on the dance floor let out a cheer at the sight of me coming to dance. They know from previous years of these functions that I don't do this.

Surprisingly, I am able to keep up with Beth. It helps my nerves knowing half the people around me are three sheets to the wind and probably won't remember my two left feet come Monday morning.

I don't even know the song that's playing. Some new, Pop release probably. Unless it's viral in a four year olds world, or on Country radio, I probably wouldn't know it.

"You know as a rule, I don't dance." I lean into whisper in Beths ear. She has her back to me, her curvy hips swaying to the beat, if she was any closer to me, her ass would be grinding right up against me. This is dangerous territory when we are surrounded by our coworkers.

I know over the music, no one will be able to hear our conversation, but I just want to be close to her. I see the bumps appear down her neck as she reacts to my warm breath on her neck.

"Yet, here you are, dancing with me." She peers at me over her shoulder. I bury my nose in just below her ear and breath her in, committing the fruity scent of her perfume to memory.

"I'd do just about anything for you." I say it at barely a whisper, I'm not even sure if it was loud enough for her to hear over the music.

"Good to know" she says with a contented smile.

At that moment, the DJ decides to give us the true Spring Fling, high school experience when he fades the upbeat pop song into a slow love ballad and calls all the couples to the floor. I recognize this song, it's one of those songs everyone knows, and you can belt out the words while you slow dance with your partner.

Most of the other couples make their way to the floor as the starting notes to Amazed by Lonestar start to play. Beth slowly turns around to face me, and there is a look on her face that I don't recognize. She almost looks sad.

"What do you say, reckon we pass as a couple enough to dance to one of the cheesiest love songs of all time?" I say as I reach out with my palm flat, waiting for her to place her hand in mine.

Slow dancing, I can do. It's just swaying back and forth, you don't even have to move your feet.

"I, uh..." She hesitates and clears her throat. "I need to use the bathroom." And before I even register what she has said, she is gone.

Well, that was weird.

I'm not going to stand and sway to a love song by myself, so I head back to the bar. Preparing to have the cocky bartender laugh in my face. But when I lock eyes on him, he just gives me a sympathetic smile. He almost looks like he has tears in his eyes as well. Shit, what have I missed?

"Don't take it personal. All the slow songs in the world, and he had to pick that one." Nate says while he mindlessly wipes clean some glasses.

"Am I missing something here?" I look over at him.

"It was her first dance song at her wedding. Griffin chose it ironically, but it holds up. I guess, even more now." Shit... and I just insulted the damn song right to her face.

"Should I go and find her?" He turns up one side of his mouth in a sort of sympathetic smile and shakes his head.

"Just give her a minute. If she isn't out by the end of the song, I'll send Abi in. She will be okay. She just doesn't like people knowing she has emotions."

I'm not sitting around waiting for her to come out. Fuck that, if she needs to be alone, she can tell me to my face, but if it's comfort she needs, then I'll be the one to give it to her.

I cross the room heading towards the bathrooms, I'm about halfway, the song has just ended and has ramped back up into some more Pop crap. When I see the door to the ladies' room open, and Beth steps out with Caroline behind her. Beth is smiling, Caroline rubs her arm gently, in such a motherly fashion.

Damn, that woman is both of our guardian angel tonight. Caroline looks over and catches my gaze, before pointing me out to Beth and giving her a gentle nudge in my direction.

As Beth approaches me, I take her straight into my arms, her head falls to my chest, and her arms go straight around my waist, we hold each other so tight for a moment while the party carries on around us. She pulls away slightly and looks up at me "Can we get out of here?" She says.

"I thought you'd never ask."

Chapter 16

BETH

Well, that wasn't how I pictured the night going. I wanted to dance, have a fun time. Tease and flirt with Mason. Get to enjoy being out in the open and be able to act like a couple.

Instead, I copped a fair smack of reality right to the chest. I was already nervous about tonight and then when that song, of all of the songs, came on. Just as I finally got Mason onto the dance floor. Any amount of confidence I got back just shattered.

We get to Masons truck in the parking lot, and he opens my door for me. He holds my elbow as I climb up, my feet are killing me in these heels, so before he closes the door, I tell him I just need to kick them off.

He runs his hand down my leg, and grabs them, pulling them off for me. I let out a moan because damn, the instant relief. I wiggle my toes and stretch my ankles a bit.

Mason just watches me, one hand still resting on my ankle. I can tell he is conflicted. He wants to be turned on, but I think he is hesitant after what just happened. I don't blame him, because... Same.

He closes my door and rounds the truck to climb into the driver's seat. He doesn't start the engine yet, we just sit there for a minute in silence, in the dark. "Are you okay?" He asks, his voice almost sounds defeated.

"Yeah, I'm fine. I'm sorry, it's just there are still little moments like that that catch me off guard every now and then. There are always little firsts that I still experience without Griffin. They just always seem to come at the worst times." I let out a breath I didn't realize I was holding.

I really am feeling better now that I'm not in a crowded room. I feel like my head is a bit clearer away from the thumping music.

"If you need some time... or space..." He starts. I turn in my seat to look at him.

"Mason, you know how I took that week to think about whether or not we were a good idea? And I said I looked everywhere for a sign that it was right? My reaction in there just now was because I felt like I finally got my sign. So yeah, I freaked out. And I ran. But then, Caroline followed me, and you know what she told me?"

I keep my gaze locked on the side of his head, he is avoiding my gaze at all costs. He is just staring straight at the steering wheel. He shakes his head and gives a slight shrug of his shoulders.

"She told me that she also believes it was a sign." I watch as his face sinks to a whole new level. I reach out and cup his face in my hand. He finally chances a glance my way and I can't hide my smile.

"She believes it was Griffin, sitting wherever he is, having a good old laugh at our expense. And maybe even his blessing that you could make me as happy as he did. Because you know what else Caroline told me?" I watch as his eyes fill with so much hope where seconds ago there was hurt. He shakes his head.

"Fireworks, on New Years, right? You know how I feel when I see fireworks? Amazed, Mase."

He looks like he is the one with tears filling his eyes now. So I continue "now, ask me how I feel about you?"

"Beth... you don't have to do this." I reach out and rest my hand on his forearm.

"Ask me..."

His gaze is locked on mine. "Mase, you've been coming to my house for months, mowing my lawns, fixing leaky taps and broken steps, doing me all sorts of favors, even when you know I can do them myself. Sometimes I don't even ask, you just do them. You answer your phone every time I call, even when it's the middle of the night, and I'm only calling because I'm lonely. You don't judge me for that. You simply listen and talk me through it. I am amazed by you, Mason. By your smile, by your sense of humor, by your kind heart." I give his arm a squeeze and come to rest my hand on his bicep.

"Fuck... I don't even know what to say, Beth. You always find a way to leave me speechless." I rub my hand from his bicep up to his neck, resting my fingers in his cropped hair at the nape of his neck, gently rubbing circles.

"Take me home, Mason Clarke. Please."

He starts the truck and pulls out of that parking lot. It's my hand on his thigh this time, rubbing the same small circles that he did on mine on our drive here. I know where his mind has gone. He will think I'm too fragile now, He will doubt whether I want him.

I'm going to leave no doubt. Because there is no doubt in my mind. I want this man.

He hates dancing, and yet he danced, for me. With me. We've been teasing each other for weeks, and he was just going to let all that go because he thought I might need space. I need the opposite of space.

We pull into my driveway, and he cuts the engine. He hesitates, he is clearly still unsure. So I fling my own door open and jump out. I turn back around and look at him, he hasn't even taken his seatbelt off yet.

"Well, you coming?" He looks at me like he can't believe I'm inviting him in. He hesitates again.

"I, uh… I. Yeah, I mean I want to, but... are you sure?" I level him with a serious glare.

"Mason, you have been teasing me and flirting with me mercilessly for months now. I'm telling you I'm ready and now you want to be sure? I'm ready. I'm willing… and I'm not above begging."

The side of his mouth lifts up in a half smile. I can tell he doesn't want me to see it. He wants to act like the perfect gentleman. He doesn't want to remove the kid gloves. But I've come to know him well over the last few months, I'm pretty sure, I've come close to snapping his self-control with that line.

He still hasn't moved though, so I need to take it up a notch. At this point, I'm glad my driveway goes all the way down to the back of my house, and I'm glad it's dark.

I take a couple of steps back and untie the side of my wrap dress slowly, while his eyes grow wider and wider by the second. I drop the strings that tied the whole dress together, and so naturally the dress begins to fall open.

I see the exact moment his composure gives out. I've never seen him move so fast. He is out of his truck like a shot out of a gun.

I turn to run towards the house, but he catches me in about six steps. He bends slightly and wraps his arms around my waist, just below the curve of my ass and throws me over his shoulder, caveman style.

I let out a playful squeal, followed by a full-on belly laugh. He drops me back to my feet when we reach the door. "Open the door, now." He demands.

"Okay, Okay, keep your pants on…" As I turn away to unlock the back door, I peer back over my shoulder before adding "actually, please, please don't…"

I push the back door open and drop my shoes on the floor. My dress is already gaping open, so I turn to face him and as he kicks the door closed, I let the straps of my dress fall down my shoulders, before I drop the whole thing to the floor.

I start gradually walking backwards, towards the living room, hoping we might at least make it to the couch before we make contact. I stand in front of him wearing a matching white lingerie set, that I bought with this exact purpose in mind. To make his face look like that.

His eyes are running up and down my body and his tongue darts out to wet his lips. He is slowly advancing on me, closing the gap one small step at a time.

I stop backing up and let him get closer. I can see the strain behind his zipper. His dress pants look uncomfortably tight. "Seems awfully unfair that I'm standing in my kitchen in my underwear, and you're fully clothed." He starts fiddling with the buttons on his shirt as he slowly walks toward me.

"The only thing that's unfair, is how fucking hot you look in that matching set. Seriously Beth, how am I supposed to look you in the eyes at work ever again, knowing what you've got going on under there?" I huff out a breathy laugh.

"Well, even the playing field then."

He stops directly in front of me. My breath has picked up almost to a pant and I can feel my heart just about to jump out of my chest.

"You have until the count of three to match my level of undress, or I'm doing it for you" He gives me a shit eating grin.

"Beth, I don't think that's the punishment you think it is."

"1…." He undoes the last remaining button on his shirt, and drops it to the floor. "2…." He undoes the button and lowers the zipper of his pants. "3…." His pants hit the floor, along with my jaw when I'm left staring at his toned body. You can tell the weather has warmed up, there are no tan lines to be seen.

Damn, I'm actually jealous of the farm animals that get to see him walking around without a shirt on.

I bite my bottom lip, purely so that it makes me pick my jaw up off the floor. I take a few deep breaths in, because this is it. There's no backing out now.

He closes the last few inches between us and cups his hand around the back of my neck, his fingers entwined in my hair and pulls me in to a deep, passionate kiss. I immediately let out a groan because this feels exactly like the two make out sessions we have managed before.. but this time, I know there are no interruptions.

Right time, right place.

My mouth instinctively opens to his and he takes the opportunity to explore my mouth further with his tongue. My hands are around his waist, rubbing his lower back, but after a few seconds I hook the tips of my fingers into the waistband of his boxers.

He lowers his right hand from the back of my neck, bringing it around so his hand cups the side of my neck, and his thumb grazes along my collarbone, as he devours my mouth.

His other hand slides down my body, over the curve of my breast, my breath hitches as he pauses over the peak of my nipple. This lingerie set might be sexy as hell but it's paper thin, and doesn't leave much to the imagination.

His mouth follows the path that his hand just embarked on, as he lays kisses all the way down my jaw, neck, chest and comes to stop right at my hard peaks.

As his mouth went south, so did his right hand and I feel one rough knuckle trace a gentle path over my stomach, down to the top of my thigh, and as he brings it back up he brushes over my wet panties. Right where I desperately need the friction.

I let out a desperate moan. I haven't been touched by a man in almost two years. Even before Griffin died, he was too sick for these kinds of activities for a while. I've been self pleasuring for too long. I forgot what it was like to have someone do it for you.

"Mason, I need you." He brings his hands around behind me and lifts me up so effortlessly. My legs instinctively wrap around his waist. Just like that first night we made out. *This is happening.*

He begins walking towards the stairs, he is skipping the couch and going straight for the bedroom. We don't break our kiss for a second. There is only a couple of very thin layers between us, so while he walks, I make the most of the added pressure from having my legs around his waist.

I can feel his thick, hard length pressing right where I need him. I start to grind my hips into him. He lets out a short chuckle "Greedy girl, so impatient."

He kisses my neck, as he reaches the top of the stairs, he stops and turns me so my back is to the hallway wall. He kisses me so much deeper and grinds his hips right into me. My head falls back against the wall, opening my neck up for him.

He takes the opportunity to kiss and gently bite my neck, which just drives me even crazier. "Please take me to the bedroom, now Mason."

"But I'm having so much fun watching you come apart for me, right here Beth."

"Mason, please. It's been so long since I've been touched. When I say I need this, I mean it. I need you." He nods his head, before resting his forehead on mine.

"Whatever my girl wants, my girl will get." He lays another deep, exploratory kiss on my lips and continues on walking towards my bedroom.

He lays me down on the bed and I can feel his length pressing into me as he hovers over me. "Relax Beth, we have all night. And I'm going to need every minute of it to do the things I want to do to you."

He returns to teasing my entire body with his mouth. I lift up on my elbows and he reaches around to unsnap the clasp of my bra with one hand. He pulls it off and drops it on the floor, before running his tongue between both of my nipples, he sucks one into his mouth and releases it with a loud pop sound. He lets out a moan and says "Fuck you're perfect."

His hands have wandered down and are rubbing over the top of my panties. Which I'll probably just have to throw out at this point. He looks me dead in the eye as he slides them to the side before slipping a finger in behind the thin fabric.

He runs it through my wetness, before pulling it away. "Don't you fucking dare tease me like that. I'm done playing games, Mason." I say, narrowing my eyes at him.

He still doesn't break my gaze as he sucks his finger into his mouth "So fucking perfect." I close my eyes and let out a moan. I don't think I've ever been this turned on in my life.

He returns his finger but this time he goes straight to my clit. I get a jolt of pleasure that springs me to life from my head to my toes. Every inch of me is tingling.

My hips buck forward, chasing more pressure, more friction. "Please, Mason. I need more."

The pad of his thumb takes over while one of his fingers slowly slides inside me "Oh fuck, Yes!" I cry out. I didn't realize just how much I've missed this.

"You want more, Beth?" I don't even have words, I just nod.

"Say it Beth. Tell me what you want."

"Yes, Yes, I want more." He slides another finger inside me and straight away he finds my G spot. He strokes against it and I swear it only takes mere seconds before I'm coming apart underneath him.

My whole body stiffens and then shudders as I fall over the edge. He slowly removes his fingers as I come down off my high, Still shivering from the endorphins. He comes up to kiss me gently on the mouth, "Fuck you are so beautiful, Beth."

Fucking hell, I can't believe that just happened.

Chapter 17

MASON

Holy fuck, that was the hottest thing I've ever witnessed. I've dreamed about this day for so long, and it finally happened. The way she begged, the way she came apart on my fingers. It was exactly how I'd imagined it.

I sit up on the edge of the bed, and I feel her crawl to sit behind me, she runs her fingers over my bare back and brings them around to run over my ribs, exploring the ridges of my abs. She continues down to run her hands up and down my thighs. "Stand up" she whispers as she kisses the back of my neck.

"Beth, no. You don't have to, not tonight."

"I wasn't asking. Stand up." Jesus Fuck.

I stand in front of her and she moves to take my place on the edge of the bed. Her face is about in line with my stomach, she starts to lay kisses over my abdomen, as her hands continue to run up and down my thighs.

She rubs circles at the tops of my thighs, each time she is edging closer and closer to touching my aching dick. "Theres one thing you should know about me." She says as she looks up at me with those emerald green eyes.

She brings her hand to cup my dick through my boxers and I jolt. Fuck. This might be all over before she even fully pulls me out. "oh yeah, what's that?" I say as I stroke her cheek with the pad of my thumb.

"I learnt a long time ago, that the secret to a good blow job, is to enjoy giving them. So in the bedroom, I don't ever just take. I like to give, as much as I like to receive."

Fuck me. I didn't think it was possible, but she just got one hundred times hotter. I don't even fully process what she just said, She yanks down my boxers and my raging hard cock springs free. Moisture already leaking from the tip. The way she is looking at my dick, then up at me.. Yeah, I give myself a few seconds here, and that's probably being generous.

She takes my length in her hand, and strokes me up and down a few times, before she drops to her knees and runs her tongue along the underside of my throbbing cock. With a deep groan, she twists her tongue around the head, and pulls her tongue back into her mouth, tasting me.

"Fuuuck. Baby, do you have any idea how fucking hot you look on your knees?" She just smiles before taking me fully into her mouth. All the way back until I feel the narrowing of her throat. She moans again and the vibration from her throat sends shivers down my spine.

I grab a handful of her hair, and it takes everything in me not to unleash and fuck her mouth into oblivion.

Slow down Mason, plenty of time for that. Let her ease into it.

She hollows out her cheeks and sucks so hard I think I actually see stars. She moves her mouth up and down my shaft, as her hand follows the same rhythm.

"Oh fuck, baby. You better stop now, or I'm coming down your throat." I let out a deep groan that comes straight from my chest. I'm trying to hold it back because I don't want this to end.

"Do it baby. I want it all." That about does it. Her words send me over the edge.

I use the fistful of her hair to hold her in place as my orgasm plows through me, releasing straight to the back of her throat. My legs are shaking and I don't know how I'm still standing. I watch as she catches every last drop of my come and swallows, hard., before she looks up at me with the sexiest smile on her face.

"Fuck, Beth. Get up here." I pick her up, her legs returning to being wrapped around my waist, where I'm quickly realizing is right where they belong. I kiss her so tenderly. Fuck, this woman owns me.

I carry her into the bathroom to clean us up. I sit her on the counter, and just take her in for a minute. Thinking about what I just did to her. What she just did to me.

She is still in her panties, although being white lace, they are covering nothing. Her make up is smudged, I'm sure at least half of her lipstick is on my dick, the rest looks like it's on my neck.

I pull her back up to stand and turn her so we are both facing the mirror. I stand flush behind her, my hands instinctively go to her tits, the perfect handful. I bury my face in her neck, as she leans her head back on my shoulder.

One of her hands reaching up to tangle in my hair, holding my head tighter into her neck. Fuck, I'm already starting to harden again and she knows it.

"You're so beautiful, Beth." She turns in my arms and throws her arms around my neck, pulling me in for a kiss.

"Mase.." She says as she breaks our kiss and stares directly into my soul. "You can say no to this if you're not ready. But I'd really like to take this further."

I rest my forehead on hers and let out a quiet scoff. "Now, why would I ever say no to that?"

"I just wanted you to be sure." This woman can't just take what she wants.

"Theres one tiny problem. I don't have.. I didn't bring.. anything with me." She looks up at me with a smile.

"What are we, 15? There's some in the top drawer." She laughs as she walks back into her bedroom, she stops at the door, takes her panties off, throws them back at me, then keeps walking.

I don't even look at what I grab, I just reach my hand in to the drawer and start grabbing and hope to god I've got a condom in there somewhere.

I was only a couple of steps behind her but she is sitting up on her knees in the middle of her bed. It stops me dead in my tracks.

Fuck, I knew she would look good naked, but this is something else. She is curvy in all of the right places, and I spy the faded stretch marks on her hips, and C-section scar along her pelvic bone.

Fuck I love the female body. The things it can do.

Theres no questioning whether I'm ready for another round. I am locked and loaded.

I walk slowly to the bed, meeting her in the middle. I wrap one arm around her waist and pull her into me in a deep kiss. I lay her down on her back, so I'm laying between her spread legs. I continue to kiss up and down her neck and chest, paying special attention to her peaked nipples.

Her hands are running all over my body, still exploring every inch. She reaches for the condom and rips the foil without even breaking our rhythm. She grabs my length and gives a couple of firm tugs, before she rolls the condom down. "Beth, I need to ask. How do you want this to go?" She looks like her confidence is wavering. She's nervous.

"Um, it's been a long time. At this point, I'm sure I'm a born again virgin. So maybe, lets start slow and see how it goes from there? If that's ok with you?" I look down at her from where I'm hovering my weight above her, and shake my head.

"This has absolutely nothing to do with me, and everything to do with you. You're in control, baby." She just nods and pulls me further down so most of my weight is resting on her.

She is absolutely soaked, "I'm ready, Mason. Please, fuck me." She says while she is nodding her head in approval. I line myself up with her entrance and slowly push in. She gasps and I stop because I can't tell if that hurt her.

"Fuck, please don't stop. You feel so good, Mase. More. Please."

She is so tight, I need a second to adjust so I don't blow in five seconds flat. "Give me a second, baby. It's been a minute for me too." She rubs her hands right up my back and my whole body shivers. I begin to thrust in and out, just gently at first. Waiting for her to give me the go ahead to speed up.

She wraps her legs tight around my waist and tilts her hips backwards, opening herself up to take me in deeper. Fuck me, I feel like my head is spinning. This is nothing short of euphoric.

"Harder. Please." I will never get sick of hearing her beg for what she needs. I increase the speed of my thrusts and feel her gripping me tighter with every one.

"Yes Mason that's it... I'm going to…" and then her whole body shudders and that's it... I'm a goner as well.

We both hit our release at the same time and ride it out together. She cradles my face in her hands and my arms are resting either side of her head. I lay a gentle kiss on her lips, "That was every bit as perfect as I had imagined."

I walk to the bathroom to dispose of the condom and when I come back she is tucked under the covers with a sleepy look on her face. If I didn't know any better, I'd say that's the face of contentment.

I lean over and press a kiss to her cheek, before I bend over to pick up my boxers and put them back on. She lifts her head to see what I'm doing "I hope you're not putting those on to leave."

****

149

I wake to the sound of a phone ringing in the distance. I blink my eyes a few times. Fuck. What time is it? II's bright out, it must be late.

I look over beside me and Beth is just starting to stir. I didn't intend to sleep over, but there's no way I was saying no to this woman. I lay a couple of gentle kisses on her shoulder, because I've realized it's her phone ringing from the living room where she dropped her bag last night.

I see the moment Beth realizes as well, because she jolts up. "Shit, what time is it?" she says, startled.

"I don't know, my phone is out there with yours." She sits up and I can't help but lay back and admire her as she sits on the edge of the bed. She walks to her closet and grabs an oversized T-shirt. I recognize that shirt, it was Griffins football team, a fact that I thought would make me feel jealous, but it makes me smile.

She rushes downstairs to the living room and a moment later I hear her talking on the phone. She comes back to stand in the doorway and looks at me, with a sort of sad smile.

"That was Will. Logan is getting a bit homesick so I'll have to go and pick him up soon. I said I'd just have a shower and be right there. You could come with me if you want?" I get out of the bed and walk around to wrap her in a hug.

"I'd love to, but I really should be heading out to the farm. Calving season is in full swing, and it's been full on." She looks up at me with a playful pout. "But, I could come with you to the shower first."

I waggle my eyebrows at her, which gets her laughing. I pick her up and wrap her legs around my waist again and carry her to the bathroom.

We take turns washing each other, until the water runs cold. I watch her get ready for the day, her hair piled on top of her head in a bun, and she opts for a simple white tank top and a long, almost silky skirt which hugs to her perfectly and almost looks like butter. Weirdly, I find watching her get dressed just as sexy as her taking it all off.

We leave the house, and as I go to get in my truck, she kisses me goodbye, I turn her and have her pinned against the door of my truck, one of her legs comes up to my waist and I grab her behind her knee.

"Fuck, Beth. We don't have time." I break the kiss, as hard as it is, her kid needs her, and I have work to do. "I'll call you later."

Chapter 18

BETH

Considering I didn't get much sleep last night, I feel like I slept like a log. I have become so used to sleeping alone, I missed the comfort of having a warm body in bed with me. The soothing white noise of someone else's gentle breathing.

Damn Will for calling so early, but duty called, I guess.

I stop in at the coffee shop on my way to Wills house. It's a bit of a tradition the night after someone has Logan for a sleepover, that I bring them a cup of coffee. It feels like the least I can do for all the favors they do for me.

When I pull up out the front, Will has Logan on a bike, teaching him to ride. I recognize the bike. It's the same one both Will and Nate learned to ride on so many years ago. Dad must've kept it all these years. Will has taken the training wheels off on one side, trying to ease Logan in to riding without them. The look of sheer joy on both of their faces brings happy tears to my eyes.

He's going to be okay. It takes a village, and the village has got us.

Getting out of the car, I walk to Logan and ruffle his hair "Looking good, Pal. You'll have the other one off in no time!" He just smiles and laughs, before riding off back down the driveway.

I extend the coffee over to Will and he places the palms of his hands together in a prayer motion while mouthing the words 'Thank You!' before taking the steaming cup of coffee from me and wrapping his other arm around my shoulders briefly.

"So, how was the big Spring fling night?" he nudges his knuckles holding the coffee cup playfully into my ribs and he is very closely mimicking the shit eating grin that only our younger brother is capable of pulling off.

"Has that little shit been gossiping about me already? Does he ever sleep?"

"Relax, he hasn't said anything.. Although, now I think I need to message him and find out why he hasn't." We start to walk towards his front porch where he has a couple of deck chairs set up.

Wills' house is located at the top of one of the many rolling hills in town, he gets the best sunset views from here. His porch also has a good lookout over his yard, so we can watch Logan while we drink our coffee.

"It was a really nice night." He brings his cup to his mouth.

"I bet it was" He takes a sip to mask his smile.

"Oh, grow up." I extend my foot out, kicking him in the shin.

"How was your night, was Logie good for you?"

"He is always good for me. He told me he was feeling a bit sad about his birthday coming up."

"Yeah, I know. I've been trying to decide what to do for it for weeks. He says he doesn't want a big party, because it will make him sad that his dad isn't there. But it's his fifth birthday, he needs something special."

Will leans forward, resting his elbows on his knees.

"Lucky for you, he told me what he wants." My eyes widen at that.

I've been trying to gently coax out of Logan what he thinks would make his birthday fun and special, and he hasn't been able to tell me anything. It's only a week out from his birthday and I still have no clue.

"He told you? Will, please, spill. I need to know." He puts his coffee cup down on the outdoor table in front of us, and with a shrug of his shoulders he says "He wants Philips Friday. Simple as that. He said that's where he feels most happy. I asked him if he was sure he didn't want a big fun party with his friends from Preschool. You'll love his response to that." Will raises his eyebrows at me with another wide smirk on his face.

"Please don't make me beg, Will. Just spit it out." I sit forward in my chair, the anticipation just about eating me alive.

"He said the only other people that make him feel that happy are Rosie and Mason. So he asked if he could invite them to Philips Friday, for his birthday. I said he would have to check with you." I sit back in my chair.

While I feel this sense of relief that Logan sees Mason and Rosie that way. I also wasn't quite ready to expose Mason to all of my family in one place like that. I shake it off because, I would literally walk through fire to make that kid happy.

"Well, it sounds like you're going to meet Mason and Rosie sooner than I anticipated."

✳✳✳✳✳✳✳✳✳✳✳✳

I'm in the kitchen, beginning to cook our dinner when I hear my phone ping with a message. I open it and it's a selfie of Mason with a tiny, slimy, very freshly born calf.

Beth: Oh, so cute! The cow is a bit slimy though.

Mason: Haha, very funny. How was your day?

Beth: It was good, we just chilled out. I have something to ask you and you can absolutely say no.

154

Mason: You know I probably won't say no to you, but please, go on.

Beth: It's Logans birthday on Friday, and I've been racking my brain, trying to come up with something special for him for the first birthday without his dad. Turns out he only has 2 requests.

Mason: You're not about to ask me to dress up as a clown or something, are you? Because if you are, I take back what I said.. I might say no to you just this once. *laughing face emoji*

Beth: Scared of clowns, noted. No, nothing like that. He actually doesn't really want a party at all. He has just asked for a normal Philips Friday, because that's where he feels happy. But he said that you and Rosie also make him happy so he wanted to invite you as well.

Mason: And are you ok with inviting us?

Beth: I mean, it's a little sooner than I anticipated, but it was bound to happen sooner or later, and it's Logans birthday. So it's up to him. But yeah, I would love for you guys to come. I think I've warned you enough about my brothers that you're prepared for it.

Mason: As long as you're comfortable with it, we wouldn't miss it. Can I bring anything?

Beth: Please don't. It's my dads thing to cook a big feast for everyone, he gets offended if anyone tries to help or take away from his time to shine. The only rule is to wear something comfy, and bring your competitive side because there will be games.

Mason: Done, and done.

****

I'm actually leaving work at a normal time, I could get used to this, it actually isn't so bad, I haven't dropped behind in my work, but I'm getting to spend more time with my family.

Today, I couldn't concentrate anyway. That's also becoming a habit I'm keen to shake.

I wanted to take the whole day off and spend all day with Logan for his birthday, but he insisted he wanted to go to preschool with his friends, so we spent all night last night decorating some cupcakes for him to take with him and share with class. He was happy, especially when I pulled out the little dinosaur figurines I bought to put on the tops of them. He was ecstatic that his friends would be getting a cupcake and a toy.

We settled on me finishing early and picking him up on my way home so we could have our own little celebratory dance party and he could open some presents before we go to Philips Friday.

The birthday dance party is a tradition Griffin started when we first moved in together. The birthday boy or girl, picks five songs, and we all wear party hats, or crowns and just dance it out in the kitchen, which is usually decked out with streamers and balloons.

We also would often do the same thing on a Saturday morning, after enjoying a bit of a lazy lay in, usually I would be in the kitchen making us some coffee and breakfast, Griffin would always put on some music to start off the day which usually always ended up with the three of us dancing around in our pajamas. It was the perfect way to start the weekend.

Was.

We haven't done it since Griffin died.

Maybe it's time we start that back up again.

Logan and I have danced around the house to Baby Shark, The Floor is Lava song, some Dance Freeze game, the one he calls the Happy song from that movie with the little yellow dudes in it. But his fifth song choice took me a little by surprise.

Shake it Off by Taylor Swift.

Usually if I try and play anything by Taylor Swift, he tells me he doesn't like it, he would rather 'cool music.'

Okay, teenager.

I ask him why he chose that song and he looked at me like it was the most ridiculous question in the world. "It's Rosies favorite song. She said it makes her feel happy when she is sad, and it works!" I smile and shake my head at him.

The realization hits me that the Clarke Family have really turned us both around.

Logan opens his birthday presents, I'm well aware I went way overboard but I couldn't help myself. Nothing felt like enough.

His favorite, surprisingly has been a pair of Baby Alive dolls, that make crying noises and actually drink their bottles. He and Rosie love role playing parents so I thought it was time he had his own babies, instead of using a teddy or a dinosaur.

He got so excited when he unwrapped them, he couldn't wait to show her. I snapped a photo and sent it to Mason so he could show Rosie.

I stand to start picking up his disposed wrapping paper so we can get ready to go to Philips Friday. "Mama.." Logan says as he is yanking on my arm to pull me down to his level. "Yeah, bud?"

"Do you think Rosie could have a sleepover tonight? I really want to show her my babies."

"I don't know, bub, I'd have to check with Mason. It might be a bit short notice." His head instantly drops in disappointment, before he looks up at me through his thick black eyelashes, shooting me a sheepish grin.

"Mason could have a sleepover too, and then Rosie can come."

Son of a gun, got me there.

"I'll ask, but no promises. C'mon it's time to get changed into your comfies."

He runs up the stairs and I shoot Mason a text.

Beth: The birthday boy wishes to extend an invitation to Rosie to sleepover tonight, And Romeo himself, said maybe you could come as well. I'm not sure whether to be happy that he is so okay with us, or concerned at the slyness that he knew if you were here, it would be a higher chance that Rosie was allowed to come. Anyway, no pressure if you don't want to, I've told him it might be too short notice. I have a couple of camping mattresses so the kids could have a lounge room camp out.

Mason: Would be frowned upon to refuse the birthday boy. I'll pack us a bag.

I drop my phone down on my bed and head into my closet to get into my comfy clothes. I stand there for a moment and take a deep breath in, calming myself because today is a lot.

I haven't even had time to fully wrap my own head around this. Logans first birthday without Griffin, Mason (and Rosie) meeting my family. And now their first sleepover. Officially, anyway.

I take another big exhale as I look up at my wall of pajamas and comfy clothes. I reach out for my favorite pair. Well, shake it off, I guess.

Chapter 19

MASON

Theres a knock on my door, exactly to the minute she said she would be here. Beth is such a stickler for routine. I doubt the woman has ever been even a minute late a single day in her life.

I open the door to see her standing there, hair piled in a messy bun on top of her head, a few strands pulled out to frame her face, as I run my eyes down her body I notice she's wearing… pajamas?

Pale pink shorts that only just cover her ass. And a matching pale pink, button up T-shirt with Mickey mouse on the top pocket. She immediately bursts into laughter.

"What are you wearing?" she says in between giggles. I'm wearing my usual, wrangler jeans, the clean ones, and she said to dress comfy so I've opted for a plain black cotton T-shirt. It's comfy, but still makes a good impression on her family.

"What am I wearing? What are you wearing?" I look her up and down. I never expected to be turned on in the presence of Mickey Mouse, but I guess there's a first for everything with this girl.

"I said to dress comfy. It's a Philips tradition to dress as sloppy as possible. Now, I know you own sweatpants. Go put some on. Just please, not the grey ones, my future sister in law will be there." She brings her hand to her mouth to hide the fact she is still giggling.

I feel a swift smack to my ass as I turn to go back to my bedroom and rethink my whole outfit, which already took me half an hour to decide on, feeling like I needed to meet some happy medium between comfy and respectable. I turn back to look at her but she is already distracted.

"Hi, Rosie Girl!" I hear Beth exclaim. Now, Rosie - She understands comfort. The girl has taken to choosing her own outfits, which usually means she is wearing approximately half of her wardrobe at any one time.

Tonight, she has a pink cowboy hat, because she has decided that she would like to give farm life a chance, and needed a hat like Daddys farm hat. A bright yellow T-shirt with a multi-colored sparkly unicorn on the front, a pair of purple bike shorts, some rainbow stripy socks, pulled up to her knees. Paired with her bright green Crocs.

She is so bright that I'm sure you can see her from space, but she definitely looks comfy, and happy, so we roll with it.

I return to the living room, dressed in some black track pants, and I've kept the black Tee. I'm carrying an overnight bag with a change of clothes for Rosie and I for the morning. Beth has already taken Rosie out to the car to see Logan and get her strapped in.

I put our bag in the back, offer a fist bump and a happy birthday wish to Logan, and just as Beth finishes buckling Rosie in, I grab her by the waist, push her gently against the back of the car and kiss her firmly, but break it way sooner than I would like, mindful that the kids can see us, and are definitely laughing at us right now.

"Hi." I say. She just looks up at me, taking a second to catch her breath.

"Hi yourself." I take a few steps to the side to open her door for her, she gets in the drivers seat and I walk around to the passenger side.

"Hey Rosie, Logan told me your favorite song today." Beth says, while she is scrolling through her music streaming App. I look at her with a look of both shock and a little bit of fear.

"Don't you dare." I say trying to hide a playful smile. She looks back at me with a flirty smile on hers and her eyes are all tease.

"Hey, drivers choice for music. Fair warning, my car is my stage. And I like to perform." She fucking winks at me. Before the starting bars to fucking Shake it Off start.

When we pull into the driveway of Beth's dads house, her childhood home, so she tells me. I stand beside the car for a minute, admiring the design of it.

It's classic, but has been kept so well that it somehow looks brand new at the same time. It's clean and white. Stained wood shutters on the windows on both the first and second floor. Polished timber decking on the huge wrap around porch, and the few steps leading up to the front door, which is painted bright red.

I can see why Logan feels happiest here. I haven't even stepped foot inside yet and I know, it's a home. There's a lot of love in these walls.

Beth takes a deep breath in as she opens the door. Rosie has gone a little bit shy and is holding hands with both Beth and I. She isn't usually the shy type, but lets be honest, she is definitely feeding off my energy.

When we walk in, we are met with three sets of eyes that all stop mid sentence and turn to look at us.

Logan takes off running into the house which immediately breaks the silence as everyone crowds around him to wish him a Happy Birthday and smother him in love. Like I said, a lot of love in these walls.

Will picks Logan up and Logan immediately tries to put him in a headlock, although the little guys arms barely make it around his neck. Beths dad and Nate approach us in the doorway, Nate wraps Beth in a hug while her dad, Hank reaches out to shake my hand and officially introduce himself.

Nate nods his head and greets me with a "Hey, man." Funny, I was expecting to be called lover boy or something. He drops to his knees and says "and you must be Rosie, I've heard so many cool things about you Rosie, my name is Nate, I'm Logans fun Uncle."

Logan comes running back over to us and grabs Rosie by the hand. Dragging her into the house. Will approaches us and reaches his hand out for a handshake "Hey, Lover boy, I'm assuming?"

There it is.

Beth snickers and Nate bursts into a full on belly laugh. Hank shakes his head and starts to walk back into the kitchen, but not before he also stops to introduce himself to Rosie as well.

Beth takes me by the hand and leads me in as well, just like her son just did to my daughter.

The noise and chaos that ceased when we walked in has resumed. Hank is doing five things at once in the kitchen but when Beth offers to help, he tells her "Hell no." So we just take a seat at the table and observe, I rest my arm casually around the back of Beths chair.

Logan is explaining to Rosie how tag team wrestling matches work. Apparently he is just glad to have a fourth person back to even out the field again.

The door opens again and one of the most petite women I've ever seen walks through the door, Nate immediately jumps up from his stool at the kitchen counter 'Olly!!' and runs to the door to wrap her in a big bear hug "I missed you so much sweetie pie. Did you have a good day at work?" He is smothering her in kisses.

I look over at Beth and she is trying to hold in a laugh "and he calls me Lover boy?" I whisper for just her to hear. She bursts out in laughter. Which is the most infectious sound I think I've ever heard. I rest my forehead on her temple as we both laugh.

"Something to share with the class, Elizabeth?" Nate turns to look at Beth, levelling her with a stare that I'm sure he means to be intimidating. But after that display, I'm not sure I'll ever see him as intimidating ever again.

"Nope, nothing… Sweetie Pie." She says while trying to hold in her giggles. She straightens up for long enough to introduce me to Nates girlfriend, Olive. And before I know it, I'm eating the most amazing homemade pizza I've ever had, Hanks Specialty apparently, and Logans birthday request.

We watch Logan open his presents, and then Bella calls in on Facetime to sing Happy Birthday, I'm introduced to her boyfriend, Brad, who frankly seems completely uninterested in the fact that it's Logans birthday, then we have cake for dessert. Rosie comments that it's the best chocolate mud cake she has ever had. Again, a special recipe of Hanks, I'm told.

You can tell his food contains as much love as his house does.

Once we are all full to the brim of food, I'm told it's game time. As it's Logans birthday, he gets to pick the game. He gets a devilish grin on his face as he runs to the cupboard and pulls out Twister.

Will and Nate start to move some furniture so they can set up the mat, Olive keeps the kids occupied and I hear her complimenting Rosie on her rainbow fingernails, and sparkly shirt. I smile at how they have all welcomed Rosie in tonight.

Growing up I was always so jealous of people with big families, and full houses like this one. Our house was always so quiet. My parents were always working around the farm, usually starting before sunrise and not finishing until dark.

I usually helped out in between school, but my sister kept to herself a lot. I always wanted different for Rosie. I wanted her to have that big family dynamic. Just like this.

Beth heads to the kitchen to wash up the dishes so I go and help her. Hank is still perched at his spot at the head of the table, he leans back in his chair, smiling as he observes his sons play with the two kids, and then I notice his gaze settles on Beth for a moment.

She looks up like she senses him looking at her, and they just smile at each other before he gives her a wink, she ever so slightly nods and if I'm not mistaken, she blushes. Then returns to the sink full of dishes, smiling down at them.

I love witnessing this family dynamic, I'm sure I just witnessed a father and daughter who were bonded in unmentionable trauma years ago, have a silent conversation that no one else was privy to.

As a father, I hope I have that kind of bond with Rosie when she is grown up, minus the trauma, hopefully.

When the game is all set up, we all come to sit on the two large couches in the living area, The kids go first at playing. This certainly isn't a game for an almost 40 year old man.

Olive spins the wheel and instructs the kids what move comes next, while Will and Nate help the kids identify their left from right. They both fall at the same time, in a heap of high pitched giggles and flailing limbs, so we call it a tie.

Logan asks if he and Rosie can play teams against his uncles next, and I can see now why Beth said to bring my competitive side. Even at five, Logan brings out a whole new level of smack talk as soon as his uncles accept his challenge, and of course, they give it back to him.

We all watch as these two enormous men, take on a kids game, against two little kids who are hopped up on chocolate cake.

Within minutes, Nate and Will have turned on each other and are taking turns trying to slap each others limbs from underneath the other. Logan whispers something to Rosie and before we know it, the two kids are jumping on top of them so they all go crashing to the ground, in fits of laughter.

"Just like you two to lose to a couple of toddlers." Beth says as she helps Logan and Rosie up, while nudging Nate back down to the floor.

"Oh, think you can do better Beth? Put your money where your mouth is. You and Lover boy versus Me and Olly.. Be warned, Olive is very bendy, right, babe?"

Olive elbows him in the ribs, before scolding him for being inappropriate in front of the kids. "Well, Olive might be bendy, but she is paired with Pooh's friend Heffalump, so I think we will be okay."

Beth turns to me and grabs my hand to pull me off the couch. "Don't let me down, cowboy." She turns back around, keeping our hands entwined, so her back is flush against my front. I get a noseful of her shampoo and decide I better put some distance between me and her ass before I really earn the nickname Lover Boy.

Will picks up the spinner and the kids perch themselves one on either side of Will so they can help him spin.

We get all kinds of tangled up. And me trying to put distance between Beth and I fails tremendously, because now she is bent over in front of me and I have her ass just inches from my face. Her shorts weren't particularly long to start with, so now that she is bent over, they are even shorter.

I avert my gaze, and consider dropping to the floor to put myself out of my misery.

Nate is the first to drop. Granted, Beth hooked his wrist with her ankle when she went to move it, and sent him tumbling, but she called that karma for him trying to do the same thing to Will earlier. We are in a rather awkward position and I'm struggling to hold on.

I'm on all fours, but with my back to the floor, sort of like a crab. Beth is also on all fours, but she is now leant over the top of me, her face leaning into my chest as her feet are on one side of me, and her hands on the other. If she was to drop now, she would be laying flat on top of me, right here in front of her family.

Its Olives turn. "Right hand, red" Rosie says. Olive reaches, and if she was a few inches taller, she would probably make it, but she stretches too far and her feet slip out from under her.

We win. But there's only one way out of this position and that's going to be to drop. Beth shoots me a cheeky grin and winks before dropping her weight onto me and I crash to the ground, my arms wrapped around her waist, as she lies on top of me.

In that moment I think both of us forget there are other people in the room, namely her family. She just stares into my eyes, and it takes everything I have in me not to kiss her. My hands are on her lower back and I feel my cock twitch at the sight of her, with her hair messed from being bent over and twisted around.

A throat clears and it becomes obvious we have been laying here a second too long. I look up to see Will whispering in Rosie's ear, right before both kids come running over to pile on top of us.

Chapter 20

BETH

We get home and get the camping beds set up for the kids, while they play with Logans new baby dolls.

It's late, but because it's Logans birthday, we decide to put on a movie for them to watch while they fall asleep. They are tucked in beside each other on the floor. Mason and I sit on the lounge, I look down and we have two sets of peering eyes on us.

"Daddy, are you going to have a sleepover in Beths bed?" Rosie asks while raising both of her eyebrows at Mason.

"Oh, I thought I was going to sleep on the couch here to keep an eye on you two rascals." He says as he leans forward to tickle them both.

"Logan is five now, and I'm nearly five. We just want to have a fun sleepover. You can go and have a fun sleepover too." Mason looks at me with a fake shocked expression, his mouth gaped open in an O shape, before looking at Rosie with the same expression.

"Well excuse the heck out of me for cramping your style, Honey Girl." Rosie starts giggling, so Logan joins in.

Mason stands from the couch and reaches out his hand to me. "Well, come on Beth, you heard the kids, lets go have our own fun sleepover." He turns his back to me before bending at the knees and saying "c'mon, jump on."

He hoists me up onto his back for a piggyback ride and takes off up the stairs with me clinging on for dear life. The kids both giggling at the ridiculousness.

When we get upstairs I wash my face and we both stand at the sink brushing our teeth. This feels like such a strangely intimate task, so domesticated. But I'm not scared of it. I don't feel that overwhelming guilt that I expected to feel. I feel happy. I feel at ease. The kids certainly seem happy.

I wondered if Logan would be uncomfortable with this, especially today of all days. But he was laughing the loudest of everyone.

I lean into the sink to spit the toothpaste, and when I rise back up, Mason is staring at my reflection in the mirror.

"You did such a good job making that boys day special Beth. I don't think I've ever seen him smile that big before." He comes to stand flush behind me and wraps his arms around my waist. He nuzzles his chin into my neck and runs kisses along my neck and shoulder. I get instant goosebumps as his stubble grazes over my soft skin.

"I don't know if anyone has told you lately, but you're doing an amazing job." I smile, and almost start to cry.

No one has told me that lately. I constantly feel like I'm failing and always question how I could be better. I wonder if I'm too strict, or not strict enough. Am I fun enough? Do I work too much?

I think Mason and Rosie coming into our lives have at least relieved some of that pressure. There is no doubt he has fun when they are around. And I've never been more tempted to leave work on time when I watch the blue eyed, wrangler cladded farmer currently staring at my reflection walk out the door.

I turn in Masons arms to look up at him, I loop my arms around his neck and pull his mouth to mine.

"Thank you. I think I needed to hear that." I say in between kisses. His hands have slid around and are resting on my lower back. As we stand in the middle of my ensuite bathroom, in silence, we slowly start to sway back and forth. Almost like the slow dance we didn't get last week.

For a man that doesn't dance, and here he is, twice in a week, dancing. This time with no music. Just us.

I climb into my bed, and Mason takes his shirt off and then his pants, leaving him in just his boxers. I sit up, motionless, just watching him undress, admiring the ways his muscles tense and release with every movement.

He slides into bed behind me, wrapping an arm around my waist and pulling me tight into him, his head buried in the crook of my neck. I love the feel of his warm breath running down my neck.

"Hey Beth, I just wanted to pre-warn you, it's coming into summer which is a pretty hectic time on the farm, so I might be a bit extra busy in the next few weeks. We have had a bumper season with crops, and we are hoping to start harvesting next weekend. It's all hands on deck, a couple of my cousins are coming across from Snowy Creek to help out, and my dad will probably get some friends together to help. But I just wanted to apologize in advance, I might be a bit MIA."

I turn slightly to look up at him, "You don't have to apologize for that Mason. We both have lives. Is there anything I can do to help? I haven't got a lot of experience with farming machinery, but one of our uncles lived on a big farm and I remember from when I was young we all used to go out to help however we could, and Griffins folks have a small farm, so I've been around it all a little bit."

"Beth, you don't have to. I don't expect you to take on my lifestyle just because we are seeing each other." I fully turn to face him now.

"Mase, why wouldn't I? It's your life, and I'm interested in everything about you. God knows you have done enough to help me out, it's the least I could do. It's been years since I've had dirt on my boots, it might be nice to be back on the land."

"I mean, my Mama could probably use a hand preparing crew meals, if you're happy to help out in the kitchen. My sister usually helps, but we are harvesting a bit earlier this year, because there is rain forecast. So Leah can't make it. I'm sure she could use the extra hands. Only if you don't mind being left alone with a woman you don't know yet."

"If you can put up with my brothers, I'm sure I can handle your folks. I'd love to help out, however I can." He takes my face in his hands, and rubs his thumb along my cheekbone.

"Okay, I'm sure they would love to meet you. Let me ask you this, how do you feel about camping?" He holds my gaze, obviously trying to gauge my honest reaction.

"I haven't been in a long time, but I used to love it. On your parents farm?"

"Yeah, it's easier for us to camp out there instead of coming and going back into town. I will be dusty and exhausted by the end of the day, so the less time spent driving, the better. But also… I have somewhere that I'd really like to show you. I think you will really love it."

We lay in my bed talking until the early hours of the morning. I go down to the kitchen to get a glass of water just after midnight and the kids are crashed out each snuggling their babies. It's the cutest thing.

I go back up to bed and Mason is sitting up in my bed, his shirtless back resting against the headboard, sheet lazily draped over his hips. His hand rests on his head, running his fingers through his strands of short, dark hair.

In the low light of my bedside lamp, he is just the perfect amount of chiseled muscle. He looks at me with narrowed eyes, and I can't tell whether he is tired or really turned on. "Kids asleep?" He asks.

"Yeah, they are tuckered out. Dutiful parents both co-sleeping with their babies." As I take a few steps towards the bed, he reaches his arms towards me so I walk around to the other side of the bed. He pulls me down on top of him, so I'm straddling his hips.

Okay, yep, definitely turned on.

He grabs both sides of my face, nesting his hands in my hair at the nape of my neck. His eyes run all over my face, from my eyes to my lips, and back again. "Good. How about we make this a really fun sleepover?"

His big, calloused thumbs are running down the length of my jaw. I swallow, and just nod my head. "I was hoping you'd say that." He says as he lowers his mouth down to meet mine in a passionate kiss. He runs his mouth along my jaw to my earlobe, and straight down my neck.

His hands run down over my shoulders, down to grip my hips, before one snakes up under my shirt, stopping when he cups my breast. I am only wearing a thin lace bralette, being comfy clothes and all, and I watch as his head rolls back slightly, looking up in pure lust. I feel him begin to harden underneath my hips and I'm sitting right in the perfect position.

As he continues to kiss me and flick my hard nipple between his calloused fingers, I slowly begin to grind my hips against his erection. A moan escapes from me, which draws one out from him. "Fuck Beth, you always know how to test my restraint." He looks at me with nothing but fire in his eyes.

"What are you trying to restrain?" I tease as I continue to grind over him. He levels me with a steady gaze and I know I'm pushing him.

"Baby, if only you knew the un-gentlemanly things I've thought about doing to you when I'm alone in my shower." He blushes, almost like he is embarrassed with his confession.

"So tell me." I run both my hands down his chest, smoothing over his sparse smatter of chest hair, and the hard edges of his pecs.

"Like laying you down, having you spread wide so I can absolutely devour your pretty pussy. Or turning you around, bending you over the edge of your bed and driving into you until you're screaming my name."

It's me blushing this time.

I bring my hands back up to his face, running my fingers through his hair. "And why do you feel you need to restrain that?" His gaze hasn't stopped roaming my face and my body, but at that it snaps up to my eyes.

"It's been a long time since both of us have been in a new relationship. Just trying to remain respectful, I guess." His mouth lifts on one side, a sort of half smile. Like he is trying to convince himself why that's a good idea.

"Can I be really honest for a minute?" Uh-oh. His face drops to a look of worry. I lay a couple of kisses on each cheek and the tip of his nose. He just nods.

"I have a piece of vibrating silicone in my drawer that has been giving me respectful orgasms for about two years now. So *respectfully,* please, take the kid gloves off and fuck me like you mean it."

That's all he needs, He looks up to meet my gaze, searching my eyes, trying to comprehend what I've just said.

"Fuck it." He says and I swear I physically feel his restraint snap. If I thought I saw heat in his eyes before, that was nothing on what's there now. He is hungry.

He has my shirt over my head and flung on the floor before I even blink. He flips me over onto my back so hard I'm surprised I don't get whiplash. His body rests flat between my legs, he has my arms pinned up above my head, one of his hands holding both of mine in place. His face is so close to mine, but he isn't kissing me. He is breathing so heavily, matching mine.

"You're sure?" He says, and I swear his crystal blue eyes are staring straight into my soul.

"Do you need me to beg? Because I will." A devilish grin crosses his face.

"Maybe next time. Keep your hands right there."

He begins trailing kisses down my neck, across my shoulders and chest, trailing his tongue over the peak of my breasts. My stomach hollows out as the warmth of his breath mixes with the cool air hitting the trail of kisses.

He continues his way down, stopping at the top of my shorts. I feel his fingers hook in under the waistband of my shorts and panties. With one swift tug he has them down to my knees. He lets out a groan of approval.

"Fucking hell, you're so goddamn gorgeous laid out for me." He continues to lower my shorts, one foot at a time, I step my feet out of them. He discards them on the floor, before he grabs one ankle and bends my leg at the knee before putting my foot flat on the bed, not far from my ass cheek. He repeats the process with the other leg.

Well, he wanted me spread, that's exactly what he has achieved. I swallow down a gulp, because that means I know what's coming next.

"Your hands stay right where they are, you hear me?" My breath hitches with excitement. I have no words so I just nod.

He grabs the back of my thighs and pushes my legs back towards my chest, and before I even fully register the movement he is running his tongue right up my center and holy shit. I think I see stars in that moment.

He circles his tongue over my clit once before pulling his tongue back into his mouth, and looking me straight in the eyes. "So fucking sweet." My eyes are as wide as saucers.

Where has this side of him been hiding?

He wastes absolutely no time, his face is buried right back between my thighs, like a man of his word he absolutely devours me like he is the one that has been starved for two years. "Mason, I.. I need to.." I can't even get the words out before I'm tumbling over the edge into the abyss of my release.

My thighs squeeze the sides of his head as they spasm through my release. "Fuck, Beth, that was so fucking hot." I just silently laugh because, yes. Yes it was.

I finally reach my hands down to bring his face back up to mine. I pull him down to kiss me. "You like tasting yourself on my lips, baby?" I don't even break the kiss, just nod my head.

Fuck it has been so long since I've been treated like this, just been able to enjoy sex.

I run my hands down his sides, and bring one hand between us to cup his rock hard erection. It feels so hard I imagine it must be painful.

"No way, Beth. I know what you said last time, but if you touch me right now, this will be over before it begins. Besides, tonight is about fucking you like I mean it, remember?" He smiles that cheek splitting, cheeky grin and winks, before he rises off me.

He grabs me by the knees and pulls me to the edge of the bed, before grabbing me by the hands and pulling me to stand, meeting me with a kiss, he finally removes my bra and drops it to the floor. I hook my fingers in the waistband of his boxers and tug them down.

Fuck I don't think I got a chance the first time to fully appreciate his body. I run my fingers up and down his ribs, over his hips, tracing that V line before dragging my nails down to his thighs. He lets out a guttural moan, as I bring my hands back up, towards his throbbing, erection standing proudly between us.

He grabs my wrists, stopping them in their tracks. He turns me around and leans me forward to plant my wrists flat on the bed. I feel him kick at my ankles. A sign to widen my stance.

"That's my girl. Fuck you look amazing bent over for me. Don't move."

I feel his warmth leave my back and hear him pad away from me, into the bathroom. He emerges seconds later, condom in hand, gently stroking himself. He stops for a second, "Just gonna need a second to take all this in, baby."

"Did I mention I have a vibrator that can take your place at any second?" I peer at him over my shoulder, as he rolls the condom down his steely length.

"Yeah, but your vibrator won't tell you how good you look stretched around it. I will." Theres that smile again. I feel his hand in the middle of my back, pushing me further down toward the mattress so my elbows are resting on it. I feel so exposed, in the best way.

I feel Mason line the head of his cock up at my entrance. I push back into him, needing to feel him. "Fuck…" We both cry out in unison.

His hands are gripping tight on my hips. He stills inside me for just a moment, letting me adjust to his size, before he gently begins thrusting. "Fuck you feel so good, Mase."

He rubs a hand over the curve of my ass before squeezing just hard enough that it hurts, but doesn't distract from the pleasure currently coursing through my body.

He leans over me, pressing his chest into my back and grabs a handful of my breast, his thick muscular arm wrapping around me so he has both breasts covered with one arm, and he pulls me back up to stand. His thrusts haven't broken his steady rhythm.

His hand slides up from my chest to gently wrap around my throat, not putting any pressure at all, but just enough to feel the perfect amount of being manhandled. My breath hitches, and I feel my walls start to flutter and tighten around him.

"Your vibrator can't do that, can it?" He whispers in my ear, before laying a chaste kiss right behind my earlobe. He snakes his other hand around and immediately finds my clit. There's no hiding how close I am.

"I need to see you." He pulls out and I let out a moan and plant my hands back down onto the bed at the sudden empty feeling and the frustration of being so close to the edge.

He sits on the bed and scoots back to the headboard, the same position this all started. "Sit. I want you to ride me and I want to watch you come apart." I look up at him through the strands of my hair that have fallen in my face.

"Oh you mean, you're actually going to let me? Not just take me all the way there and then pull out?" He reaches out and grabs my wrist, pulling me to him.

"Don't tempt me, baby. Get over here."

With my arms around his neck, his hands on my hips, he lowers me down his length until he is completely buried inside of me. I watch as his eyes roll to the back of his head and he lets out a deep groan, straight from his chest.

"God yes, Mase, you fill me so well." I say as I begin to grind my hips along him. His grip is tight on my hips, and he takes some of my weight as he pushes me up and drops me back down on him.

"Fuck Beth, I can feel you dripping down me."

I just close my eyes because my orgasm is fast approaching. "Let me see it, Beth. Now." That's all it takes, I shatter. My body shudders and flings forward onto his chest, heaving to catch my breath.

He pumps his hips a couple more times underneath me, before he drops his head into the crook of my neck and lets out a shuddering moan through his own release.

He lifts me up, cradling my face to look him in the eyes. "Next time you reach for that vibrator, you call me first. Even if I can't get here, I want to see your face when you come at every opportunity." I feel my blush spread from my cheeks down to my chest.

Cute that he thinks my vibrator will ever live up to that.

Chapter 21

MASON

I wake up to the sound of two sets of small feet running up the stairs, I force my eyes open and Beth is still sound asleep beside me, I quickly thank the lucky stars that we had the sense to put some clothes on after we were done with our fun sleepover activities because we are about two seconds away from having innocent eyes on us.

I lean in and press a gentle kiss to her temple and leave the bed, hoping I can contain the noise that is about to rain down on us.

I get to the door just as the kids round the corner. "Shhhh. let's let Beth have a bit more sleep, c'mon, let's go get some breakfast."

The woman can sleep all day after the things she let me do to her last night. That exceeded every dirty thought I've ever had about her.

We get to the kitchen and the kids request pancakes. Okay, that I can do.

I sift through Beths pantry finding all of the ingredients, the kids want to help, so I set up at the kitchen table, the kids pour the flour and milk in, and crack an egg each. I'm impressed neither got a single piece of shell in the mix.

We take turns mixing the batter, before I tell the kids to go and play while I take care of cooking them.

I'm about three pancakes into cooking when Logan comes into the kitchen, "Mason, do you think you could put some music on the speaker? Me and my daddy used to have a dance party while we cooked breakfast."

I crouch down so I'm at his eye level. I'm not an emotional man, generally. But this kid asking me to partake in a tradition he had with dad, has me swallowing the lump that has formed in my throat.

"Absolutely I can, do you have any song requests?" He shakes his head.

"You can pick, as long as we can dance to it."

I find a generic 'family dance' playlist on my streaming app and play it "Yayy! Dance Party!" I hear Rosie squeal.

I watch the two of them wiggle their hips and spin and twirl, giggling and squealing. Rosie looks up at me, "Cmon Daddy, you have to dance with us!" I shake my head and flip the batch of pancakes in the pan.

"Now, Honey girl, you know Daddy can't dance."

"Please Mason.. It's so much fun." That's Logan again, he is tugging on the hem of my shirt, trying to pull me into the middle of the room, their makeshift dancefloor.

"Fuck it" I mumble under my breath so the kids can't hear me. I wonder how many times this boy and his mother will make me say that.

I flick the gas stove off, and take both of the kids by the hand and we dance in a circle, I spin them both a few times, they take turns standing on my toes so I can sway them and walk them around.

When a particularly boppy song comes on, we are really just hitting our stride, and starting to feel ourselves, I'm mid pirouette, when the most beautiful woman in the world catches my eye.

I don't know how long Beth has been standing on the landing of the staircase, watching, but even from a distance, I can see tears free falling down her face, but is she… smiling?

We lock eyes and just stare at each other for what feels like hours, but is probably mere seconds. Logan clued me in, I know this was a Griffin thing. I just hope I haven't overstepped by saying yes to the kid.

"Mama!!" Logan finally spots her and goes running over to her. I pick Rosie up in my arms, pulling her in for a hug as well. Before I start walking towards Beth.

When I reach them, I put Rosie down at the bottom of the stairs, and Beth and Logan step down to meet us. I pull Beth into my chest and lay a soft kiss in her hair. "Logie wanted a dance party.. I hope it's okay that I did that."

She just shakes her head and wipes away her tears, "Are you kidding me? This is a tradition I've wanted to start back up, every weekend I turn the speaker on, and then can't pick a song, because nothing feels right. It always feels like something is missing. So imagine my surprise, coming down the stairs to… Laughter, and music. And you shaking your ass. You don't dance, yet in the last week, you've danced with me. And you've danced with my son, because he misses his dad. You… you're amazing, Mason. Thank you, for this."

I finish making the pancakes and we all sit to eat breakfast, we keep the music playing in the background and the kids randomly burst into song and dance while they eat.

When we finish, the kids go to play quietly while Beth and I clean up. We are working together loading the dishwasher and wiping the counters down. When fuck me, you can't make this shit up. What song comes on over the speaker?

The same song that exactly one week ago had Beth running away. Today, makes her laugh and run her hands around my waist, while she slowly starts to sway.

I turn in her arms, so we are face to face, hand in hand, as we were about to be last weekend. We sway back and forth to Amazed by Lonestar.

"Definitely a sign." She says as she is looking up at me with bright eyes, she lowers her head into my chest.

The kids come running in halfway through the song. "It's Daddys song!" Logan says. Beth breaks away from me, before turning to grab Logan and lift him to her chest, holding him in a variation of the position we were just in, she starts swaying back and forth with him in her arms.

It's a beautiful moment between a mother and her son. So I crouch down in front of Rosie, looking her in the eyes, I hold out my hand, with my palm flat facing up. "Excuse me Miss, could I have this dance?" She just giggles and throws herself into my arms and we copy Beth and Logans movements.

****

Monday morning rolls around and I'm not even ashamed to admit I'm clutching at straws, looking for any excuse to walk into the office to see Beth. I can't get her out of my head. Her face is burned into the backs of my eyelids. I have a bit of a stockpile of expense receipts so I take them in for the girls to file.

I walk in and I've definitely interrupted a conversation. Abi and Beth both turn to look at me trying to cover up the fact they were clearly just giggling like schoolgirls. I look between the two of them, suspiciously.

Abi clears her throat, straightening her shoulders "Good Morning, Mason. How was your weekend?" she lifts her coffee mug to her lips, hiding her smile.

"Good thanks Abi, and yours?" I tilt my head at her, willing her to break back into a fit of giggles so my suspicions can be confirmed that I think they were talking about me, or at least, my weekend activities.

"Pretty boring, actually, nothing fun to report from me."I turn my attention to Beth, hoping she will confirm.

She has sucked both her lips into her mouth, her face is as red as a tomato, holding back her giggles. She pulls her water bottle towards her and wraps her lips around the thick straw and she hollows her cheeks out as she takes a long sip.

Oh, fuck me. Didn't need that image in my head right now.

I just shake my head and start heading towards the door before I really give them something to laugh about.

"Well, this has been fun. I'll let you ladies get back to.. whatever it was you were giggling about."

****

The second half of the week, I'm mostly out on job sites. My team is pretty self sufficient, I've been learning a lot more of the back of house processes lately, preparing for John's eventual retirement, but I still enjoy getting out on site, and getting my hands dirty.

I miss seeing Beth when I'm not around, but we are pretty much constantly texting back and forth. We have managed to make a decent plan for the weekend.

She is going to go to Philips Friday as usual, but she will leave Logan there with her dad, and we will travel out to the farm that night. We will stay at the main house for the first night, so Beth can meet my parents and to get a good nights sleep before the first big day of harvest, but then I plan to take Beth camping on my hill.

I call it my hill, because I own a part of the family land. My portion contains this steep rolling hill, that has sweeping views out over the river, where I took Beth and Logan to go fishing.

The river bank is lined on both sides with Poplar trees, which follow every bend and turn in the winding river. It's particularly beautiful when all the leaves start to change color and the river is shadowed by magnificent shades of red, yellow and orange.

My plan down the track is to build my forever home here, right on the top of the hill so I have the best outlook over the river and further beyond back towards town. Ever since my separation, I've been thinking it's time to start building.

I find it so quiet and calming, just sitting on top of the hill, and I'm hoping Beth will get as much peace out of that as I do.

Chapter 22

BETH

Mason arrives at my dads' house at 7.30pm. Nate is just leaving for his late shift at the restaurant, and Logan is getting ready for bed. He asks Mason if he can come out to go fishing again, and Mason says as soon as harvest is done, he would bring everyone out to go fishing for the day. That makes Logan happier.

I give him a goodnight kiss and cuddle, and he gives Mason a hug goodbye. I'm not sure when they graduated from a fist bump to a hug, but I look up at my dad and Will, and they both have the most sincere smiles on their faces.

Masons farm isn't too far out of town, but it's dark by the time we get on the road. His hand is rubbing up and down my bare thigh, playing with the ragged hemline of my cut off denim shorts. We get to the outskirts of town, past where the streetlights end. We are only minutes from the turn off into his property.

Its pitch black outside, nothing but the stars in the sky. He pulls the car over to the shoulder, and abruptly shifts the car to park and yanks on the handbrake.

He reaches over and puts his hand around the back of my neck, pulling me in for a deep kiss that feels so desperate it almost feels violent. His tongue finds its way into my mouth almost immediately.

One hand stays at the back of my head, holding me in place while the other runs down my arm, making goosebumps appear in its wake.

When he breaks the kiss, my lips feel hot and swollen. I just look at him because even one kiss feels like he has rocked my world. "Fuck, I needed that. Pretty soon, we will be in front of my parents, and I won't be able to just do that whenever I want to. So I just needed to get that out of my system." He releases me, and then turns back to put his hands on the steering wheel.

"Seriously, you're just going to kiss me like *that* and then expect me to face your parents in mere minutes, knowing how wet you've just made me?"

He looks at me, smiles, fucking winks. "That's exactly what I'm going to do, baby."

He shifts the car back to drive and pulls back onto the road. I rub my hands over my face. What the hell have I got myself into this weekend? And why do I feel like this is going to be like being 15 again and sneaking around to play 'just the tip' when his parents backs are turned.

****

"Oh Beth, it's so nice to meet you. We have heard so much about you and that little man of yours." Masons mother, Elsie greets us at the front door, immediately wrapping me in the warmest of hugs.

The front porch light turned on the minute we turned from the dirt road to the gravel driveway, about a hundred yards from the main house.

She glances at Mason over my shoulder and reaches her arm out to give his shoulder a squeeze. "Hi Ma," He says as he grabs her arm.

185

Elsie ushers us in, where we find Mason's dad, Henry, just pushing to stand out of his armchair. I can tell that's his spot, it's a worn, leather armchair that looks as though it's almost as old as he is.

"Hey Pops. This is Beth. Beth this my old man, Henry." I reach out my hand for him to shake it, feeling a bit awkward.

"None of that, girly. Get over here." He waves me over to him, and wraps me in a hug just as warm as his wife.

"It's good to finally meet the reason my son has pep back in his step." I blush at that.

I was nervous to meet his folks. Not knowing their thoughts and feelings on Hannah and their separation. But I couldn't have asked for a warmer welcome.

Henry gets Mason a beer from the fridge, while Elsie fixes me a cup of tea. I stand in the living room and take in the house for a moment,

It has some of the highest ceilings I've ever seen. The walls, covered in a deep brown wainscoting, adorned with family photos, as well as some photography which I recognize as being landscapes of their property. One of the bending river and another of the sun setting behind the old barn structure we passed on the way in.

"It is so generous of you to come and help out Beth. Very unexpected, but we appreciate it so very much." Elsie says, we have all settled in the lounge around their stunning coffee table, which I can't help but notice it looks homemade.

Each of us sipping our beverage of choice. Henry is back in his armchair, Elsie in the matching one across from him and Mason and I are side by side on the two seater couch in between them.

Mason's arm rests casually along the back of the couch, and his thumb gently rubs my shoulder. We make small talk and I get to hear so many stories about Mason as a boy. Until Henry decides to call it a night. It will be a long day tomorrow for everyone, so we all decide to follow his lead and turn in.

Mason leads me up the long hallway to what was his childhood bedroom, but has since had somewhat of a makeover. There are still some photos and sporting trophies lining the shelves, but it now has a queen sized bed and some photos of Rosie, as well as a basket of Princess dress ups and some dolls and accessories.

We share the bathroom just as we did at my house, he sits and watches as I wash my face and brush my hair, before tying it up in a messy bun. We both brush our teeth while constantly smiling at each other. It's one act that I never thought of as being romantic by any stretch of the imagination. But feels fun, and almost playful. That sounds so ridiculous.

I pull back the covers to climb into bed, and he does the same on the other side of the bed. He lies on his back, and I curl into his side, his calloused hand running across my back, playing with the straps of my pajama tank top.

My head is resting on his chest and I can her his heartbeat so soft and steady."Thank you for being here Beth. You have no idea what this means to me. To my family." A smile crosses my face. And I realize, I don't want to be anywhere else but in his arms.

Mason's alarm sounds at 4.30am. It's still dark out, but I guess that's farm life. He reaches over to turn it off, before cuddling back into me for just a moment. I feel his impressive morning wood pressing into my lower back and damn, I wish we had time for me to do something about that.

"Good Morning, beautiful" He rasps in my ear, his voice like gravel, still half asleep.

"Any day I wake up with you behind me is a good day." He lets out a breathy chuckle as he lays a gentle kiss on my cheek before rolling over and standing from the bed. It's then that I get a glimpse of the aforementioned morning wood.

I don't think I'll ever get used to be being this turned on by just looking at the man.

He stands tall, wearing just a pair of black boxers, that look uncomfortably tight. He leans back to stretch his arms over his head, yawning at the same time. He looks back at me and I've one hundred per cent just been caught out checking him out, but I don't even care.

"That way you're looking at me right now, Beth. Save that for later." He leaves the bedroom, headed straight for the shower. I get out of bed, and start getting myself ready for the day.

Moments later he emerges from the bathroom, with just a towel wrapped around his waist. Oh heaven help me.

I excuse myself to get myself showered before my wandering hands get us into trouble. He smacks me on the ass playfully as I walk past him.

When I come out of the shower, fully dressed, I head to the kitchen. Mason has traded his trademark baseball cap, for a well worn cowboy hat, I can't decide which I prefer on him. He has paired with a dark blue, lightweight, long sleeved shirt, and his worn out Wrangler jeans, that as usual hug his ass perfectly. My eyes go straight to it.

I have to shake my head and remind myself that we are in his parents house.

He rounds the kitchen counter to stand beside me, handing me a cup of fresh brewed coffee. He put his other hand on my hip and lays a gentle kiss on my temple.

"Time for me to head out. See you ladies a little bit later."

I walk further into the kitchen where Elsie is already pulling her apron on and digging through the pantry for ingredients.

"Okay, Elsie, put me to work." I sip my coffee, and she hands me a spare apron. It's well loved, and when I tie it around my waist, I look down at it and it is embroidered with the words "Mrs. Clarke" on the chest.

Huh, that's… not what I was expecting at 5am on the first day here. I feel tears start to prickle in the corners of my eyes, but I shake them off, because it's just one of Elsie's aprons. It's not like it's a marriage proposal directed at me.

Settle down there, big girl.

Elsie and I work like a well oiled machine. We bake cookies and muffins, both savory and sweet as snacks for the whole crew. We make trays upon trays of sandwiches and fruit platters, as well as cut up cheese and some cold cuts and pack everything into small containers to disperse between everyone.

We also make up a big batch of lasagna, a pasta bake, a big beef stew and some fried rice which will all be kept in the house and served later tonight for dinner once the day is done.

I actually enjoy the time I have to get to know Elsie, I get an insight into her life on the farm, I learn more about Mason as a kid and also learn a bit about Leah, Masons sister.

This place is full of so much history for their family, and it's easy to see why Mason loves it so much out here and dedicates so much of his time to looking after the place.

It's almost lunch time and we have managed to make a lot of the food needed for today already. We are just starting the clean up process, I'm wiping down the counters, when Elsie looks up at me with a gentle smile.

"Beth, I know you will probably get sick of hearing us all thank you for coming. But it really does mean the world. This place is Masons life, the red dirt is bred into him. But Hannah, well, you could take the girl out of the city, but you couldn't take the city out of that girl. They loved each other for a good while there, but this was never her thing. She never made the effort. So when we say it means a lot to us that you're here, it's not just for helping me out with the food. It's for making him happy. For putting in the effort."

I just smile and wrap my arm around her shoulders in a one armed hug, still holding the cleaning wipes in the other hand. "He makes it easy, and there's no where I would rather be."

She smiles a satisfied smile, while looking down into the sink full of dishes. She opens her mouth as if to say something, then closes it again. She takes a deep breath and then looks back up at me. "I know the last year or two hasn't been easy for you. Mason has told us a bit about your husbands illness, and passing. I can't imagine how hard that must've been for you, and for Logan, who I'm looking so forward to meeting one day, by the way." I give her a weak smile, I don't know where she is going with this.

"I guess what I'm trying to say is, I know I only met you a few hours ago, and I know you and Mason have both had your doubts about moving on, but a mothers instinct rarely misses. And I see the sparks that you and Mason share. It's rare, that connection. Despite both of you having your pasts, I'm happy you have found each other."

God dammit, Elsie. I came here to cook, not cry.

"I appreciate you saying that Elsie. I am very much enjoying spending time with Mason, just taking it day by day and seeing how it goes, I guess. And Rosie, she's a blast all on her own." We both share a chuckle at that.

"You know, when Henry and I were dating, many, MANY years ago now. I was in much the same position as you now. In a new relationship, staying in this very house. Dying to be together but trying to be respectful of his parents. We were quite young at the time and Henrys dad made sure we slept in separate bedrooms, at opposite ends of the house, and made it known he slept with his shotgun by his bed in case he heard any midnight footsteps. So there was absolutely no funny business… at least not in the house anyway." She nudges an elbow into my side and turns back to the oven, laughing to herself.

She makes a point of looking at the watch on her wrist. "Oh would you look at the time? Time to deliver the lunches out to the field, those boys will all have worked up quite the appetite by now, I'd say. Would you be a dear and run them out to the field? You can drive the farm truck, keys are by the door. Follow the dirt road all the way to the end, then turn left and head towards the big dust clouds." She winks at me and then nudges me in the direction of the door.

I follow Elsie's directions and at the sight of the truck rolling into the field, the half dozen trucks and combine harvesters all come to a stop, and the operators all jump down from their respective cabs and drivers seat and make their way to the back of the farm truck to help me unpack the fold up table, and the large tubs containing their lunches and some ice cold water.

It's unseasonably warm for being so early on in summer. I look around the small sea of unknown faces. Henry is there and introduces me to a few of the men. A couple of Mason's cousins, and some friends. I recognize one or two of their faces from around town. I have yet to lay eyes on Mason though.

Henry catches on immediately to my eyes scanning for the one person missing. "He's down in the back corner of the field, the stubborn bastard wants to finish his section before breaking for lunch. No idea where he gets his hard headed qualities from. You might as well take his lunch to him. Might cheer him up a bit, seeing your face, I think living in town has made him soft. Grumpy bastard can't handle these early mornings anymore."

I love Henry's gruffness. I grab one of the lunch packs, a couple of bottles of icy water and jump back in the truck. Looking forward to seeing him even if just for a minute.

I head out into the field, and immediately see the dust cloud at the other end of the field. He must see me coming because he stops the Combine harvester he is driving just I put the truck in park and jump out. His face lights up.

I see him pick up the handheld radio, I assume he is communicating to the driver of his companion truck to break for lunch.

I walk the few feet between the truck, and he opens the door to the harvester and gestures for me to climb up. He takes the keys to the farm truck and tosses them to the other driver and tells him to go and get some food.

The harvester cab is more spacious than I was expecting. I take him in as I climb the steps into the cab, dirt on his pants and boots, dust covering almost every other visible inch of him. He stands from his seat, and takes the food from my hands, placing it down on the floor beside his seat.

"Look at you getting dusty out here in the fields. I'll have you driving this thing soon enough."

I look down at my own body, my boots are covered in dust, and even my legs are looking a little orange with a light covering of dust.

"I think my boots almost fell apart in shock at the concept of actually getting dirty. It's been a while."

He sits back in his chair and drags me down to straddle his lap, running his hands all over my body, starting at my thighs and running up over my hips.

I'm only wearing a simple pair of denim shorts, and in this position they have ridden a fair way up, leaving most of my thighs exposed. He moves to kiss me, but I pull away. "You don't want to kiss me right now, I'm sweaty and dirty."

"Baby, dirty has never looked this good." He cradles my face in his hands and pulls me in to kiss me, hard and deep like we haven't seen each other for days, or weeks, instead of just a few hours.

I instantly feel him harden beneath me, his hands run down to my lower back. I lower my head to kiss down his neck "Fuck, Beth, You're playing with fire here baby." I pull away and look him in the eyes, running my fingers through his short hair.

"At the risk of ruining this mood, by bringing up your mother… But I'm pretty sure she just told me to come and do this."

He gives me a quizzical look, "Do I even want to know?" I shake my head. "Fuck it, I don't even care."

He kisses me again, this time much more desperate and hungry. I roll my hips over his ever impressive erection that is still digging into my ass.

I don't break his kiss as I rise to my feet, he follows and I tug him over so he is sitting in the second seat, away from the steering column and control panels.

Now that we have a bit of extra room, I drop to my knees between his, and fumble with the button and zipper of his jeans, pulling them and his boxers down just enough to release his angry looking erection, already leaking moisture from the tip.

I give the tip a few slow strokes, before running my tongue all the way along his shaft from root to tip. I circle my tongue around the tip, flicking it back into my mouth to savor his salty taste. He groans and drops his head back against the back of the chair. He reaches a hand out to grab a handful of my hair.

"Fucking hell, where did you come from?" I barely even let him finish his sentence, I hold eye contact the entire time I take him into my mouth. All the way to the back of my throat.

I can't even breath for a moment but it's worth it to see the pleasure in his eyes. Hear it in the long, deep groan that erupts from his chest. I know we probably don't have a lot of time so I don't waste a second of it.

I hollow out my cheeks and suck, hard. Just like I know he was picturing me doing the day he walked in on Abi and I giggling in the office a few days ago. I saw his blush when I sipped my water through the thick straw. I know he pictured himself as that straw.

I get myself into a steady rhythm, my mouth and hand working in sync, bringing him closer and closer to the edge with each stroke.

His grip on my hair is tight, and he is putting more and more pressure on the back of my head, he is gently thrusting into me, chasing his release. "Fuck me Beth, I'm so fucking close."

His breathing turns erratic and with just a couple more strokes he unleashes, spilling his warm come straight down the back of my throat. I look up at him through my thick eyelashes, and he watches me as I swallow every drop down.

With a chuckle, he hooks his thumb and forefinger under my chin, pulling me back up to his eye level, He gently kisses me "A guy could get used to this kind of lunch break."

That was without a doubt, the hottest thing I've ever done. We just get his pants back up before a voice comes over his handheld radio "Hey Mason, is it safe to come back to my truck now, or am I going to catch you with your pants down?"

He laughs and shakes his head "You thought your brothers were bad, wait till you meet the owner of that smart little mouth, my youngest cousin, Bentley. He'd give Nate a run for his money in the shit talking stakes."

He grabs the handheld radio of its base and pulls it to his mouth. "Very funny, smart ass. You can get back to work, whenever you're done mouthing off."

He looks at me, as I am fixing my hair, and shuffling back towards the door. "Hey" he grabs my face and pulls me back into his chest. "This isn't over." He winks at me and smacks my ass as I climb back down out of the harvester.

Chapter 23

MASON

Well, this is shaping up to be the best harvest in years. And I'm not talking about the crops. The fact that the girl of my dreams just pulled up and sucked my dick in the cab of the harvester. It can't get much better than that.

I get hard all over again just thinking about the sight of Beth stepping out of the old farm truck. Oversized, blue linen shirt, partially tucked into the waistband of her denim shorts, buttons done just right to show off just the right amount of cleavage. And those boots. I think I'll keep them. I love them. I love everything about her. I love her.

Fuck, where did that come from?

The rest of the day drags, and it's late afternoon by the time we all call it quits. There are still some everyday jobs to be done around the farm, Herds of cows to be fed out and barn stalls to be mucked out, plus a nice surprise to set up for Beth.

My parents two Palamino horses, Barney and Billie don't get ridden a lot anymore. They are nearing an age where they will be old to ride. I'd love to teach Rosie to ride one day, but it has been baby steps to even get her out here.

I've just finished mucking Billie's stall out, and I take a minute to give her a few pieces of licorice, her favorite treat. While I give her coat a bit of a brush out.

Horses can be so instinctual when it comes to human emotion. They seem to be able to sense when you're happy, or when you're sad. I used to love when I was having some teenage emotional crisis, I'd always come and vent to whichever of our horses was in need of some attention. They become like big lap dogs when you give them a bit of loving.

"Hey Billie girl, you and Barney got it pretty good, huh? Living the good life with each other, getting all the treats." She lets out a low nicker. She knows it.

She nudges her big head into my neck, like she is trying to give me a cuddle. I hear my dad approach the stall in the fading daylight.

"The hell you doing in here cuddling with my girl, when yours is waiting up at the house for you?" He unlocks the gate into the barn stall, gesturing for me to exit. He clips it shut behind me, before reaching up to pat Billie's nose. "You got it bad, boy. No one would blame you for being scared of that."

I take my hat off my head and run my hands through my hair. He slaps me on the shoulder. "Don't let your head get in the way of your heart, son. She's special. I could tell months ago. Your mother knew the minute you walked through the door last night. You love her. Look after that."

I haul ass back to the house. I can't wait to get Beth back in my arms. I'm taking her camping tonight. I roped Bentley in to helping me set up the perfect campsite before I came down to the stables.

Everything is set up, we have rugs to lay out under the stars and a big bell tent set up with a ridiculous amount of blankets and pillows, Bentley went back up to the house where I had already had some wine, cheese and crackers organized. So he has raced back and set those up for us as well.

The kid might be a smartass, but at twenty-three years old. He's one hell of a wingman. It's perfect. The girl that has bought happiness back into my life, in the place that brings me peace.

When I get back to the house, Beth is sitting cross legged on my parents old porch swing, sipping a cup of tea. She looks comfortable. Content. Like she belongs here.

She gets up and sits the cup of tea on the porch railing when she sees my truck approaching the house. She gets to the top of the porch steps, and stops, leaning her hip against the hand railing. I run out of my truck as soon as I stop it. She senses the urgency and meets me halfway, leaping into my arms, her hands around my neck as our lips crash together in a passionate kiss. Like a scene from a fucking movie, just missing the pouring rain.

"Beth, I don't want to ruin this mood, but I think we have an audience." She turns to look back at the house just in time to see Bentley and my mother quickly pull their heads back behind the curtain of the window by the front door. Beth lowers her legs from my waist and we walk toward the house arm in arm.

I can hear the chuckles from inside through the front screen door. In their defense, they have both been a good wingman/woman in their own way today. Although I'm sure not going to be high fiving my Mother for her part.

I load a bag each for me and Beth into my truck and lead her by the hand down the front porch steps, we say goodnight to my folks, and I help her up into the front seat.

I round the front of the car into the drivers seat and pull out a blindfold from my pocket, and hand it to her.

"What is this?" She looks at me while raising an eyebrow.

"It's a blindfold." She shakes her head.

"Duh, but why am I holding a blindfold?"

"Well, it would be entirely more useful, if you put it on, instead of holding it." I take the blindfold back off her and drape it around her eyes.

"Relax, remember I said I have something I want to show you. But I want to see your reaction. So, just trust me. Okay?" She just nods her head.

The spot I have chosen on the hill is secluded enough that we will feel like we are entirely alone. It's a small mercy because having Beth blindfolded is doing all sorts of things to both of us. Who knew something so simple, would feel so sensual.

She is all hands, the whole way, so thank God it's only a couple of minutes drive from the house to the hill. Her wandering hands have my dick standing at attention under my jeans, it's not the most comfortable situation to have while driving.

I put the car in park, then round the car to open her door. Perfect timing, the sun is just starting to set. I take her by the hand and help her step down, shut the door, then take her by the hips, standing flush behind her, I untie the blindfold, and pull it away from her eyes.

She is absolutely speechless, her mouth drops open, the sight of the sun setting, the gorgeous tent, the picnic rugs set up.

I can tell she is trying to find words but is legitimately gob smacked. "Holy… Mase… What? How?"

I just laugh, wrapping my arms around her and kissing a gentle kiss to her shoulder. "So you like it then?"

"Like it? Mason, I think this is the most beautiful thing I've ever experienced. How on earth did you have time for this?"

She turns in my arms. To look up at me with her fierce green eyes. "Let's just say I owe a couple people some favors."

I sit on the picnic rug and she crawls to sit in between my legs, her back resting on my chest. We snack and have some wine each as we watch the sun disappear below the surrounding hills. She tells me all about her day, learning some of my family recipes, and hearing all of the embarrassing stories about me from my childhood.

"Well, I don't know about you, but I'm sweaty and dusty and gross from a long day in the field. I'm gonna go cool off, and freshen up in the river." I push out from behind her and start making my way down the hill toward the river.

This side of the bank has a really sandy shoreline, where there is no current. It's the perfect place to swim. "Oh, I wish you had've told me we'd be swimming. I didn't bring anything with me."

I turn back to look at her with the widest smile, holding my hands out wide in a sort of shrug motion, "Baby, neither did I." I pop the button of my jeans, so she knows I'm serious. "Race ya?" I lay down the challenge.

Beth smirks and then takes off like a shot out of a gun. Fuck me, I underestimated how fast she was. I catch up to her within a few strides and throw her over my shoulder, carrying her the rest of the way while she giggles, and tries to smack my ass.

I drop her back to her feet, when we near the banks of the river, but keep my arms wrapped around her, pulling her body in close. I kiss the top of her head. "Thank you for being here with me Beth."

"You can thank me by taking your clothes off. But Mason…. leave the hat on, can you?"

"Yes, Ma'am. I'm gonna need you to hold it for me for a second though, okay?" I hand her my hat and reach behind my neck to take my shirt off.

When I look back at her, she has my old worn-out hat on her head. "Now Beth, I hope you know the rule about wearing a man's cowboy hat."

She steps up to me and lowers the zipper on my pants that suddenly just got a whole lot tighter. Looking up at me from under the brim of the hat. "Of course, I know the rule about wearing a man's cowboy hat."

She lowers my pants, taking my boxers with them, I toe my boots off and kick my pants to the side. She doesn't break eye contact with me as she places my hat back on my head.

I fumble over the buttons of her shirt, before pushing it back over her shoulders. It hits the ground just as I begin fiddling with the button and zipper of her denim shorts. She toes her boots off and I drop her shorts to the ground, leaving her in just a thin red lace bra and matching lace panties. Fuck I'm glad I didn't know that's what she was wearing under there when she came out into the field this afternoon, I would've torn a hole through my favorite jeans.

I take a step back to look at her. Really take her in. This beautiful girl stripped almost bare, in my favorite place in the world.

"Off, now." I say to her in a low raspy voice, as I point to her underwear. She turns and walks away from me, heading for the water.

She unclasps her bra, removes it, holds it out beside her and drops it, then without even missing a stride, lets her underwear drop before stepping out of them. The perfect trail of Beth leading straight to the water.

The fuck am I doing still standing here with my dick in my hand?

In a few short strides I'm at the water's edge. She dove in headfirst, so I quickly follow suit, wading into the water behind her. The water is refreshingly cold, I remove my hat long enough to dunk my head under the water, and immediately feel so much cleaner.

I reach for Beths hand and pull her into me, her arms go straight around my neck, and her legs immediately wrap around my waist. My hands instinctively fall to cup her perfect ass.

This is dangerous territory, my cock twitches nervously at being right up against her bare. She kisses me, pulling her body in so there is no space whatsoever between us.

I can feel the hard peaks of her nipples pressing against my body. I'm not sure if it's the cold water or the fact that she is turned on, and I don't even care. I just want them in my hands, in my mouth.

I lift her slightly so her full breasts are just above the waterline. I bring one hand up to cup one breast, before lowering my face down to bring her hard peak into my mouth. She takes a sharp inhale and then lets out a moan at the sudden change in temperature.

My hand on her ass squeezes into her flesh, which reactively makes her grind her perfect pussy over my painful erection.

Fuck, I'm in trouble here.

"Beth, I think we might need to cut this swim short. I need to be inside you." I say in between flicking my tongue over her pert nipple.

She shifts her hips in my arm, and I think she is going to remove her legs and climb down so we can head back to the tent, but she doesn't. She lines herself up on my cock and lowers herself down my length. "Holy Fuck! Beth…"

She looks at me, her chest heaving with heavy breaths as she slowly starts to grind her hips. "Sometimes you just have to take what you want, Mason."

I feel like a bumbling teenager that is losing his virginity for the first time. "Are you sure about this Beth? I have condoms up at the tent."

She strokes the side of my face, still lightly grinding her hips. "Mason, we're both consenting adults, right? I track my cycles. It's a very, very, VERY low risk right now. But if you want to, we can head back up. It's up to you, but I'm good." I look at her face, searching for any hint that she isn't as okay with this as she says she is.

Nothing, she is rock solid. Fuck, how did I get so lucky?

I take a few steps back into shallower water, so I can lay Beth down against the sand bank, I keep one arm behind her, elevating her off the bottom slightly. The sand has given me a bit of traction, so I start thrusting into her harder, watching her full tits bounce and sway in the water, her head rolls back,

"God yes, Mason. Just like that." Fuck I love hearing my name fall from her lips. Almost as much as I love feeling her squeeze my cock when she comes all over me.

I kiss her deep, reaching down with my free hand, my thumb rubs circles around her swollen clit. I watch it happen in slow motion. Her eyes roll back, her mouth falls open, and she squeezes. She moans. She shatters. All around my bare cock.

"Beth, can I come all over these perfect tits?" She looks up at me, still not even fully recovered from her earth shattering orgasm. "You can come wherever the hell you want to."

We switch positions so her tits are right in front of me and I'm stroking myself. It only takes a matter of seconds after the pure ecstasy of fucking her bare for the first time. I blow my load all over her perfect chest.

"Fucking hell. Letting me fuck you bare, and then sitting in my water wearing my come? Be careful Beth, you're starting to look like you're Mine."

Chapter 24

BETH

"Be careful, Beth, you're starting to look like you're mine." The words came from his mouth in such a moment of passion. And I know he probably didn't mean anything by it. Hell, I love seeing his restraint snap when our clothes come off. Him saying things like that though? Scares me a little.

I am starting to feel like his. He is starting to feel like, mine. This thing is starting to feel very real. Everyone around us can see it, feel it. I know we both can feel it.

I think I've been living in this fairyland of wanting to see how things go. I still don't know if I've waited long enough after Griffins passing, or after Mason's separation, to be in this deep. I carry this guilt with me every day, and I just don't know how to stamp it out.

We get out of the water and Mason produces two towels from a bag next to a massive, old poplar tree by the banks. The man thought of everything.

We dry off and walk back up to the tent, which is adorned with solar powered fairy lights that have switched on now that night has completely fallen. It's even more beautiful from afar.

Collecting our discarded clothes along the way, and laughing back and forth. He makes this feel so easy. Which makes my mind go even crazier.

I just can't get my head around these new feelings. I thought Griffin was it for me. And now, Mason comes out of the blue, and does things like this, and says things like "You're starting to look like you're mine." What chance do I stand against that? How do I rid myself of the guilt for falling for someone other than my dead husband, even though he gave me his blessing a thousand times over before his passing?

Let it go, Beth. Just enjoy this night for heavens sake.

We get back to the tent and he passes me my bag, we get dressed, and sit out on the picnic rug. Elsie packed us up some dinner to bring down, so we enjoy that and then lay out in silence staring at stars. It's been a long time since I was far enough out of town to be able to see the stars like this. It's easy to forget just how many are up there. How small we are in this world.

"I can hear you thinking, Beth. What's on your mind?" Mason says. I have my head laying on his leg, using his thigh as a pillow, while his fingers are brushing through my hair.

"It's beautiful out here. Just so peaceful. It's easy to see why you love it so much. I've needed this level of peace on so many occasions in the last twelve months. Thank you. For bringing me here." I have a lump in my throat, that I swallow down hard, before I go to water and spoil an otherwise beautiful night.

He sits up, so I follow suit, he pulls me in so we are facing each other. He cups my face in his hand, rubbing a thumb along my jawline. "You know, I've heard it said that grief is the greatest measure of Love. And that the bigger the grief, the bigger the love. It's okay to miss him, Beth. You loved him for so long, and your time was cut short. You don't need to feel guilty about it, or hide away from it.

"This piece of land has seen me through some pretty shitty times, but somewhere, between the grass, the trees, and the water. I always manage to find clarity here, somewhere." He kisses my forehead. "I bought you here because I know it could offer you the same thing. Peace. Clarity." He gives me a gentle smile, and my heart is absolutely pounding.

"I'm going to head in, we have another early rise in the morning. You take all the time you need." He doesn't kiss me this time. Just squeezes my shoulder and stands to walk into the tent.

I take probably the deepest breath in I've ever taken. And blow it out with force. I lean back on my hands, laying back to take in the expanse of stars above me.

He's right, Griffin would've loved this. He loved the outdoors, and nature. I miss him. Especially in moments like these. I throw a smile up to the sky, hoping Griffin is up there somewhere catching it.

I give myself a couple of minutes before heading inside. Mason is already laying in the makeshift bed which looks like a couple of air mattresses covered in a nest of blankets and pillows, he has a light blanket draped over his hips, he is shirtless and has one muscular arm resting underneath his head, the other laying across his stomach.

"You okay?" He lifts the blanket he is under so I can climb in next to him.

"Yeah, just having a moment, I guess. When the world is quiet, my mind seems to get loud. I guess I haven't had a lot of quiet lately." He wraps his arm around me, and rolls to his side so my back is flush against his chest, and his strong thighs are cradling my legs.

A few traitorous tears slip out of my eyes, if Mason notices he doesn't say anything, just squeezes me tighter and within seconds his breathing evens out and he is softly snoring.

✶✶✶✶✶✶✶✶✶✶✶✶✶✶

Masons alarm sounds just as early as yesterday. He groans as he rolls over to shut it off. I don't think we moved all night, he is still holding me just as tightly as he did last night.

205

We do a quick pack up of all the blankets and pillows and load them in Masons truck. He says he will send Bentley down later to get the tent and mattresses. So we head up to the house for some coffee and breakfast before he heads back out to the fields.

His hand is on my thigh the entire drive back to the house and when we pull up in the driveway, he reaches over to unbuckle my seatbelt, before hooking his finger under my chin and forcing my head to turn towards him, it's still dark, the sky is just barely starting to lighten.

"You look beautiful this morning." And then he lays a gentle kiss on my lips before he exits the truck and opens my door for me.

He takes my hand and walks me up the front porch steps, and into the house, never dropping my hand. I take a seat at the dining table and he makes me a coffee and grabs some toast for both of us.

He lays a kiss on my temple as he puts the toast down in front of me on the table before taking a seat next to me.

Henry is seated at the end of the table catching up on yesterdays newspaper. Without even peaking out from behind it he says "Good night camping, kids?" I try to hide my blush. I really try, but I feel it creeping up my chest.

Mason sucks his lips in between his teeth before answering "uh, yeah, Pops, it was a beautiful night out."

Henry shifts the newspaper down now, glancing between the two of us "Uh-huh. Bet it was." I am mid sip of coffee and just about snort it out. Mason squeezes my thigh under the table.

Elsie comes over from the kitchen, collecting Henrys breakfast dishes and returning to the kitchen. Henry raises from his chair "Well son, lets get out of here, this shit aint gonna do itself." He goes via the kitchen to give Elsie a quick peck on the cheek. It makes me smile.

I vaguely remember my parents having a relationship like that when I was very young before everything went down.

Mason stands but leans back down to kiss me, mimicking what his father just did to his mother, except he pauses near my ear and whispers "You delivering lunch again today?"

I elbow him in the ribs and giggle "You heard the man, get out of here."

My second day with Elsie is just as enjoyable as the first. I become like her Sous Chef, I wash and chop what feels like a metric ton of vegetables and fruit. I weigh out all of her baking ingredients, flours, sugars, butter, milk and she has me go out the back to the chicken coop to collect some fresh eggs for her.

I feel like I just looked death in the face when I came face to face with their big, scary looking Rooster. He chased me down on the way in and the way out. Mean Fucker.

I didn't even realize how many hours had gone by, we spent most of the morning talking about me. She asked me about Logan, about Griffin, about my siblings. She thinks she might have met Nate once at Just In Thyme. She said he makes a mean Margarita, which sounds about right.

We even talk about my mother and her issues, and the fact that I haven't seen or heard from her since just before my twelfth birthday.

Usually when I talk about my upbringing, people's reactions always feel judgmental or you can feel a sense of pity, like they can't possibly understand what would possibly make someone give up the rights to four kids and just leave. But Elsie doesn't have that tone of judgement in her voice.

She just listens, and at the end of the conversation she hugs me, and commends me on being able to support my younger siblings through all of that, when I was still just a kid myself.

I find it comforting, finding these maternal moments along the way, with other 'mother figures' in life. This one coming with someone that I met just over 24 hours ago, but feel like I've already bonded with like we have known each other for years. Or like I'm part of her family.

Thinking back on what Mason said yesterday about grief being the greatest measure of love. It's not lost on me that in my case, my grief seems to have bought so much new love into my life.

Elsie and I both take a drive down to the fields for lunch time today, to catch up with everyone and see how it's all going.

They have all made great progress, but still not enough. Mason decides to take the week off work to help get it finished before the weather is forecast to change next week.

He will still drive me home this afternoon, but then I probably won't see him for a while, and probably have limited phone contact as Mason will be so busy, and the reception here is patchy at best. We seemed to get decent service in the tent last night and I received a couple of photos of Logan from my dad and Will. He is being spoiled rotten with those two in charge, I'd be surprised if he even wants to come home tonight.

****

I'm exhausted by the end of the day, and I haven't worked half as hard as Mason has. On the drive home, his hand rests on my thigh, and I stroke his knuckles and hold his hand the whole way. The mood feels a little somber after such a playful, fun weekend. It's like we can't take our hands off each other, knowing we won't be seeing each other for a little while.

He pulls into the driveway at my dads house, where I left my car, and Logan on Friday night. He cuts the engine but doesn't move to get out.

"I know it's been said a million times already, but thank you for coming this weekend Beth. Everyone really enjoyed getting to know you. And it sure made the long days worth it, knowing you were there waiting for me at the end of it"

208

He lifts my hand to his lips and kisses the top of my hand before holding it in his hand and resting it on his lap. "I had a really good time. I enjoyed being back outdoors, in the dust, and the water." I wink and blush slightly at that.

"I need to get something off my chest, and I want you to know that this changes nothing between us." He looks straight down at the trucks steering wheel, like he is avoiding my gaze.

"What is it, Mase?" He has me a little concerned, and I think he must sense it because he shifts in his seat to face me as best as he can with his big frame in the bucket seat of his truck.

"Beth, I think…. I Love you."

No… No, no, no, no… Fuck….

"Mase…." I say on the exhale. I shift my hand out from under his.

"I know you need more time. But I couldn't keep walking around with this big feeling in my chest, and not say it out loud. Life is too short, Beth, you taught me that. So, I just needed you to know. Because I think you feel it too, and even if you aren't ready to say it, or open yourself up to completely feeling it yet. It's there. I see it, I feel it. And I'll be right here waiting for you whenever you are ready. Whether that's next week or next year. I don't care. It's on your time now, Beth."

Fuck, here come the waterworks. I breathe in and nod. I need to get out of this car, like now. "Goodnight, Mase, I'll see you soon." I bite the inside of my cheek, trying to will away the tears that are prickling the corners of my eyes. I squeeze his hand, but we don't kiss goodbye.

Chapter 25

MASON

Henry Mother Fucking Clarke. I'll kill him. 'Don't let your head get in the way of your heart.' He said. What sage advice that turned out to be.

I'm pretty sure I just sent Beth into a full fucking tailspin. Fucking idiot. As soon as the words left my mouth, I wanted to stuff them straight back in.

I knew it was too soon. I knew she wasn't ready. I have absolutely just freaked her the fuck out. And I'm heading straight back out to the farm and I know I will have limited contact with her from now until at least next weekend, probably even the Monday after that when I'm back to work, so I can't even go and beg her to unhear the words.

Fucking idiot.

When I get back to the main house at the farm, I cut the engine of my truck and sit there for a minute. I rest my forehead on the steering wheel, banging it gently a couple of times. Thinking maybe it might knock some sense into me, although a good time for that would've been half an hour ago before I dropped the L word on Beth when I knew she was already in her own head. I immediately pull out my phone.

Mason: Beth, I'm sorry. I shouldn't have said anything until I knew you were ready.

I watch my phone as those three little dots that indicate she is writing back appear. And then disappear. And then appear again. When ten minutes go past and a response hasn't come through. I put my phone back in my pocket and head inside.

I have no appetite but hopefully a cold shower and a comfortable bed will ease my mind.

"Everything okay, Darlin'? We missed you at dinner." Trust Elsie Clarke to spot a life crisis a mile away.

She pokes her head through my bedroom door just as I'm climbing into my bed. This feels exactly like it did when I was a teenager having girl troubles.

"I don't know, Ma. I have a feeling I might've just stuffed things up with Beth. I, uh, told I loved her and then watched as she completely freaked out, but I couldn't stop it."

She sits on the edge of my bed, resting a gentle hand on my knee. "I don't think you've ruined anything. I think she needs time to process what you've told her. She has been through a lot, not just this year, but her whole life. I can't imagine she loves easily. Let her have a moment to breathe, and get it all straight in her head. She loves you back Mason, trust me."

I know deep down she is right, but it doesn't help the immediate panic right now. I let out a deep breath and give her a weak smile. "Thanks Ma."

She pats my knee a couple of times and gets up, heading for the door. She stops at the threshold and turns to look back at me. "You make each other really happy. It's really nice to see you with that big cheesy grin back on your face. Goodnight, son."

She turns the light off on her way out of my room and I get myself comfortable in bed. I toss and turn a few times, trying to get comfortable around this pit I feel in my stomach. I pick up my phone to double check if Beth responded. Nothing.

Mason: Goodnight, Beth. Sweet dreams xx.

∗∗∗∗∗∗∗∗∗∗∗

It's been a long few days, it's Wednesday now and we are over halfway done with harvest. We are aiming to be finished by Friday, which will be the perfect timing as heavy rainfall is expected this weekend, plus it means I get to go home in time to pick up Rosie.

The days have been sweltering hot, so every afternoon, a few of the crew have been heading down to the river for a swim to cool off. Today, I can't bring myself to get in the water.

I sit on the bank because everywhere I look down here now, I see her.

Where we laid on the rug and stared at the stars, where we slept wrapped up in each other all night. Where our clothes landed as we stripped them off each other. Where I laid her down and fucked her exactly how she asked. Fuck. She is everywhere.

I have made a point of sending her a text message every morning, and every night. Even if it's just to say Good Morning, or to see how her day was. I sent her a couple of photos of things I thought she would like.

I managed to get some tack on Billie and took her for a ride yesterday evening, so I snapped a couple of photos along the trail I rode. It's probably lame, but I came across some bright wildflowers that just reminded me of her, so I made sure to tell her of that.

I haven't had a single message back. I know my service has dropped in and out but messages would still come through. I must've done a real number on her.

Since I'm here, where I know the phone service is good, I try calling her. She doesn't answer, she should be finished work by now, and it's late enough she would be home with Logan.

It's taking every ounce of willpower not to get in my truck and drive to her house. Just to make sure she is okay. Just to hear her voice or see her face. It's been three days, this is so pathetic. Giving her her space might be the hardest thing I'll ever do.

I get her voicemail "Hey Beth, it's me. I just wanted to check in to see how you are. I really miss hearing your voice. I really miss…. All of you, if I'm honest. Anyway, you don't have to call me back but I just wanted you to know I'm thinking about you. Goodnight, Beth."

I run my hands over my face and get in my truck, headed back towards the main house. I decide I'll have an early dinner and early bed time. I just want this day over with, then I'm one day closer to seeing Beth again.

Mason: Good Morning Beautiful. Have a good day at work. I should be back in town tomorrow night, I'd love to see you. Let me know xx

Nothing. As usual, no response. My god, what have I fucking done? At this rate, I might be headed back into town to check into the local psychiatric facility.

****

Friday lunch time and we have finally done all we can do with harvest. Even though I want to run as fast as I can and get my ass back into town to see Beth.. Okay, and Rosie too. I take a bit of a drive around the farm first and make sure there isn't anything else I can do around here. I don't plan on coming back out for a while.

If I have my way, I'll be tangled up in Beth for the foreseeable future.

As I reach the stables for a last minute pep talk with Billie, I see my dads truck parked near the door. This should be good. I consider not even going in, not wanting more shit advice.

"Just checking in before I hit the road, Pops. You need anything?" I almost shout it as I enter. He sticks his head up over the wall of Billie's stall.

"I need you to go get your girl. Honestly son, stop doing everything for everyone else and do something for yourself for once." I shake my head and look at my boots, scuffing my toes against the dusty barn floor.

"Yeah, no offence, Old man, but your stellar advice is the reason my girl hasn't spoken to me all week." He exits Billie's stall and clips the gate shut, she lets out a low whinny, no doubt protesting the interruption to her coddling.

"Your mother took a bit to come around to the idea of me too. Now look at us, almost fifty years later, dishing out life advice to our dumbass kids. Give her space, just…. Not too much. The sparks you two have are undeniable. Don't let that go."

Why does everyone keep saying that?

"So I've heard. Thanks Pops. You making it in next weekend for Rosie's birthday party?" I shake his hand and pat his shoulder at the same time, like a typical manly farewell.

"Wouldn't miss it, especially if it means we get to meet the famous Logan… assuming he will be there?" He raises his eyebrows at me.

"I hope so. See ya then, Pops. Take it easy, yeah? You've earned a rest old Man." He pats me on the shoulder and pushes me towards the door.

The drive back into town feels like it takes hours, instead of just twenty minutes. My mind is rushing. Do I text Beth? Call her? Or just go home and wait it out?

I do the responsible thing and go straight home. I unpack my bags, and shoot her a quick text

Mason: Hi. Just checking in. I'm home, just going to grab a shower. Would love to see you, or I could call you tonight when you're home from Philips Friday? I'm really worried Beth. Just want to hear from you. xx

I toss my phone down on my bed and head into the bathroom. I just stand and let the water run over me for a good twenty minutes.

When I emerge from the bathroom in a billow of steam, with just a towel wrapped around my waist. I check my phone immediately. I'm not sure why I expected today to be any different from any other day this week, but I have to keep some hope in the fact that she will come around.

I sit on the edge of my bed for another few minutes, just staring at my phone. Willing it to make a noise, signal a message or incoming call. Anything.

I check the time, it's almost four. Everyone at work will just be leaving, and Beth will still be there. Fuck it. I need to see her.

I throw on some jeans and a black T-shirt, throw my boots back on and jump in my truck. I drive to the office but the gates are locked up. No one is here.

Okay, she must have actually finished at normal time, she has been doing that a bit lately. I drive to her house, but her car isn't there either. Maybe she went to Philips Friday early?

Maybe I shouldn't be doing this. I should just give her the space she clearly needs.

Tell that to my bleeding heart.

I have an hour or so until I have to pick Rosie up from Hannah, I can't sit at home alone any longer. So I do what I almost definitely shouldn't do, and drive to her dads house.

I sit in the driveway, wringing the steering wheel under my sweaty hands. Her car isn't here either. At this point though, I just need to know she is okay.

I get out of my truck, wiping my clammy hands down the front of my jeans, and head to the front door. I knock and I hear movement inside before the door opens and I'm greeted by Will.

"Mason? Hey man. What, uh… What are you doing here?" He reaches out his hand for me to shake and pulls me in for a bit of an awkward bro hug. I hear everyone else inside the house go silent. Waiting for my answer.

"I uh – I don't know, actually. I just got back into town, and I was really hoping to see Beth, but.. She obviously isn't here."

He narrows his eyes at me, tilting his head to the side. "You don't know?"

Well that makes my stomach drop to my fucking toes. "Know what? She hasn't written back to any of my messages or answered any of my calls all week. I know I fucked up, but I just need to talk to her. I need to know she's okay."

He opens the door wider and gestures for me to come in. Nate and Olive are sitting side by side at the dining table, his thick arm snaked around the back of her chair.

Olive gives me a timid little wave and Nate gives me a sympathetic smile and nods his head at me "Hey man, good to see you again."

Hank calls from the kitchen "Mason, welcome back, can I get you a drink?"

What's going on? Theres no smart ass comments, no joking around. "I'm okay, thanks Hank, I have to pick Rosie up soon. Can someone please tell me what I don't know? Is Beth okay?"

Hank comes over, gives my shoulder a firm squeeze and tells me to sit down. I take a seat, opposite Nate and Olive, next to Will and Hank takes his usual seat at the head of the table.

"Beth has taken Logan to Cedarvale for the week." Hank says and they all give me a look, like that should clear everything up.

"I'm sorry, I still don't understand?"

"She really didn't tell you?" Nate pipes in. "She hasn't written back to any of my messages or returned my calls since I dropped her off here on Sunday. I… I said some things, and I think I freaked her out. Which, clearly I have if she felt like she had to be five hours away when I got home."

I push up from the table, and scrub a hand over my face, before I start heading for the door. I knew I shouldn't have come, I never even let myself think that she didn't want me in the same way.

"Mason, sit back down." Hank has put his stern words on, and I feel like a little kid that just got caught with his hands in the cookie jar right before dinner.

I turn and they all have such stern, yet sympathetic expressions on their faces. Well, I'm not about to argue with the three of them giving me their serious faces.

I sit back down in my chair, with my face in my hands. At this point it's as much from embarrassment that I came here.

Will is the first to speak "I don't know what went down between you and my sister on Sunday, it's not unusual for Beth not to keep us in the loop of her private life. But Mason, I can assure you, Beth going to Cedarvale has nothing to do with you and whatever shit you've put your foot in."

The side of his mouth turns up. I know he is trying to lighten the mood a little bit. And maybe it's working. Although I still need someone to hurry up and spit out the rest of this story.

Hank takes over, "She has gone to visit Griffins folks. Tomorrow would've been his birthday. They have a whole little memorial thing planned on the family property. Planting some trees or something in his honor. We didn't ask for the details, she didn't want any of us to go. She wanted it to just be her and Logan and Griffins parents."

Fuck… …

I let out a breath that comes out so harshly it almost sounds like a sob. Feels like it too. My whole chest and stomach goes into it. I'm not sure whether to feel relieved that maybe she isn't upset with me, or feel like a dick for being such a selfish, whiny baby all week when she has been going through some real shit.

It never even crossed my mind that something like this might be going on. It explains her reaction under the stars. God, I'm such a dick.

"She didn't tell me. Any of it. I thought I freaked her out. I thought she was avoiding me. I feel terrible."

"Don't take it to heart, I'm sure if we didn't know what the date was, she wouldn't have told any of us either. That's our Beth, hard headed to a fault. You'll learn." Hank claps me on the back and returns to the kitchen.

I look to Will and Nate who are giving each other shit eating grins, and look like they are trying to hold back laughter. They look at me and realize I've caught them "Dude, what'd you say to her to make you think you freaked her out that bad?" They burst out in laughter.

"That's enough you two meatheads. It's none of our business." Hank shouts from the kitchen.

I look back to them and they look like they are trying to kick each other under the table. I see why Beth get so exasperated by these two. They are like the two most overgrown children on Earth.

"Hank is right, it's none of your business. But because I know you two will give her hell trying to get it out of her. I told your sister I love her." They both stop what they are doing.

Olive looks over at me and I swear she has hearts in her eyes. "Oh My God, that's so cute! I'm so happy for you."

Will gives me a scowl and Nate makes a fake gag sound. I look back to Hank and he keeps his head down chopping vegetables, but I don't miss his smile.

"Well, I better hit the road, go and pick Rosie up. Thank you all. I was going crazy staring at my phone. I'm glad I came."

They all stand to see me out. "You're welcome to come back for dinner with Rosie if you want Mason. We love having you both around." Hank offers out his hand for me to shake.

"Thanks, maybe another night, it's been a damn long week."

Chapter 26

BETH

I'm just putting Logan to bed when my phone pings with a message. I don't have to look at it to know exactly who it's from.

I know I've been immature by shutting him out. He hasn't given up. I've woken to a message from him every morning and haven't been able to go to sleep until I get the goodnight message from him every night. I've missed a few calls from him, I screened a few of them purely because I don't know what to say to him.

I liked hearing him say those three words. The timing was just… off. I shouldn't be holding it against him, he couldn't have known.

I feel guilty for still not contacting him, but selfishly, I just needed to come here and deal with this day first. Logan needed my undivided attention.

Logan is out cold within minutes, he is exhausted but truth be told, I think he just naturally sleeps better here. He feels closer to his dad, and I don't blame him, I do too.

We are both sharing Griffins old double bed while we are visiting for the week, so it's a bit of a squeeze. Logan's head is resting in the crook of my elbow, rendering me nap trapped, when my arm goes dead, I finally roll my arm out from under him to look at my phone.

Mason: I'm sorry. I had no idea. I mean it now more than ever, take all the time you need. I'll be here when you're ready. Goodnight my sweet girl, I'll be thinking of you tomorrow xx.

Well, looks like the cat is out of the bag. I wonder which one of the weak ass males in my life was the one who ratted me out. I'll bet it was Nate. I guess there is no point running from my feelings anymore.

Beth: Thank you. There's no way you could've known. I'm sorry for not telling you, it's just something I needed to deal with on my own. Thank you for understanding. xx

****

The following morning, we go ahead with our little memorial as planned. Griffin would've loved this. Logan and I in the dirt, digging some holes to plant trees for him.

He loved the outdoors, he loved everything to do with gardening.

It's been almost a year since his passing, and we all finally decided that we would plant some trees on the family property and spread his ashes under them, so we could all come back and visit him here, but also so it would be like he was helping them grow.

We considered waiting a couple more months and planting them on his anniversary, but the weather has been ideal for planting, so the time was right for his birthday.

It's a long, emotional day for all of us. I didn't get a message from Mason this morning. I think that is out of respect. And I appreciate it. Guilt would probably have killed me.

I feel awkward enough being back with Griffins parents Rob and Heather while I've been involved with another man. I have no idea how to bring it up with them.

Today is definitely not the day for that. I'd like to avoid it this whole trip, but I also don't want them finding out on the grapevine either.

The week goes by quickly, Logan has loved spending time with his Papa and Mimi. I need to make an effort to get out here more often. Maybe now with Griffin at rest here, we will have even more of an excuse.

It's our last night here before we head home tomorrow, we take some picnic rugs out to the house yard and lay down and look at the stars. I flashback to doing this with Mason just two weeks ago. This time it makes me smile. I can't put my finger on what has changed in me. But I feel at ease.

Logan points out a few different constellations that he learned from Rob this week, being out of town and being able to see them all so clearly.

While Logan and Rob soak up the last few hours together for a while, I join Heather on the camping chairs she has set up. She suffered a horse-riding accident 15 years ago and has a long term back injury so she doesn't get down on the ground.

As we sit side by side, she reaches over and takes my hand and thanks me for bringing Logan out for the week. Heather has always treated me like her own. It's always been a huge comfort for me to have that maternal figure for the last twenty or so years.

She was even in the room when Logan was born. I think things like that have bonded us as though she is my own mother.

I spoke to Rob and Heather together last night after Logan went to bed about me seeing Mason. They were happy for me and said they remember Griffin joking that Mason would be good for me when he is gone. Of course he did.

They were both excited to meet him one day, and of course, Logan told them all about Rosie and Heather definitely teared up, watching his little face light up with sheer happiness.

I expressed my guilt at moving on, and shared all my doubts about it being too soon, and getting hurt and then Logan gets hurt as well. But as expected, Heather just took my hand and said "Only time will heal those scars Beth. And you know what they say, misery loves company. Don't go through life alone. Griffin didn't want that for you, and neither do we."

It's getting late and Logan is falling asleep beside Rob on the picnic rug. Rob picks him up and carries him inside to bed. Heather looks over at me, she reaches out once again and takes my hand, like only a mother can.

"I know you're leaving early in the morning Beth. I have something to give you. Wait here a second?" She says, as she pats the top of my hand and walks back into the house.

She re-emerges a moment later, with an envelope in her hand. "You don't have to open it now, whenever you're ready." I give her a questioning look, and then I look down at the envelope she has just handed me. My hands start to shake when I recognize the handwriting on the front of the envelope. It's Griffins.

She gives me a gentle pat on the shoulder and turns to leave. Rob has made his way back out and is standing at the top step on the front porch with his hip propped on the railing.

When Heather approaches him he holds out his hand to her, and they both stand arm in arm just watching me for a moment before heading inside.

I sit for what feels like hours staring at this envelope. "What the hell, Griff?" I whisper to no one.

We are leaving early in the morning. It's Rosies birthday party tomorrow morning. Something that I had thought about skipping in the last week. Because I'm a coward and didn't want to face Mason in an environment when I don't know anyone else. But the invitation has been on the fridge for weeks and Logan has been counting down the days, so I can't let him down.

We have a five hour drive ahead of us to get back in time for her party tomorrow afternoon, we need to leave by seven AM.

And now I am going to sit here and stew over whether I have the strength to read this. I also don't have the strength not to. I need to know why Heather waited until now to give this to me.

With a deep, steadying exhale, I turn the envelope to open it and the minute I pull the letter out I immediately feel the tears form in the corners of my eyes. I don't think it even matters what it says, the tears will be falling thick and fast.

My Darling Beth,

If you're reading this, it means I am gone, and you're officially back on the market. It also means that you have started seeing someone else and you're having doubts. I knew this day would come which is why I had to pen this letter to remind you.

You are far too hot to be alone for the rest of your life, it would be a damn shame for that ass to be walking around with no one to appreciate it.

Okay, now that I have you smiling, I'll get serious for just a second, because we both know a second is about as long as I can muster.

You filled up my life with Love from the day I met you fresh out of high school. You don't love easy, Beth. But you love big. You love hard. It wouldn't be fair to you, or frankly the rest of the world to bottle that kind of love up.

Set it free, honey. Let it burn so bright that I can see it from wherever I have ended up.

Logan deserves a happy mama, You deserve all of the happiness in the world. And you are happiest when you are giving out that big, hard Love.

It's okay, Beth. It's Okay.

I Love You. Thank you for filling my life with so much big, hard love.

Now, go get him, tiger. Your Happily Ever After is waiting Princess.

Griff xx

P.S It better be a certain fox of a contractor that I'm encouraging you to go after. Anyone else would be second best.

Chapter 27

MASON

It's the day of Rosies birthday party and we haven't heard the end of her excitement all week. Oh, to be five and this excited for your birthday again.

We are just having a party in the backyard at Hannahs house, family and a few of her friends from Preschool. And Beth, hopefully.

Planning this party has been a true test of just how amicable my split with Hannah is. I think we have passed the test with flying colors.

Everything is perfect. Princess themed, of course, just as Rosie wanted. The party starts in about an hour. The only thing I care about now is if Beth shows up.

I haven't spoken to her since my message last Friday. When I got a response from her, I decided to finally give her the space that I knew she needed, and let her soak in the time being with Griffins family and in his space. She hasn't said she isn't coming so I'm hoping she still shows. Although, if she does I'm not sure how I'm going to stop myself from touching her.

Hannah picks up on my nervous energy and has been sniffing around all morning for the gossip. "Are you sure you're okay, Mase? You know we are still friends right? You can trust me?"

I level her with a gaze, her calling me her friend felt weird. But somehow, also nice. Like we are just so okay with this new normal. "Yeah, I'm fine. Just nervous. I really thought I fucked things up with Beth, so I don't know if she is going to show. God, but I want her to."

"Okay, I know I said we are friends, but I swear to god, if you make out with another girl in front of me at our daughters birthday party, I might take it back." She smiles.

I know she's joking. Or I think she is. God dammit I don't even know what is real at the moment. "I'm sure she will be here, Mase. Relax." She gives my arm a reassuring squeeze as she walks past me ferrying food and drinks out to the backyard.

My parents are the first to arrive, carrying the biggest present my dad could carry with his own two hands. Way to make it obvious Rosie is the only grandchild, Pops.

I greet them both at the door, I don't even get to say my hellos before Rosie comes running through the house and barrels straight into them in a wide hug. "Papa, Grammy!"

"Here she is! Happy Birthday, Baby!" My dads face lights up the minute he lays eyes on her.

"Come see my castle!" I take the oversized present from my dad and Rosie takes them both by the hands and leads them to the backyard to show them the inflatable princess castle we have hired for the day. I watch as Hannah meets them both with a kiss on the cheek and a hug on their way through.

I have to take a second to take everything in. This is the first time having everyone in one place since we separated and I thought there would be some awkwardness but there just isn't.

An hour and a half later, the backyard is swarming full of kids, and parents alike. It's like half the town was invited to this thing.

There's still two people that aren't here though. My hope is fading fast. Maybe she just isn't up to it after Griffins memorial.

I head to the tables where Hannah has set up a huge punch bowl and jugs with a rainbow of assorted drinks. It sits side by side with a table overflowing with food. Of course, this is where I find my dad hovering as well.

I grab a cup and half fill it with ice. I'm halfway to putting a ladle of punch in when I see a little dark haired flash run through the yard "Rosie!!!!" I'd know that little flash anywhere.

"Logie!!!" I hear Rosie scream from somewhere within the ridiculous castle.

My heart immediately picks up pace as my eyes frantically scan the backyard trying to see where he came from. Hannah appears by my side out of nowhere. "Told you she would be here."

At least, I think that's what she says. I can't hear a damn thing. I can no longer see anyone else in this backyard either. Because Beth just appeared from around the side of the house. Sorry, but no one else exists right now.

She is like a mirage in a desert. Part of me had definitely convinced itself that I wouldn't see her again. She looks fucking gorgeous.

She is wearing a white floral sundress that hits her right above the knee and hugs her gorgeous figure just perfectly. Her hair is down, running down her back and fuck, she looks like summer. So fucking gorgeous.

We lock eyes across the yard. She gives me a small smile and a shy wave before she breaks my gaze. She turns her head slightly to look at the woman approaching her from the side. Elsie Clarke, running interference already. God Dammit.

I watch my mother wrap her arms around Beth in a warm, welcoming hug like they have known each other for years. I want to go to her. I want to wrap her in my arms like that, where she belongs. But for some reason my feet won't move. I'm glued to the spot. Punch ladle still in mid air.

From beside me I hear my dad scoff, I look over to see him lower his head, shaking it as he looks down at the ground. Again, I'm not sure my hearing is working properly but I'm sure I hear him call me a Dummy before he walks over to greet Beth as well.

Hannah takes the ladle off me and puts it back in the punch bowl. Before taking the plastic cup out of my hand and setting it on the table. That snaps me out of whatever daydream I'm in. "She really rattles you, huh?" She gives me a cheeky smile. I think she might actually be enjoying my pain.

"This last two weeks really have, yeah. I honestly thought I had stuffed it all up before it even really got off the ground. I just, need to know where I stand with her."

She puts her hand on my shoulder. "I'll tell you what, let's do the cake first, and then you can try and steal a moment away with her and talk to her if that's what you want. Put us all out of our misery."

She stalks away back inside the house to fetch the cake. My parents still have Beth occupied, God only knows what my dad is talking to her about but she throws her head back laughing, so that's alright with me.

I have no idea what I even want to say to her. I don't think there is anything I can say. I think she needs to do the talking right now, and that means I can't rush her.

I approach the castle and yell out "Cake time!" and in a split second there are small bodies flying past me, racing to the empty table where the kids have sensed the cake will be placed.

Logan is the last kid out of the castle, almost like he was hanging back waiting. I help him to climb down and as soon as his feet touch the ground, he wraps his arms around my legs in a tight hug.

I kneel down so I am at his level and his arms wrap around my shoulders. I wrap my arm around him, almost completely engulfing him. "I missed you and Rosie."

He lowers his head down onto my shoulder, nuzzling into my neck. "I missed you too, bud."

"Now that we're home, do you think we could go fishing soon like you said?" I pull away from him to look him in the eyes.

"Absolutely we can. Should we ask grandpa and your uncles to come too?" I watch as his eyes widen like big saucers.

"Can we? That would be so cool!!" I stand back up and grab his hand as we walk towards the rest of the party

"We will have to check with your mama, but I think it will be okay."

I glance around the yard again, and immediately lock eyes with Beth. I notice her eyes look glassy.

She has got a plastic cup clenched in her hands, held tight to her chest. She is still flanked by my parents at either side. She gives me a very subtle nod of her head, so subtle that I can't be sure whether it was real or if I imagined it.

Hannah brings the cake out and we all sing Happy Birthday, we snap a few photos with the birthday girl, and then kids go back to playing.

Logan didn't let go of my hand the entire time, until Rosie basically pried him off me to go back to playing. Every time I looked over at Beth, I caught her watching me. Or maybe she was watching Logan, again, I can't be sure.

I finally have a minute to myself, so I see it as the perfect time to go and talk to Beth for a minute. At least say a proper hello.

I head to the table and get myself a cold drink and fill a fresh cup up for her as well. Just as I start to head towards her I look up and see… Oh god, here we go..

Chapter 28

BETH

"Hey Beth! Thanks so much for coming. Logan looks like he is having a blast. Rosie hasn't stopped talking about him, she's been so excited to see him again." I swallow hard as Hannah approaches me.

I know Mason has said their split was amicable, but I'm still nervous. I felt weird about coming to her house in the first place and now she is approaching to talk to me one on one.

I gulp down the excess saliva that has filled my mouth thanks to my bundle of nerves. "Hi Hannah. Thanks for having us. Rosie is just beautiful. The feelings are very mutual between the two of them. They are very cute together."

She tilts her head slightly "I know it's absolutely not my place to say… But you and Mason are too. I said for a long time before we split that I saw something between you two." I let out a nervous laugh.

"Let me guess, a spark?" She meets my smile, before she places a gentle hand on my forearm.

"I know this situation makes you a little bit uncomfortable, but I promise you, it's fine. Mason being happy is one of my top priorities. And in these last few months, he has been happier than I've seen him in years, thanks to you. Well, maybe except for the last couple of weeks. I'm almost ashamed of how entertained I've been by his inner turmoil."

I bite on my cheek nervously. I don't really have a response for that. "Look, I've already toed the line by even talking to you about your relationship, so this is no doubt going to be like taking a running leap over the line. But he loves you. And if I'm not mistaken. You feel the same way about him. I see the way your eyes have tracked him around this yard. The way you teared up when he interacted with Logan."

I nod, very gently. I don't even know if anyone can even register the movement. "Beth, the past is in the past. I can't imagine what you've been through, or how you must be feeling. But I know a good thing when I see it. And for what it's worth, I think you'd be mad not to see where that can go."

My eyes lock on Mason who is watching from across the yard. I see his parents trying to have a conversation with him, and he is absently nodding, but his eyes haven't left mine since Hannah approached me. He looks, scared? Worried? I can't place it.

"Thanks Hannah. I appreciate you saying all of this. I was nervous coming here. Not really believing you would actually be okay with all of this. I still have a lot to figure out, but I agree, it's worth seeing how it goes. If you'll excuse me, I think there is someone else that might need to be in on that conversation." I grab her elbow and give it a gentle squeeze and leave her with a grateful smile.

As I walk across the yard towards Mason, I watch as he dismisses his dad with a half wave, and Henry looks like he has just been slapped, until he turns and sees me walking towards them.

Elsie promptly grabs Henry by the arm and pulls him out of the way so Mason and I have a clear path to each other. He takes a few long strides towards me.

He looks damn good today. His signature baseball cap has returned and he has it turned backwards, it's hot, but I miss the cowboy hat already. His tight blue T-shirt clings to every muscle and ridge on his body, and his casual gym shorts cling perfectly to his thick thighs.

"Hi." I look up at him when we meet in the middle of the yard. He reaches up and tucks a piece of hair behind my ear, not really making full contact but enough that I feel his heat, and goosebumps prickle over my bare shoulders.

"Hi yourself. Thanks for coming."

"Wouldn't miss it for the world. Wouldn't have been allowed to even if I wanted to." We both let out a small chuckle.

"Yeah, your kid has already convinced me to take him and your whole family fishing. He made sure to hit me with the I missed you first though so there was no way I could say no. I might've just been emotionally blackmailed by a five year old."

I lower my head and shake it, not being able to contain my smile "Yeah, sounds about right, the kid really knows how to get what he wants."

We smile at each other like giddy teenagers for a few seconds before his gradually drops. We both open our mouths to talk at the same time "I think…" We both stop.

"You go ahead" he says and gestures his hand for me to continue.

"I think we need to talk. Do you think you could come over tonight?" I watch as his face sinks. I probably phrased that in the complete wrong way, but I can't say what I need to say in the middle of his daughters birthday party.

"Uh… yeah, I can come." He lifts his hat off his head and rubs at the back of his neck before putting his hat back on.

"7.30? after bed time okay?" He just nods his head and I can tell he is nervous. Well, I just hope that what I have to say is worth his current anguish.

****

234

We call in to see my dad on our way home from Rosie's party. Logan is hopped up on cake and sugar. I almost feel relieved when I see Nate's car in the driveway. That's one way for Logan to burn some energy, trying to beat up his 6 foot 4 uncle.

"Hi Darling girl! Welcome home." My dad wraps his arms around me when I walk into the house. This is home. Wherever this man is, I'm home.

"We missed you both this week." I head to the fridge and grab a bottle of cold water.

"We missed you too."

"We aren't the only ones that missed you. Have you seen Mason yet?" I narrow my gaze at my dad, giving him the best suspicious look I could muster.

"So you're the weak link that ratted me out? After I kept your secret all this time." He holds up his hands in a fake surrender.

"Now Darlin' you didn't see his face. Someone had to tell him. He was going out of his mind." I hear a throat clear from over my shoulder.

"Secret? What secret?" I turn to look at Nate, who is wearing his signature shit eating grin. Oops. Now I'm in trouble.

"Um, no, nothing. No secret. You must've misheard." I shake my head while I suck my lips in between my teeth, effectively zipping my lips shut.

Nate averts his gaze to our dad and points an accusatory finger at him "What are you hiding from me, old man? And why does Beth get to know, and I don't?"

I can't hold it in, I let out a snicker. Nate snaps his gaze to me "I heard that Elizabeth. Tell me what you know."

He steps toward me, and I know what's coming. My little brother is a pest. Always has been, he fights dirty. He knows which buttons to press on each of us to get us to talk.

He knows my weakness, the ticklish spot at the junction of my neck and shoulder, he knows if he puts the right amount of pressure on that spot I will drop to the ground immediately. Even at almost ten years older than him, he could always beat me in a fight because of that one weakness.

He makes a pinching motion with his thumb and forefinger and I'm flinching instinctively already.

"Come on, Beth, out with it." I look at my dad, and back to Nate who is slowly, torturously approaching me.

"Fine I'll talk. I came early to Philips Friday one day and accidentally cockblocked dad and his lady friend."

Nate pauses, fingers still in the pinching motion, but suspended in midair. He turns and points his finger at dad. I think he might be in shock. Well at least he wasn't the one walking in on them.

"You… you have a lady friend, and you didn't want to tell us?"

Dad lets out an exasperated sigh and shakes his head "I don't need to tell you lot every detail of my private life. But yes, I have been getting back out there. I figured it was about time. If Beth can get back on the horse, then so can I."

I look at my dad and give him a teary eyed smile. Look at us, just two broken hearts, healing. "Can I ride a horse mama? Can Mason teach me how?"

My eyes widen and I take a deep breath in and hold it for a moment. "One thing at a time, kiddo. How about you master fishing first?"

✱✱✱✱✱✱✱✱✱✱✱✱✱✱✱✱✱

I've just put Logan to bed when I hear a knock at the door. My stomach does a little flip and I feel my pulse race. Now is the moment. Take what I want. My next chapter stands on the other side of my front door.

I open the door and Mason has his forearm resting on the doorframe, with his forehead resting on his arm. His ear-to-ear grin splits his face, it's contagious, so immediately my face mirrors his.

"Hi." It's about all I can muster in this moment. The butterflies have worked their way up to my chest and I need to take a second to catch my breath. I step out of the way so he can walk into the house. He hesitates slightly and I watch as he balls his fists up beside him.

I know that look, he is trying to restrain himself. He wants to touch me.

"Thanks for coming. I owe you an apology, Mase. I shouldn't have ghosted you like that." He turns around to face me, there is about two steps between us, and we are now standing facing each other.

"Beth, you have nothing to apologize for. I'm sorry I said what I said." He steps towards me and reaches out to cup the side of my face.

I take a deep breath in and blow it out with more force than I intended to. "I'm not the best at talking about my feelings, but I'm going to give this my best shot. I do owe you an apology because I absolutely freaked out and instead of talking it through like an adult, I shut down, and froze you out. You didn't deserve that, and I'm sorry."

He opens his mouth to start talking back. I lift my index finger to his mouth, indicating that I'm not finished.

"Honestly, I never imagined I would ever hear those words from another man again. And it just caught me so off guard when I was already in my head about it being Griffins birthday. I still have this sense of guilt that no one could possibly live up to what Griffin and I had, and some days I almost feel like I'm betraying him by diving into this with you. Moreso because, as much as I had told myself that we were just taking things day by day. I knew deep down that this was something bigger than that. More than just getting to know each other or messing around. I knew eventually I would fall head over heels for you.

"This last week spent with Griffins parents, back at his house, in his space. I was nervous. I thought it would be easy for me to sink back into the past and want to wallow in that. He was my first true love, and I feel greedy in thinking that I can have more than one true love in this lifetime. In going back there, I think this part of me was still looking for some kind of sign. Some form of validation, or closure, I guess."

I have surprised myself in being able to get all of this out without crying. I don't think I can say the same for Mason because his eyes look glassy. He clears his throat, "and did you get it? Closure, or a sign?"

I step towards him, closing the distance so our bodies are touching. "I didn't get a sign, no." Okay, now I'm just baiting him.

I watch as his face falls. "I got a flashing billboard that could probably be seen from Mars." His face lifts and the look in his eyes shifts from sadness to disbelief.

"I'm sorry, I don't think I understand what you're trying to say?" I turn away and walk towards my bag that is at the bottom of the staircase. I grab out the envelope and give it to him.

He takes a second to read it. I watch as a single tear falls from his eye, landing directly on Griffins letter, and then his mouth turns upward into a half smile, and I know he has read the last line.

"Turns out Hannah wasn't the only one who saw something between us."

"Beth… I've watched you over the last few months as you regained your happiness. The spark in your eyes when we are messing around, the way you laugh when you watch the kids play together. The way you light up when my daughter wants to do girly things with you. The sense of ease you get after the kids go to sleep and we can just talk. You, Beth, you light up my god damn world. You captivate me. And while I know Griffin was the lucky son of a bitch who got to be your first true love. If you let me, I'll happily spend every god damn day living in that mans shadow, giving you all of the happiness you deserve. The happiness he wanted for you."

He wraps his arms around my waist and pulls me close. "There's just one thing wrong with that." I say as I look up, getting lost in those baby blues.

He tilts his head and looks at me with a confused look on his face.

"You're not a shadow, Mason. You're the light. You, and Rosie, you came into my life at such a dark time, and you ignited something in me, and Logan, that I thought didn't exist anymore. You bought that big, hard love back into my life. And I…"

I have to swallow down the lump in my throat. Of course, it would be too good to be true that I would've been able to get through this whole thing without crying.

"I Love you, Mason." Well, at least we are crying together now.

Before I even get a chance to gauge his reaction to that, his mouth crashes onto mine, with his arms still wrapped around my hips, he hoists me up so my legs wrap around his waist. Where they belong.

"I love you too."

Epilogue

BETH

18 months Later

All my fears and doubts turned out to be for nothing. All those signs I spent so long searching for, have continued to pop up in the most mundane ways in the day to day.

By the end of last summer, Masons lease expired on his small rental house, so he moved into my house, while he started to build his dream home on his piece of land on the farm.

Along with the help of his dad, his cousin, Bentley, and a few of the guys from work, It was finished construction and we all moved in over this summer.

I'm not sure whether it's more his dream house, or mine. He wouldn't let me see the progress over the last couple of months of construction and design. He asked for my opinion, but I wasn't allowed out here to see it. Which sucked because Summer on the farm has become my favorite time of year, I was keen to relive the first time he bought me swimming out here at harvest time, but that wasn't allowed this year, because that would mean seeing the house.

When he finally revealed the house to me it was absolutely breathtaking. It took in elements of my house, the one I built with Griffin, my childhood home, and the main farmhouse here as a nod to his childhood home.

It was like all of our favorite places rolled into one. But the house itself wasn't the best part.

The front yard boasts a beautiful sunken fire pit, surrounded by heavy, dark timber bench seats built in, which has become a favorite place to sit out in during the cooler nights.

The front porch is lined with rose bushes, including the Adams roses from my house that Mason dug up and re-planted out here.

Around the back of the house, Mason had hand built a kids wonderland, a castle fit for a princess, and a pirate ship sand box fit for a little pirate, or the perfect place to dig up dinosaur fossils. The kids both went absolutely nuts when they saw it.

Overlooking the play areas, there is a mini house, a small studio apartment, purpose built for grandparents. The first people to stay there were Griffins parents when they came to visit shortly after we moved in.

The house itself has five bedrooms, plus a study which has gradually turned into a toy room, a master suite that is almost laughable, it's so expansive. The adjoining bathroom has a bath that is big enough for two and sits in front of a floor to ceiling, one-way vision window that looks straight out over the river. It's absolutely beautiful to soak in right at sunset.

Five bedrooms at first seemed excessive but we both liked the idea of having a couple of spare rooms, and they have come in handy for the times when my Dad and brothers come out to go on their monthly boys fishing trips, which usually end in a few too many beers and my brothers, my son and Mason rolling around in the grass trying to put each other in headlocks. Some things will never change.

Last week we celebrated our first Christmas in our house, and we hosted everyone here, Masons family, my family and Griffins family. It was absolutely magical to see everyone come together so seamlessly and fill this new house with laughter and so much love.

I surprised Mason early on Christmas morning before the kids and our guests woke up. I bought him in his coffee and a small gift containing some dry mix and ingredients for cookies. I attached a little card saying "Cookies aren't the only thing baking this Christmas" and I wish I recorded his reaction because I don't think I've ever seen his eyebrows shoot up so high.

Tonight is New Years Eve, and we are hosting my family here. I'm not sure how Nate managed to get the busiest night of the year off work, but he did. He seems a little off tonight, and I have a sneaking suspicion I know why.

My dad finally got the confidence to bring Sadie around and I've lost count of how many times I've watched as Will and Nates heads have just about exploded as they try and keep their smartass comments in.

Even Bella is here. It's the first time she has been home in almost three years. None of us miss how gaunt she looks, and the light that seems to have dimmed in her eyes. But I can see it sparking back to life after even just a few days back home.

Will somehow has acquired some fireworks to set off down by the river at midnight, the kids are busy toasting marshmallows on the fire, I'm pretty sure they have both had at least a dozen each, and I'm just standing on the front porch, hip resting on the railing, taking in the view. Basking in the happiness and looking forward to doing this for so many years to come.

Mason comes jogging up to the porch, the sun is just starting to set, and we have just the perfect view over the rolling hills from our front porch.

He grabs me by the hip and pulls me into him, pressing a gentle kiss to my temple "This is your five minute warning that the kids have requested the last dance party of the year, so I'm going to get the speaker because who am I to say no to them?" I laugh at him and shake my head.

"I'm just grateful they were happy to share their Christmas present, I don't think I'd have coped with two, and I know you would've got them one each if they asked."

Oh yeah, did I mention, the kids wanted a pony for Christmas? Not sure how Santa fit Frankie in his sleigh but a little chestnut Shetland pony appeared in the barn on Christmas morning anyhow.

"Still would if they asked." He smacks me on the ass and continues on his way inside. I make my way back down to the fire pit.

Olive is pouring a few glasses of champagne, she passes one to my dad and Sadie. Nate and Will are happy sipping their beers. As I approach, she reaches a glass out to me, and I discreetly shake my head. Her eyes go wide as saucers, and I can see her working overtime to stifle her excited scream.

I bring my index finger to my mouth in a 'shh' gesture and wink at her. Thankfully she is probably the only one around here that can keep a secret.

Mason returns with the speaker and to my surprise, everyone gets up to dance. Rosie, bless her soul, who has developed a little bit of an infatuation for my brother, immediately asks Will to dance with her. The disappointment in Logans eyes clearly feeling like he has been replaced. Thankfully Sadie steps in and takes him for a spin, and has him giggling in seconds flat.

My Dad has Bella in his sights, I can see the concern for her laced in his eyes.

Get in line, Pops.

Never in my wildest dreams did I think my life could end up this picture perfect. That I would possibly feel this level of happy again.

We are nearing midnight and suddenly the fire pit has emptied out. My dad has retired into the guest house, I don't think he has made midnight on New Years Eve in at least ten years. So Sadie has followed him.

Will has gone down, getting ready to let off his fireworks, Bella went down to help him. Nate and Olive left an hour ago, saying they were just heading off for a walk. I assume Nate would end up down by the river, not missing an opportunity to mess around with fire.

Leaving just the four of us around the fire, the kids have lost a lot of energy, I'm surprised they have lasted this long, the marshmallows have helped though, I'm sure.

Logan has perched himself on Masons lap, head resting on his broad chest, Mason runs his hand mindlessly up his back and Logans eyes are heavy and struggling to stay open.

I look at the time, 15 seconds to go. We get the kids up, trying to muster a little bit of excitement.

"3,2,1…. "

The fireworks explode from down the hill, and I hear Wills laughter carry up the hill over the bangs and whistles. Such a child.

The kids laugh with pure glee, jumping around like they weren't just almost asleep in our arms. Mason and I both laugh and he hooks his fingers into the belt loops of my jeans. Pulling me in close to him, he wraps his arms around me, swings me around to dip me into a deep kiss.

"Happy New Year little Mama." I can't wipe the smile off my face at that. "Happy New Year, Daddy." .

We are broken from our sweet moment when Nate and Olive re-appear from around the corner of the house, Nate holding Olive tightly at his side, his forearm almost shadowing her entire body.

"Oh gross, cut it out you two. Where is everyone?" Nate says.

"Happy New Year to you too, little brother. They are either asleep or down the hill being pyromaniacs. Why, what's up?" I raise an eyebrow at him and glance between him and Olive.

"We're engaged!!"

Acknowledgments

Well, you made it to the end of my very first book. The first person I want to thank for making this dream come true is you. By reading this book, and maybe going and telling your friends/families/social media followers about it, you are supporting this Indy authors dreams and making me want to keep doing this.

To my main hype girls, the bookish babes, Em, Monique, and Jess for the limitless, blind support. No matter how ridiculous I am you girls are always behind me to offer a gentle nudge and a "yaass girl!" Thank you for sharing all of your opinions and feedback, and being completely unbiased.

To my husband. Thank you for supporting my book buying habit, that turned into this book writing dream. For holding my hand through the shit-storm that has been our life. Thank you for relieving me of the design duties for the covers of these books, but still accommodating my demands.

And finally, to my son and Niece. The biggest inspirations for Logan and Rosie. I hope you both never stop being unapologetically yourselves

Keep reading for a sneak peak at the next installment of the Philips four.

Get ready for Nates story

Rumors Fly

Coming November 2024…

Chapter 1

NATE

Whoever said you can't have your cake and eat it too, was a liar. Life is fucking good. Don't get me wrong, I've had more than my fair share of troubles in my time.

My mother took off and left my dad to raise their four kids, when my twin sister Bella and I were just two years old. We were practically raised by my oldest sister, Beth.

Our old man worked a lot, while we adjusted to being a single income household. So sure, I have some deep-seeded abandonment issues that come into play every now and then. But who wouldn't, right?

It's always been my number one motivator in life. I refused to let myself sink into any form of depression or mental distress like the one that took my mother away from me before I even had a chance to know her. I have a plan for my life. So far, everything is coming up Nate.

I bought my first house five years ago, when I was just twenty-one years old. It was a bit of a fixer- upper, but with some help from a few of my buddies, and my older brother, Will, it quickly became pretty close to being my dream home.

I've been working my absolute ass off since the minute I was old enough to get a part time job. I took up a paper route at about ten years old, and by the time I was twelve, I had my route as well as sweeping floors at the local barber shop.

I saved every spare penny I could, until about four years ago when, with a little help from his parents, my best friend Zealand and I opened our own business.

Just in Thyme is our very own, trendy little restaurant/bar in an old run-down boat house in town, overlooking the lake. We were driven and ambitious with what we wanted. But neither of us predicted it would be the raging success it quickly became.

Zealand and I met in Preschool, we both grew up here and were always attached at the hip, more like brothers than friends.

Zee is an only child and I of course, had three boisterous siblings so he loved the chaos of my house, and I enjoyed the quiet of his.

Growing up in Rosewood was interesting. It's a small town, with a population of about two thousand people. The narrow, shaded, cobblestone main street only has a handful of boutique stores, a supermarket, pharmacy, twenty-four-hour diner and a gas station. We also have one café, that makes probably the best coffee in at least a hundred-mile radius. People legitimately drive over an hour just for a caffeine fix from Bubbas Brew. And then there's Just in Thyme.

Rosewood has always had one bar. O'Reilly's is located right at the edge of town but honestly, if you value your life, you don't go drinking there, it's the very definition of a dive bar. It attracts all the wrong types of people, gangs, drunks and derelicts. Most nights there are brawls, sometimes worse.

I'm sure the local police force should relocate their holding cells to the parking lot, or better yet, right there in the front bar, they are there so often anyway.

Zee and I saw the opportunity and had enough passion to create a safe and welcoming environment that the residents of Riverwood could enjoy year-round. So, when the opportunity presented itself, we took it. We were completely booked out on our opening night, and there have only been a slight handful of nights since then that we haven't been full up.

It helps that Rosewoods population almost doubles every summer as tourists converge on the town to make use of our picturesque lake and expansive array of meandering rivers and streams that carve through the hills surrounding the town. The lake is perfect for all things watersports, while the rivers and streams attract fishermen of all ages and abilities.

Last summer we had to almost double our staff numbers to keep up with the increased number of bookings, and this year is shaping up to be the same, thank God there is always a bunch of college kids looking for some easy cash to fund their vacations, that are happy to wash dishes and clean tables for a couple of months.

We have worked out the perfect partnership between Zee and I, he went straight to culinary school when we graduated high school, he always had a passion for good food and wanted to make a living out of making people feel happy through his food.

I on the other hand, always had a bit of a creative side, I enjoyed experimenting and even when I was in my teens, and my two older siblings, Beth and Will were old enough to drink. I always loved seeing what concoctions I could come up with for them. So naturally, I worked on perfecting those skills so that one day, we could give Rosewood a decent place to enjoy some good food and drinks, without the fear of being beaten to a pulp, or dying.

To round it all out, I also have the girl of my dreams, Olive. We met when we were just 18. I know it's a cliché, but I just know we are meant to be. When you know, you know, right?

Almost six months ago, when we were celebrating new years eve at Beths farm, I got down on one knee and asked Olive to marry me. Of course, she said yes, because we are soulmates.

I've known from the moment I first saw Olive working at the local diner on the main street of town eight years ago, that she was the girl for me. I wasn't even hungry. Zee and I had only stopped in to get a cold drink on our way home from the lake one summer afternoon.

Three hours later we walked out of that diner having eaten our weight in fries, sampled every flavor of milkshake they served. And I got the number of the pretty little blonde waitress who blushed at me every time our eyes met across the counter. I called her that night and the rest, as they say, is history.

It's been the best eight years of my life loving on my girl, and I can't wait to see her float down the aisle like the angel she is. I can't wait to see her carrying our children, being the best goddamn mother that I know she will be. Everything about this life, I've imagined it with Olive by my side.

We are nearing the end of Spring and both Zee and I have pretty much been working seven days a week from before opening until after closing, preparing for what is shaping up to be a massive summer season. Every motel, hotel and campground within an hours drive of Rosewood is booked up, which means the town will be swarming with people young and old looking for a good night out.

The best part about Just In Thyme is the restaurant and bar areas are separate enough that we can offer a relaxed, quiet dining experience, while also catering for the rowdy bar scene as well.

Zee looks after the kitchen and the dining experience, while I look after the bar area. We haven't ever had any trouble here, not a single bar fight in almost four years. It helps that I'm about 6 foot 4 and stacked like a Mack truck. I clearly enjoy a good gym session, so I don't think anyone has been game enough to start any shit in my bar. Yet anyway.

It's late in the day, it's only Monday, one of our quieter nights, so I'm taking some time looking over my inventory in the bar, taking stock of what I'll need to order. There's a major college campus about two hours' drive from here, where most of the local kids end up going to further their educations, so it's inevitable that this place will be crawling with college kids both local and from abroad in just a couple of weeks as they all blow off some steam for the summer. I know I need to be well stocked with all the tequila and vodka I can get my hands on.

The first few years of running this place were a little tough, as a lot of those college kids were my old classmates, who never missed an opportunity to judge me for being just the 'lowly barkeep.'

It's nice now that the kids coming through now are younger, so they don't really know me and don't feel they need to look down on me for never leaving our small town.

Even though my very successful restaurant has probably landed more zeroes in my bank account than their precious trust funds have for them. But hey, who am I to judge?

As our last patron cashes out their tab, I officially close the doors for the night and see the remaining staff to their cars. I pour Zee and I a nightcap, the perks of owning the place, is all the top shelf whiskey we drink, and then we both head into the back office to place a few orders for supplies.

I have taken on a lot of the ordering lately, Zee has been caught up hiring the summer employees. Apparently, I'm not the best judge of character, although I beg to differ, because I'm sure he would hire anyone that walks in here in a tight skirt. But I have to trust him because he hasn't done us wrong yet, we have had some great seasonal staff working for us every year so far.

"How many people over the age of 23 have you hired this year?" I ask him with a smirk on my face. My family like to tell me I should have this smirk trademarked, because no one pulls off the shit-eating grin quite like Nate Philips. It comes from being the youngest of four siblings. Beth is the responsible one, Will is the strong and reliable one, Bella is the smart one. So I guess by default, that makes me the funny one.

"Funny enough, the only people older than that that are looking for summer jobs are usually just wanting to fund where their next hit comes from, so you should be happy I don't hire them. Although Mrs. Simons did apply again, so if it's old blood you're looking for, I could give her a go this year."

Angela Simons was the lunch lady at our high school. She is now well into her seventies, but every year without fail, she applies for a summer job with us. She usually comes in and pinches Zee's cheek and tells him what a good boy he turned out to be. I run and hide every time I see her coming.

With a grimace on my face, I sip my drink and just shake my head slowly. Zee lets out a breathy chuckle "Didn't think so."

We spend another hour or so chatting away and joking about old times, once we are sure we have done as much as we can for today, I decide to call it a night. I am absolutely wrecked. Working eighty plus hour weeks is quickly taking it's toll on my body. I feel like I haven't seen Olive much in the last few weeks.

She is a beauty therapist, and works for herself, offering a mobile service, pampering people in their own homes. She has built a really successful business model for herself over the years, and I couldn't be prouder of my girl for chasing her dreams.

Although it means she typically works from the morning until the evening, and I work all night, until the early hours of the morning most nights. She is usually asleep when I get home, and I'm asleep when she leaves. But we somehow make it work.

I'm so looking forward to getting home, a warm shower and crawling into bed right behind her. Her petite little frame fits so perfectly cradled in my giant arms; I know we both sleep better when we're together.

I jump into my truck. The other love of my life. A 1975 Ford F-150, with a custom paint job. It was my grandfather's car, he started restoring it before he died, so I took it over and now it's my pride and joy. I have the car, the house, the job and the girl of a lifetime. It's little wonder why I smile the entire drive home.

I walk into the house and as usual it's quiet. I assume Olive must be asleep. I can see a light left on down the hallway though, so maybe she waited up for me. "Ollie, baby? you up?" I call down the hallway as I toe off my shoes and dump my keys and wallet on the hall table.

I head towards our bedroom, where the light is coming from. I can't help but notice something feels off in the house. I just can't quite put my finger on what it is.

As I reach the door to the bedroom, I see the bed is perfectly made, no sign of Olive. Huh, weird. I would've thought she would be fast asleep by now. I head into the ensuite bathroom, still no sign of her. What the fuck is going on? As I stand in the doorway of the bathroom and stare at our bedroom, I glance over at our closet and notice it.

It's empty.

What the fuck? I reach into my pocket to pull out my phone. I pull up Olives contact and turn to walk towards the bed. I need to sit down. I take two steps towards the bed and that's when something on the side table catches my eye.

Olive's engagement ring, sitting on top of a post it note that reads. 'I can't do this, I'm sorry.'